# SWEET

"[A] riveting addition to the rising new adult category."
—*Library Journal*

"A sexy, romantic, emotional coming-of-age new adult that uses a different approach to the defining romance than the usual NA offerings. Crisp writing, indulgent humor, and a smooth, flowing story line make it incredibly easy to become fully invested in this book . . . A wonderful love story that takes us on a journey filled with love, laughter, growth, and angst."
—*Smexy Books*

"Full of steamy romance and entertaining banter . . . [McCarthy's] writing is very captivating."
—*Dark Faerie Tales*

"A wonderful second book to the True Believers series. I love the characters that McCarthy has created."
—*The Book Pushers*

"Sweet and fun . . . Erin McCarthy has a real gift with creating real stories."
—*Ticket to Anywhere*

# TRUE

"McCarthy's entry in the burgeoning new adult subgenre is a page-turning, gut-wrenching success . . . Their troubles are real, their love True, and readers will root them on past the very last page."
—*RT Book Reviews*

"A sweet, romantic, dynamic coming-of-age new adult that takes a much-needed detour from the usual emotionally draining, overly dramatic offerings . . . Crisp writing and a smooth story line make it incredibly easy to become fully invested in this book."
—*Smexy Books*

*continued .*

"By turns sweet, steamy, gritty, and heartbreaking, *True* is an outstanding read."                                    —*On a Book Bender*

"One of those books that you just can't and won't put down . . . Extremely realistic and relatable . . . [A] dramatic and beautiful story."
—*Harlequin Junkie*

"Ms. McCarthy did a wonderful job with this story."
—*Under the Covers Book Blog*

## PRAISE FOR NOVELS OF ERIN MCCARTHY

"Sizzling hot, jam-packed with snappy dialogue, emotional intensity, and racing fun."       —Carly Phillips, *New York Times* bestselling author

"A steamy romance . . . Fast-paced and red-hot."
—*Publishers Weekly*

"Characters you will care about, a story that will make you laugh and cry, and a book you won't soon forget."       —*The Romance Reader*

"Priceless!"                                                     —*RT Book Reviews*

"Quite a few chuckles, some face-fanning moments, and one heck of a love story."                                        —*A Romance Review*

"Reader's won't be able to resist McCarthy's sweetly sexy and sentimental tale."                                           —*Booklist*

"[McCarthy] is fabulous with smoking-hot romances!"
—*The Romance Readers Connection*

"Just the right amount of humor interspersed with romance."
—*Love Romances*

"One of the romance-writing industry's brightest stars . . . Ms. McCarthy spins a fascinating tale that deftly blends a paranormal story with a blistering romance . . . Funny, charming, and very entertaining."
—*Romance Reviews Today*

ERIN McCARTHY

# SWEET

BERKLEY BOOKS, NEW YORK

THE BERKLEY PUBLISHING GROUP
Published by the Penguin Group
Penguin Group (USA) LLC
375 Hudson Street, New York, New York 10014

USA • Canada • UK • Ireland • Australia • New Zealand • India • South Africa • China

penguin.com

A Penguin Random House Company

This book is an original publication of The Berkley Publishing Group.

Berkley trade paperback ISBN: 978-0-425-27551-1

An application for cataloguing has been submitted to the Library of Congress.

PUBLISHING HISTORY
InterMix eBook edition / October 2013
Berkley trade paperback edition / June 2014

PRINTED IN THE UNITED STATES OF AMERICA

10  9  8  7  6  5  4  3  2  1

Cover design by Rita Frangie.
Photo: Young couple in love © Coka/Shutterstock.
Interior text design by Kristin del Rosario.

# CHAPTER ONE

I COULDN'T GO HOME FOR THE SUMMER. I JUST COULDN'T.

Going home would mean endless worried looks from my mother, and reminders about following curfew and the dangers of alcohol and premarital sex. My father would force me to volunteer— which was *such* an oxymoron—to teach Sunday school at his church and threaten to throw out all of my revealing clothes. Like shorts. Because wearing shorts in summer was so scandalous.

I couldn't deal with it, a whole summer ruined with their good intentions and their high moral standards that only a saint could live up to. And I'm no saint.

So I lied and told them I was spending the summer in Appalachia building homes for the poor with a Christian mission group when I was actually staying in Cincinnati and working at a steakhouse. I know. That was kind of a shitty lie.

But it was the only one that would have worked, so I had gone with it and there was no turning back now. Maintaining my freedom was worth a little guilt that I wasn't actually helping people in need, though I suppose I could argue I was at least fueling the economy by serving beef. So the only thing still unresolved was where I was going to stay for a week in the gap between when I had to leave my dorm and when I could take over a sublet on an apartment June first.

I had a plan. Turning the doorknob, I stepped inside and assessed the situation. My roommate, Kylie, snuggled with her boyfriend, Nathan, who lived in the apartment. Tyler and my other roommate, Rory, also cuddling. The sap factor in the living room was huge, with Kylie on Nathan's lap, their fingers entwined, while Tyler did that weird thing he was constantly doing where he played with Rory's hair and made me want to smack his hand away on her behalf. She always seemed okay with it, though, go figure.

"Hey, Jessica!" Kylie said brightly. "Cute top."

"Thanks." I had put on the tight red tank absently, then had wondered if more cleavage would be better for what I had in mind, then had been disgusted with myself for even thinking such a thought. So then I had decided no cleavage was necessary to my self-respect and pulled a Union Jack shirt on over the tank. Appearance was such a process. "What are you guys up to?"

"I'm watching *Inglourious Basterds*," came a voice from the kitchen. "Everyone else is engaged in foreplay."

Ugh. Trying not to sigh, I turned and saw Riley Mann, Tyler's older brother, popping the top of a beer can. He was not who I wanted to see.

"Jealous?" I asked him lightly, forcing a sardonic smile. Everything about Riley annoyed me, from his sarcasm to his inability to ever be serious, to the fact that he was hot as hell and so clearly knew it. I didn't see him very often since he worked full-time in construction, which was perfectly fine with me. It was easier to breathe without his testosterone choking the room.

He shook his head. "No. Sex is not worth the headache of a relationship. And my hand doesn't expect me to text it twenty times the next day."

There was mental imagery I did not need, though I couldn't argue with his opinion that relationships were a crapload of work. I made a face. "You're always so charming. Is Bill here?"

"He's studying in his room," Nathan told me. "He has a physics final tomorrow. God, I'm so glad I'm done with my exams."

I was done, too, which was why housing was becoming something of an issue. I only had two days until I had to vacate the dorms. "Okay, thanks." I started down the hall to Bill's room.

"You're going in there?" Nathan called after me. "I'm warning you, he's in a mood."

"I'm sure it's fine. I just want to say hi." Bill had been crushing on me for six months, ever since his girlfriend from high school had dumped him for a basketball player at Ohio State. We had hooked up a few times, but I had been totally clear about not wanting to date. I was not in the market for a relationship at all.

Without knocking I went into Bill's room. He was at his desk, and with the exception of the books and papers spread out in front of him, his room was neat as usual, bed made, no sign of finals stress. Until you got to his hair. Then the tension was evident in the floppy curls sticking out in various directions, looking like he hadn't made nice with a hairbrush in days. His glasses were sliding down his nose when he looked up, and he was a very cute modern interpretation of the absentminded genius.

"Hey," he said, looking vacantly at me.

"Hey. How's studying going?" I propped a hip on the corner of his desk and smiled.

"Not bad, but I still have a lot to go through. Did you need something, or did you just want to hang out? Because I can't until tomorrow."

"I wanted to know if I can stay here with you, in your room, for a few days." Okay, so it was more like eight days, but who was counting?

"What?" He frowned. "What do you mean?" He tapped his pen on his lips and blinked up at me.

"I need a place to crash until I can get in the apartment I sublet. There's no way I'm sleeping on that couch in the living room. It's like chain mail. But I can sleep in your bed with you, right?" I smiled and used the tip of my finger to push his glasses up. "I promise I won't kick you in my sleep like I did last time."

For a second he didn't say anything. Then he shook his head. "No."

That was definitely not the answer I was expecting. "What? Why not? Okay, so I know I can't promise to have control over my limbs when I'm sleeping, but you can always kick me back. I don't mind." He couldn't be seriously telling me no. My heart rate started to increase, anxiety creeping up over the back of my neck.

"I don't care if you kick me, it's not that." Bill sighed. "Look, Jess, we both know it's no secret I like you, and you've been totally straight up with me about not returning the sentiment, and I appreciate that. Maybe it's insane of me to say no, because sometimes I do manage to talk you into hooking up when you take pity on me, but I can't share a bed with you every night for a week and not feel like shit about it. I just can't."

My jaw dropped, and I felt a hot flood of shame in my mouth, which made me angry. I hadn't done anything to feel bad about, despite what my dad's opinion about it would have been. "You make it sound so sketch. We're friends. We've hooked up when we both felt like it, not because I was desperate and you were my only option or because I felt sorry for you. I'm not that nice of a person that I'll blow you out of pity. I just like you as a friend and I think you're cute. We have fun. Apparently, I was totally wrong in thinking you felt the same way."

"I do feel the same way," he insisted. "The problem is, I feel more than that, and I'm just not into torturing myself. I want you to be my 'girlfriend.'" He made air quotes. "Pathetic, I know."

The thought of being anyone's girlfriend made me want to throw up in my mouth a little. There was no way I wanted to give a guy that much control over my emotions and my time. I had finally gotten away from that for the first time in my life.

"I'm sorry. It's not pathetic, it's just . . ."

"It's you, not me." He rolled his eyes. "I know. You can save the let-him-down-gently speech for another dude. I get it."

I had to admit, that was kind of a relief. "This is awkward," I told him.

"Probably more for me than for you," he said with a nervous laugh. "Look, you can stay on the couch in here."

"Except now it will be weird." It already was.

"No, it won't. I won't be needy or anything. I just need to have some self-preservation."

"Okay, I understand." I did. But it made it different. I couldn't casually touch him anymore. I couldn't flirt without feeling like I was leading him on, and I would have to be careful around him. I

fought the urge to sigh. Why did everything have to be so complicated between guys and girls? Curse hormones. "Good luck on
your final."

"Thanks." He gave me a smile, then he returned his attention
to his book.

I left, feeling deflated and oddly sad knowing Bill and I couldn't
quite be friends in the same way we had been. But then again,
maybe we'd never really been just friends, because I had always
known he liked me. And why did that suddenly make me feel so
guilty?

"That was fast," Riley said the second I came into the living
room, his feet up on the coffee table, expression bored. "I guess
that's why they call it a quickie."

"Shut up," I said, with more vehemence than I intended. I was
feeling bad, and I couldn't precisely figure out why Bill's rejection
had bothered me so much. I didn't need Riley judging me.

"What's wrong?" Rory asked, peeling herself off Tyler's chest,
where she was splayed like plastic wrap.

"I just don't have anywhere to stay for the next week, that's
all." I didn't want to say in front of Riley that Bill had turned me
down. It would be like handing him the material for a ten-minute
stand-up routine at my expense. No, thanks.

"You can stay here," Nathan said.

"Thanks, but I don't think that's going to work."

"Why not?" Kylie asked.

I shot her a look, hoping she'd get the hint.

"Did you and the nerd have a fight?" Riley asked. "Is he not
putting out enough for you?"

It really wasn't fair that such a beautiful face was on such an
asshole of a guy. Riley was a little shorter than Tyler, just as mus-

cular, but whereas Tyler had a certain hardness to his face, Riley had been gifted with adorable dimples and large eyes. It was almost tragic he was such a jerk-off. I ignored him, but it wasn't easy, because he seemed to take great pleasure in pissing me off. I really wanted to throw something at him. Like my fist. Right into his cocky face.

"You can stay at my house," Tyler offered. "The boys and I are going to Rory's dad's for a week, remember, so you'd have a bed to sleep on."

There was a thought, though it was an intimidating one. "Is it safe?" I asked, before I thought about how rude that actually sounded. Tyler and Riley lived with their two younger brothers in a lower income neighborhood in a house the bank was in the process of foreclosing on since their mother had died. Riley had lived in a basement before that, but once his mom overdosed, he had moved back in. I'd never been there, but I was picturing a drug-infested neighborhood with drive-by shootings and prostitutes on every corner. My parents lived in a minimansion in a small town, so I didn't exactly have street cred. My experience with poverty was limited to movies and episodes of *Cops* on my laptop. It was like a bear walking through the desert. I had no previous exposure.

"I mean, won't the neighbors think I'm breaking and entering?" I added, as a very lame cover to my initial question.

"Princess, I don't think anyone is going to think you've broken into our shithole and are squatting," Riley said, rolling his eyes. "If anything, they'll just think you've come over to score drugs."

"Rory stays with me all the time," Tyler added. "No one will even notice. People keep to themselves in our neighborhood."

"I never feel unsafe there," Rory said. "But then again, I'm never sleeping there alone. Tyler is always with me."

"I've never lived alone," I said. Even for a week, the thought had a certain appeal. No one's opinion but my own. No rules. No guilt. No feeling bad that I could never live up to anyone's expectations. It sounded awesome and scary. I wanted to try it, just to see what it would be like. "That sounds great, Ty. Thanks for offering."

"Have both of you forgotten something?" Riley asked, picking up his beer.

"What?" I said, wary. I just knew I wasn't going to like whatever he was going to say.

"I'm not going to Rory's dad's to swim for a week like a kid at summer camp. I'll be here, working. Living in my house."

Oh, God. I couldn't help it. I made a face.

The corner of Riley's mouth turned up. "That's exactly how I feel about it, princess."

"I think it will be good for you guys," Kylie said, an eternal optimist. Or suffering from massive delusions. "You can become better friends this way."

"Maybe we don't want to become friends," Riley told her. "Maybe we like not liking each other."

I almost laughed. There was a certain truth to that. I basically felt like I'd seen all I needed to see to know I didn't need to see more. But if I said that Kylie's head would explode. She was a very honest and kind person, and she didn't always get my point of view. Or anything involving math.

"How much will you even see each other? You both work and it has three bedrooms," Tyler said. "It seems stupid to sleep on a floor somewhere when there's plenty of room at the house."

"It's up to Riley," I said, because that only seemed fair. It was his house. "Maybe he wants some alone time with all of you gone."

I didn't mean that to sound quite as weird as it did.

He laughed. "Does that come right after Me Time and Circle Time?" He stood up and moved further into my space than was strictly appropriate.

It was a game of chicken, and I lost by instantly backing up. Damn it. He smirked in triumph.

"I'll be fine. I can handle it if you can."

I was playing right into him and I knew it, but I couldn't stop myself. "Of course I can handle it. What's there to handle?"

He stared at me, his eyebrows raised, a challenge in his deep brown eyes. The stubble on his chin was visible, and I could smell the subtle scent of soap and a splash of cologne. He looked and smelled very, very masculine, and I was suddenly aware of my body in a way that made me seriously annoyed.

"Bring some beer."

"I'm not twenty-one." Not that it had ever stopped me from drinking, but I wasn't going to give Riley anything I didn't have to. I did not want to feel like I owed him. It was Tyler who had made the offer of a place to crash, so if anyone deserved thanks, it was him, not his arrogant brother.

For a second, Riley's eyes roamed over my chest, like he could gauge my age by my boobs. Such a tool.

But then he just said, "You can borrow my ID."

And I couldn't help it. I laughed. "Because we're practically twins."

He nodded. "Though I am *slightly* better looking."

I snorted. "I have better hair."

"I can drink more whiskey than you."

"I'm smarter."

"I'm stronger. We should mud wrestle so I can prove it."

I bit my lip so I wouldn't throw a scathing response back at him, or worse, laugh. He didn't deserve the attention, or knowing he'd gotten under my skin, which was what he wanted.

But for a split second I wondered if I should sleep on the couch after all. Because Riley seemed to be the one person who could get an emotional response out of me, even if it was just anger.

And emotions were dangerous.

They led to being trapped, like my mother, in the pretty prison of my father's house.

I was never going to let that happen.

"I call dibs on the bathroom first in the mornings," I told Riley.

Then to let him know that he did not intimidate me, and that I was always in control, I turned and walked away.

# CHAPTER TWO

I SHOULD HAVE TAKEN NATHAN UP ON HIS OFFER FOR A RIDE. Instead I had decided that in further pursuit of independence I was going to learn how to use public transportation. What I didn't understand was that the city bus was nothing like the charter bus we took to church camp growing up. When you were a member of the New Hope congregation, you didn't sacrifice comfort in the pursuit of your relationship with God. My dad was fond of saying that even Jesus wore sandals rather than going barefoot. I didn't really think it was exactly the same thing to have shoes versus a six-thousand-square-foot house with a closet full of designer clothes, but when I had suggested this at the age of thirteen I had lost the use of my cell phone for a month.

*Since you're so quick to point out others' alleged hypocrisy,* he had said, *let me eliminate yours for you.*

Of course, in the end, all he had done was make me the ultimate hypocrite. I paid lip service to his church and its many rules and nothing more.

Eventually, when he figured out the truth—which he would, because it was becoming harder and harder to fake who I was— he would dismiss me from his life. I knew it as surely as I knew he had a flask of vodka hidden in his nightstand drawer. So when the inevitable happened, I needed to be ready. I needed to have seen the real world, or at least a bigger slice of it than the narrow view- point I'd been raised in.

So the bus.

Yeah, not such a brilliant idea when you're dragging two very large hot-pink suitcases with you and you've never ridden public transportation in your whole life.

A crusty old man drooled as he mumbled and gestured to me repeatedly. I slunk down in my seat, suitcases wedged against the window next to me because I couldn't understand anything he was saying, and I totally didn't want to understand. Two teenage boys with their jeans down around their thighs kept shoving each other and laughing as they made blow-job gestures in my direction. I ignored them. If I knew them, I would have told them off, but I figured it was possible they had guns in those insanely outdated and slouchy pants, or at the very least they wouldn't hesitate to harass me. The bus smelled disgusting, and the air-conditioning blasting only served to float the odor around. As I compulsively checked my phone for the bus route map, I kept checking the street signs every time we turned, afraid I was going to miss my stop.

I had texted Riley to let him know I was showing up around six, and he had responded with, "Yippee." The feeling was mutual.

By my estimates, it was only a thirty-minute bus ride to the nearest intersection to Tyler and Riley's house. The bus chart had arrival as 6:03, and I kept glancing at the time, wishing I hadn't worn flip-flops and shorts. I felt like bus crud was rubbing on me from the seat and floor. My heels and calves felt vulnerable.

"Hey, blond girl," one of the teenage boys said, moving from the back of the bus to drop down in the seat behind me.

That was probably me he was referring to.

Glancing at him, I said, "Hey," and went back to my phone. I didn't want to have a conversation with him, but I knew if I totally ignored him he would be calling me a stuck-up bitch. Sometimes there really wasn't a way to win as a girl.

"Where you goin'? This don't look like your neighborhood."

"I'm moving in with my boyfriend," I told him, flatly. Let him think I had a big old gangbanging, drug-dealing badass of a boyfriend.

His eyebrows shot up, and he looked like he didn't believe me. He was about fifteen, and he was more attitude than anything else, since he probably weighed less than me. I could see his ribs through his basketball jersey. "Your boyfriend lives here?"

I didn't answer because I realized the bus driver wasn't slowing down, and the street that was supposed to be my stop was just a few feet ahead. "Isn't he going to stop here?" I said, freaking out, starting to sit up and slip my purse over my head like a cross-body bag. It was too short to do that, and it cut into my armpit, but I needed both hands for the luggage. And maybe to tackle the driver if he didn't stop, because my little social experiment was over. I didn't want to be on this bus anymore. My armpits were sweating even though it was freezing from the air-conditioning because I was a little stressed, I had to admit.

The kid looked at me like I was a complete moron. "If you want to get off, you have to pull." He reached over and yanked on a laundry line–type cord above the windows and I immediately heard a ding.

"Oh." Duh. Guess the driver wasn't psychic. "Thanks." The bus started to slow down, so I started to tug my bags into the aisle, regretting the "Stop following me. Follow Jesus" sticker Kylie had bought for me as a joke and slapped on the front of my suitcase.

For some reason, I expected the kid to offer to help, since he was so clearly interested in flirting with me. But he actually slipped around my bag like it was a nothing more than an obstacle, even as it fell sideways into the opposite seat. His friend followed him. The bus stopped, and I stumbled forward as I managed to haul both bags down the aisle, yelling, "I'm getting off at this stop!" to the bus driver in case he didn't glance back.

He glared at me in his large rearview mirror, obviously impatient with how long it was taking for me to exit.

"Thanks," I said, breathless, basically falling down the stairs in an avalanche of hair and luggage. Once on the curb, I readjusted so I could pull each bag with one hand and tried to ignore the fact that the two teenagers were just standing there on the corner, looking in no particular hurry to go anywhere, belts barely holding up their pants, arms already sporting a couple of tattoos. It was hot on the sidewalk, the air a humid mix of gas fumes from the bus and a chicken restaurant. The back of my neck got damp as I started walking.

Immediately, I knew the boys were following me. So I paused and pulled out my phone, confirming the direction I was going in. Then I took a gamble and called Riley, propping the phone on my shoulder so I could keep walking. I didn't think he would answer, because I didn't know any guy who answered his phone, but I was starting to get weirded out. The neighborhood was what I had expected, and while it didn't seem anything other than a little tired and lower income, I felt very obvious as an outsider. There were empty shops, a dingy restaurant, a tattoo parlor, a Check 'n Go kiosk, and potholes the size of a Volkswagen Beetle in the road. On the side street I turned down, the houses were close together, small, some of them run down. If anyone had grass, it was burned out, brown and dusty, or it was a breeding ground for pricker weeds. Some were as high as my knees as I trudged down the sidewalk, my purse bumping my breast with each step.

Riley actually answered. "Hello."

"Hey! It's Jessica. Um, I'm almost at your house. I, uh, took the bus, and I'm on your street and well . . ."

I could practically hear his eyebrows shooting up in disbelief. "You took the bus?"

"Yeah. And I think these dudes are following me," I murmured in as low of a voice as possible.

"What? Shit." There was rustling. "Keep walking. I'll come get you."

"'K." I dropped the phone on the sidewalk when I tried to end the call with my finger still hooked around the suitcase handle. Bending down to retrieve it, I looked back at the guys.

One had a baseball hat on sideways, and now that they were off the bus they had both stripped off their T-shirts in the heat. One was tanned, the other glowing so starkly white, utterly hairless, and blinking against the sun, he looked like a baby mole. Now that I knew Riley was just a minute or two away, I felt more irritated than scared.

"Why didn't your man pick you up?" the one with the hat asked.

I stood up, spotting a car coming up the street. "He is." Relieved, I saw it was Riley as he pulled up and put the car in park.

Leaving it running, he opened the door and got out. He wasn't wearing a shirt either, and I shook my head to try to get my sweaty hair out of my eyes, wishing I could fully appreciate his chest. But I was more concerned with getting in the car and away from Beavis and Butt-Head. I was already dragging my bag off the curb when Riley stepped up, barely giving me a nod before grabbing the other one.

"Wassup," he said casually to the guys, but I could see his shoulders were stiff as he rolled the suitcase behind him and made a point of turning his back on them. They didn't look like any particular threat to Riley, given he was twice their width, and I felt better.

"Your bitch is fine," the scrawny one said.

Gee. Now my life was complete. They thought I was attractive. I rolled my eyes as I opened the back door of Riley's car and shoved my suitcase in.

"Thanks," was all Riley said. I realized he was gesturing with his left hand for me to go around and get in the car, so I did. He loaded my other bag in the backseat.

Then he stood and spoke to them in a very casual, friendly tone. "If you ever see her walking in the neighborhood again, you cross to the other side of the street, do you understand me? You don't look at her, you don't talk to her. Stay at least fifteen feet away from her, or I will fuck your shit up, no questions asked."

"Hey, we don't want no trouble," one of them said, holding up his hands and looking alarmed.

I almost felt bad for them. Almost. But the truth was, their intention had been to harass me, and that was bullshit. A woman should be able to walk on the sidewalk without taking crap.

"Good." Climbing back in, Riley turned the car around in the nearest driveway, while I yanked my purse off and stuck my right arm out the window to air out.

Lifting my hair off my neck, I twisted it into a knot and tucked it through so it would stay up for at least the drive to the house. "Holy shit, it's hot out here. Thanks for picking me up."

"Why the hell were you riding the bus?" Riley glanced over at me, and he was shaking his head in disbelief, amused. "Do you know who rides the bus?"

"Teenage boys and old men who smell like pee?"

"Exactly." He gave me a small laugh. "Welcome to paradise, Jessica."

"It wasn't awful," I told him, which was true. It had been more unnerving than really horrific. Especially now that I was in his car and in zero danger, the bus didn't seem that bad at all in hindsight. In fact, I felt a little triumphant that I had managed it on my own. Well, almost my own. I suppose without Riley it might have had a more irritating outcome, but I didn't think those guys were actually dangerous. Then again, Kylie always told me I downplayed trouble, and I suppose that was true. After all, I was moving into Riley's house in a sketchy neighborhood when I was supposed to be off building new houses for the financially needy. That was borrowing trouble with my parents, no doubt, if they ever found out.

Though as we pulled into Riley's drive, I thought probably the Mann boys qualified for the title of financially needy themselves. It was, to be totally honest, a shithole, a house that no one had cared about in a long time. Exactly what I was expecting, but as the bungalow sagged in the heat, it was undeniable.

"You've got balls, I'll give you that," he said.

"Are you complimenting me?" And why did that stupidly please me? That wasn't exactly a glowing report. But then again, I did pride myself on being strong, so that he thought it couldn't help but make me happy.

"If I am, don't worry, it's backhanded," he assured me as he parked the car. "Now why do you look like you packed to study in Europe for a year? I thought you're here for only a week."

How to explain without lying? I only wanted to keep some of the information from him, not be totally dishonest. But I didn't want him to know I was lying to my parents. "This is all my stuff from my dorm room. Well, a lot of it. Kylie took some of it home for me, but I couldn't ask her to drag all of it. It wouldn't fit in Mark's car."

"Who is Mark?"

That was what he pulled out of that paragraph? Yay. That was an easy question to answer. "He's a guy Kylie and I went to high school with who has a car on campus. He usually gives us a ride if our parents don't pick us up." Then I was immediately sorry I'd mentioned parents. I didn't want Riley to ask me about mine.

But he seemed to lose interest in the conversation in general, stepping out of the car, giving me a great view of his perfect ass in jeans that fit the way they should on a guy, not too loose, not too tight. They were riding just slightly past his hips, his back muscles clearly outlined as he twisted. Head thunk. What was I doing? I was supposed to ignore his hotness. It was a mental pact I'd made with myself over the last two days as I had packed up my room. It was the only way I could justify staying with Riley, to swear totally and on my favorite pair of Guess jeans that I would not pay attention to anything about him other than to note how annoying he was.

I opened the back door to grab the second suitcase, but he was already dragging it across the seat.

"Thanks," I said.

"No problem." He studied the sticker on it and fought a smile. "So were your little friends on the bus with you?"

"Yes. I think they were following me."

"Oh, most definitely. You stick out like a pink thumb."

"Ha ha. You don't think they were dangerous, do you?" Unless I was mistaken as to how to conceal a weapon, I hadn't seen anything on those two. Then again, their jeans had been like garbage bags, so what did I know?

"Not to me. To you? Maybe. You were smart to call me."

"Thanks, Dad." I reached for a suitcase to roll it up the driveway, but he waved me off and got both.

"Your sarcasm is annoying," he told me.

"Why? Because it reminds you of yourself?" I tossed at him, walking over the gravel and up the crumbling steps behind him. For a second, I almost questioned their structural soundness, but then I realized that would be rude.

"That's entirely possible," he admitted.

The door wasn't locked. He shoved it open and swept his arm out for me to enter. "Mi shitty casa es su shitty casa."

"You need a doormat with that on it," I told him, brushing by him, determined not to look at his chest, or his eyes, both of which were way more dangerous to my health than the dudes on the bus. My arm touched his pec despite my best efforts, and his skin was warm.

"If we had a doormat it would get stolen," he said.

I stepped into the stifling heat of the living room. There was no air-conditioning. Craptastic. It smelled like old cigarettes and boy. Sometimes I could tolerate boy but the cigarettes I couldn't. Wrinkling my nose, I moved forward, peering into a small kitchen while trying to look like I wasn't checking it out.

"You sure you want to do this?" he asked.

I glanced back to see him watching me carefully, my suitcases standing at attention on either side of him.

No, I wasn't sure.

"Rory doesn't mind it here, but Rory is in love with Tyler. For some bizarre reason, people are willing to put up with a lot of shit when they're in love. I know this place is a dump, so there is still time for you to bail."

It was tempting. The carpet was dirty brown, stained with years of street dirt and mud and who knew what else. The couch had a sag to each cushion, and it might have been a faded red plaid, but it was hard to say exactly. The oak coffee table was covered with video game boxes and an ashtray loaded with butts. There were no curtains, just a sheet that had been hung with thumbtacks. I wanted to bail, I'm not going to lie. But it was just too rude. If I had absorbed anything positive from my childhood, it was manners that popped up when I least expected them. "No, it's fine. I appreciate you putting up with this arrangement since it was Tyler's idea and you and I are not exactly best friends."

He shrugged. "No big deal. There is plenty of room with the boys gone."

"Well, thank you." That was about as gushing as I was going to get about it, so I hoped he heard my sincerity.

"You're welcome."

However, I couldn't stop myself from saying, "Can I open a window? I have asthma, and the smoke bothers me." Which wasn't exactly the truth. At all. But I was going to be coughing in another ten minutes if I didn't get some fresh air.

Riley gave me an incredulous look. "You don't have asthma. You're just saying that because you think it stinks in here."

Bingo. "What? Of course I do. Why would I lie about having asthma? And how do you know if I have it or not?" Maybe that was defending myself too passionately. I shut my mouth, cheeks just a little hot that he had busted me in my lie.

"I know because I've seen you outside in the middle of winter, I've seen you dance all night at a club, and I've seen you talk enough to make your teeth ache, but I've never once seen you use an inhaler. And you've never mentioned it before, and Tyler and Nathan smoke in the apartment all the time."

Damn it. Why couldn't he be an idiot? It would be much easier to manipulate him that way. "Fine, you're right. But I am sensitive to the smoke. Besides, opening the window will let some of the heat out."

"It lets heat in."

"No, it doesn't. How does that even make sense?" I sat on the couch and my ass almost hit the floor I sank so deep. It was like being bear-hugged by a marshmallow.

"How many houses without AC have you lived in?"

What could I say to that? "None. But that doesn't change the fact that your logic is illogical."

"That's an absurd statement. And it's true. You keep the windows closed and covered during the day, open them to the breeze at night."

"So what time can I open them? Is there like a set time? Or do they just automatically fly open at sunset?" I coughed, which was actually an accident. The smoke haze really was getting to me. Or maybe I just needed a drink of water, but either way, it was bad timing.

Riley gave a snort of laughter. "Oh, princess, you won't win any Oscars, but I give you points for trying. Look, I think we need some house rules."

"Oh, goodie."

"Let's go sit outside for a minute and we can discuss it."

Why did I feel so suspicious? I eyed him. "Why?"

"Because it doesn't stink out there. Well, not like smoke anyway."

"Are you being thoughtful?" I asked, teasing, but kind of touched.

"Yeah, I suppose I am, so you better enjoy it while you can."

Then again, I wasn't sure how thoughtful it really was when he reached for a pack of cigarettes on the coffee table and grabbed them.

Maybe a house rule could be that he had to wear a shirt, because his bare skin was messing with my head. And my hormones. He had the same tattoo as Tyler, the words TRUE FAMILY on his bicep in a tribal script. Rory had told me TRUE were the guys' initials, meant to signify their solidarity. How they were always there for one another, despite the fact that their father was in prison, and before she had died, their mother had been a negligent parent and drug abuser.

What would it be like to have a brother like that, instead of the self-serving, backstabbing one I had gotten? What would it be like to have Riley Mann loyal to you? A shiver ran through me despite the heat, and I focused on his other tattoos, the screaming skull that marched down his flank and the weird thing on his chest that may or may not have been a winged werewolf.

I followed him through the kitchen to the back door, where he took a seat at an old, peeling, and rotten picnic table. I sat gingerly on the opposite side, worried about splinters in my butt or at least getting lead paint poisoning from the chips that were clinging to my hands just from pressing my palms on the boards. Riley lit his cigarette and blew the smoke away from me. He smoked the same brand as his brother, and he looked similar enough to Tyler that there were moments that I wondered why I felt so much more on guard around him than I did Tyler. Back before Tyler and Rory were together, I had even had sex with Tyler, more than once, and yet I thought of him as a friend, someone I was totally comfortable around. My reaction to Riley was different, and it really made no damn sense.

I was attracted to him in a way I never had been with Tyler, and it was annoying.

Maybe it was because Tyler was more sincere, where Riley hid his emotions behind humor. It meant he could be thinking or feeling anything. It was both annoying and sexy.

"So, house rules?" I asked him. "I can't wait to hear where you're going with this." I was sure it would piss me off, and anger was better than sitting there thinking that he made my vag tingle.

"I don't mean to be a dick," he started.

Promising.

"But the thing is, it's my house and I should be able to do whatever the fuck I want in my own house."

Perfect. "If this is you not meaning to be a dick, I can't wait to hear where the rest of this is going."

He made a face and took another drag off of his cigarette. "*But,* while you're here, I won't smoke in the house. It's summer, and there's no reason I can't come outside. Truthfully, Tyler is the real nicotine junkie in this house anyway. I only smoke two or three a day."

That was actually pretty damn nice. Probably the nicest thing he'd ever said to me, and I had no smart-ass response to it. "Thanks."

But then I couldn't help but add, "If you only smoke two or three a day, why smoke at all?"

He made a face at me. "Who asked for your opinion?"

I was already in it. I might as well finish my true thoughts on the subject. It was one thing to ruin his own lungs, but kids never have a choice. They are forced to live like their parents or whoever is raising them. "I have to say, I don't think secondhand smoke is good for Jayden and Easton."

His younger brother Jayden was eighteen, and he had Down syndrome. He was always smiling and laughing, and he was easy to like. Easton was only eleven, and who his father was seemed to be a mystery. He was quiet and serious, and the few times I had seen him, he gave me the willies, I can't lie. But that didn't mean he deserved lung cancer at eleven years old because of his brothers.

Riley's jaw clenched, and I knew I had made him mad. "House Rule Number One: Mind your own fucking business."

"That's kind of vague," I complained. "I mean, I'm staying in your house, so I am sort of in your business unintentionally."

"How about this? You're staying here for free and I'm letting you. If you criticize the way I'm taking care of my brothers, I'll throw you and your pink luggage out into the fucking street." And he blew a huge cloud of smoke right into my face.

Okay, so maybe I had gone too far. I didn't mean to actually imply he was doing a shitty job with his brothers. Well, I guess I had in regard to the smoking issue, but that wasn't a general statement about his surrogate parenting. "Got it. Sorry."

"That about killed you to say, didn't it?" he asked, with a sudden grin.

Yes. "Of course not. I was wrong. Just because it isn't healthy for the boys doesn't mean I should point that out to you." Hm. That wasn't really a great apology. I tried to channel my New Hope bible study personality—the one that was polite and kind and nonjudgmental. But that part of me seemed to be missing whenever I wasn't in my hometown of Troy, and most of the time I liked it that way.

Riley rolled his eyes. "Rule Number Two: Don't piss me off."

"I was thinking these rules would be more like along the lines of wash your dirty dishes and lock the house when you leave. You know, specific things. I feel like you're setting me up to fail."

"I feel like you're setting me up to have an ulcer." He clutched his chest like he was in pain and grimaced. "Or have a heart attack."

I laughed. "Now who wants an Oscar?"

"I get up at seven for work."

"A.M.? Ew."

"So I would appreciate it if you don't make a ton of noise after eleven at night since I'll be in bed."

Why did a shiver just roll up my spine? It was eight billion degrees outside. Oh, yeah, I knew why. It was Riley mentioning the B word. Now I was picturing him naked with a sheet up to his waist. "Sure, no problem. I usually work three to eleven, so I'll be quiet when I come in."

"You're not planning on taking the bus back here at night, are you?" The very thought looked like it was increasing the pain in his chest.

"No. I can take a cab. It will only be, like, ten bucks."

"You can sleep in Jayden and Easton's room. It has an AC window unit."

Yes. Yes, yes, yes. "Really? Oh my God, I love you." I had been imagining sweaty sleepless nights, my thighs stuck together. "Where are you going to sleep?"

"Oh, I have a unit in my room, too. Only Tyler's room doesn't have one."

I would have preferred to sleep in Tyler's room instead of where a couple of teen and preteen boys were living, but cool air won out over a funk-free environment. "How did Tyler get so screwed?"

"Cuz he's an asshole."

"Well, that clears it up." I rolled my eyes, picking at my T-shirt to get air circulation between my boobs.

"You can use anything in the kitchen, though I'm not sure why you'd want to. But there are actually real kitchen things now that Rory's been back around. She bakes and shit."

"I won't be baking." I would rather do just about anything else, frankly.

"That does not surprise me. You and Rory aren't much alike, are you?"

I shrugged. "I guess not, on the surface. She's not big on sarcasm or teasing."

"You have those down pretty good, I'd say."

"You, too." Grinning at Riley, I added, "I feel like we should high-five here or something."

"Don't get carried away."

My tongue came out before I could stop it. But he just smiled. "In return for not smoking in the house, I'm asking you to keep your girl shit out of the bathroom."

Girl shit? "If I can't keep my shit in the bathroom, where else would it go?" I asked, amused.

"You know what I mean. I don't want to go to brush my teeth and there isn't an inch of counter space to use because you have creams and equipment and whatever."

"*Equipment?*" I snorted. "I don't use power tools to get ready in the morning. But fine, I will put my blow-dryer away after each use. And I promise to never ask you to pick up a box of tampons for me on the way home from work."

The horror on his face made me laugh. "Don't tell me you have never bought tampons before?"

He shook his head. "I'm a dude. Why would I buy tampons?"

"For a girlfriend." It seemed obvious to me.

He flicked his spent cigarette off into the yard. I could see there were literally hundreds of butts in the dirt that might have been an actual yard back in about 1965. There was such pride in home ownership at work right here.

"No. I probably would if she was, like, bleeding on my car seats, but otherwise, no."

Was he for real? "You are so ridiculous. You're not talking about a bullet wound. Don't be gross."

"You're the one who brought up tampons. And speaking of that whole guy-girl thing . . ."

Were we? I didn't think we were, but this could be interesting. "Yes?"

"If you have Nerd Boy or someone over here, that's fine, whatever, just keep it down, okay? And wash my brother's sheets the next day. Laundry is in the basement."

My jaw fell so fast and far it was amazing it didn't land in my lap. "I hadn't really given any thought to it. Since it's only a week, I think I can manage to hold off on hookups. But feel free to do whatever yourself. You don't even need to keep it down—I have earplugs. Kylie snores."

What the hell was I saying? Earplugs crammed into my cranium wouldn't drown out the sound of sex if I knew to listen for the sound of sex. The last thing in the freaking world I wanted was for

Riley to be banging some chick just a few feet and a thin wall away from me.

But why was that exactly? It wasn't like I wanted to bang him. Not really.

A horrible thought occurred to me. With the house to himself, maybe Riley had been envisioning a week of brother-free boning. Maybe he had a girlfriend. He could. How would I know? No, wait. He'd said he didn't want a relationship, so there wasn't a girlfriend. That didn't mean he hadn't been planning on a sweaty sexfest, though.

I wondered what Riley's type was. I realized I had no clue.

Then again, I wasn't sure I knew what my own type was.

"That's very considerate of you," he said dryly.

"I'm like that," I told him. "What can I say?"

"So you don't mind if I have a girl over?" He was studying me, his brown eyes indecipherable.

Yes. "No." I waved my hand. "God, why would I care? I mean, it's your house. You should be able to do what you want, right? House Rule Number One."

Riley nodded slowly. "Right. Thanks for understanding."

That was me, being a big person. I wanted to beat the shit out of myself for being so stupid. This was what being nice got you— your worst nightmare. I may want to throw beer cans at Riley on a regular basis, but I did not want to see him making out with some giggling twit on the couch. Because she would be a twit, that was a guarantee. She would also be pretty and I would hate her for it.

And now I was jealous of a fictional girl. Fabulous.

I stood up. "I need some water or something. My throat is super dry. If you think of any other rules, let me know." I needed to get away from him. "I think I'll run to the store and get some essentials like diet pop and yogurt." Possibly an air freshener or two.

"And how are you going to get to the store, princess?"

Riley wasn't easy to charm, but I went for it. I gave him a pleading smile. "I was hoping I could borrow your car?" I showed lots of teeth and pulled my shoulders up by my ears. It usually worked with most guys.

He shook his head and gave a scoff of a laugh. "You're fucking unreal. The keys are on the coffee table."

Hot damn. "Really? Thanks!" I impulsively threw my arms around his bare shoulders and gave him a half hug.

It was a mistake. He smelled like skin, and his body was hard beneath my touch. I heard a sharp intake of his breath near my ear. I pulled back quickly, my nipples suddenly tight. "Thanks, Riley," I repeated.

He just waved me off, not looking at me. "Bring beer."

"I'll try."

As I left, I saw he was pulling another cigarette out of the pack. Interesting.

# CHAPTER THREE

WITHOUT KNOWING WHO THE BED BELONGED TO, I HAD CHOSEN the one closest to the air-conditioning unit stuffed into the window. The second window was bare of blinds or drapes, so I had duct-taped my hoodie to it, arms spread out like an Abercrombie crucifix. The thought made me grimace reflexively, twenty years of religious training strong. My father would have a heart attack and die if I said something like that out loud.

The makeshift window covering was because I was pretty sure that picnic table was right outside and I didn't like the idea that Riley could be sitting out there watching me wander around his brothers' bedroom. Not that I thought Riley was a creeper, but it just made me feel better to have it covered. It would prevent the morning sun from pouring in, too.

Back from the store, I leaned against the wall on the bed and called Kylie, knowing this was too important for texting. I needed to hear that she understood how important this was. Surveying the room as the phone rang, I tried to imagine Jayden and Easton in here, and I couldn't quite picture it. There wasn't really anything personal to the room. The walls were blank, the sheets generic, the quilts old crocheted afghans in a god-awful orange-and-black color combo. I realized they might have been made to represent the Cincinnati Bengals football team, but that didn't excuse the fact that they were just ugly.

The closet had clothes hanging up, but most were on the floor in a pile. I only saw one lone pair of shoes, which made me wonder how two guys survived with three pairs of shoes between them, assuming they currently both had shoes on their feet. There was a dresser in the corner that had been painted black but was chipping off everywhere, showing the original oak stain beneath it. There were a few things on top, like earbuds, a couple of dollars in change, and a receipt for the gas station. A Twix bar and a Dr Pepper. Yes, I looked.

It was nothing like the way I'd grown up, my mother's personal doll to dress and show off, the house a tribute to God and the almighty dollar.

"What's up!" Kylie said as she answered.

Her energy amazed me. Or maybe it was her inability to ever feel depressed. I envied that about her, and sometimes wondered if we were friends because I wanted to leech some of that positivity off of her. But I couldn't be that selfish, could I? I loved Kylie like a sister and we had been friends since middle school, when we both made the volleyball team, and we had been an inseparable pair ever since. In college we had just added Rory to our friendship.

"Hey. What are you doing? You didn't drop my stuff off yet, did you?" The plan was for Kylie to take my dorm junk to my parents' house for the summer to store since they had plenty of room. Kylie's family had a typical suburban brick colonial, a decent size, but nothing like my house, plus she had three younger siblings, so their house was loaded down with sports equipment.

"No, I'll do it tomorrow. Tonight I'm going to dinner with my parents."

"Okay, cool. Remember what you have to say to my mom. My dad won't be there during the day so you won't have to see him. You have to tell my mom that I will call her from Appalachia."

"I know. No worries. I won't screw it up."

Kylie and Rory knew the truth, of course, but Kylie was the only one I would ask to directly lie on my behalf. I trusted her totally to have my back, but the problem was that with Kylie, you never knew when she might flake out. Sometimes her words moved faster than her thoughts, and she was notorious for "oops" moments, like the one in high school, when she had told a guy I just met that my dad was a minister. Or when she had told Rory we had offered Tyler money to hit on her. Or told Nathan that he shook his head like a wet dog during oral sex.

"You cannot in any way, shape, or form tell my mother that I am still in Cincinnati. Pinky swear."

"I pinky swear. God."

"Or I will be dead. I will be put under house arrest until I'm twenty-one and that is almost eight months from now."

"I know." I could practically hear her rolling her eyes.

Still sweating, I stripped off my T-shirt and stood in front of the air-conditioning, letting it blast straight onto my stomach and chest. "When do you start the internship? Next week, right?"

"Yeppers. It's going to be awesome."

Kylie was going to be working at the hospital in the nurses' station, doing their menial crap. It sounded like a whole new dimension of hell to me, but Kylie loved people, and she was excited to be giving directions to visiting family members and taking Popsicles to sick people.

There was a knock on my door, and I told Kylie, "Hang on." Then I called in the direction of the hall, "Yeah?"

What I didn't expect was Riley to actually open the door. *Yeah* didn't mean *open. Yeah* didn't mean *check me out in my bra, letting the air-conditioning freeze my sweat in stink streams down between my tits and disappear into my belly button.* I almost dropped my phone when I turned and saw him standing in the doorway, his eyes trained on my bra. Granted, it wasn't anything that wouldn't be shown in a bikini. I wasn't even showing as much, because I had shorts on, but it didn't make me feel any less naked. Especially given the way he was staring, his nostrils flaring.

"What?" I asked, irritated. Or turned on, whatever you wanted to call it.

His eyes finally lifted and met mine, but they were dark and sexy, intense. "I ordered a pizza when you were at the store. It's here if you want some."

"Cool. Thanks." I was trying to be casual about the whole thing, but then I realized that this was a perfect opportunity to lay down a rule of my own. "You probably shouldn't come in my room unless I say 'come in.'"

But it turned out it was the absolutely wrong thing to say. He grinned, and his hands slid into the front pockets of his jeans. He still wasn't wearing a shirt, not that I could blame him, given that it was ass-crack hot in the house. Now he didn't look in any hurry to retreat or to check out my chest further. He just stood there smirking.

"Why, what are you doing in here that you need a locked door and a hoodie duct-taped to the window?"

"What do you mean?" Though I knew exactly what he meant.

"You're either cooking meth or filming a sexy YouTube video."

I snorted. "No. Now go away. I'm on the phone."

"Fine. Hurry, or I'm eating the whole pizza without you." He turned, the metal-spiked bracelets on his wrist jangling as he pulled his hand out of his pocket.

Feeling flushed, I lifted my phone back to my ear. "Hello?"

Kylie had hung up. Nice.

But she had texted.

Riley? HAWT.

I rolled my eyes, but even as I tapped a denial, I totally agreed with her. Snagging my tank top, I went for a slice of pizza, knowing it would bloat me, but I was hungry. It sucked not to have cafeteria access in the university center, no matter how dicey the teriyaki beef was. Plus it seemed stupid to be ignoring Riley when I could be fighting with him. It was way more fun.

Especially when I had the satisfaction of walking into the living room right as Riley moved past the coffee table with the pizza box, triggering the automatic room freshener I had bought at the store. He jumped.

"What the fuck is that?" he asked as it misted up along his hip.

"It's an air freshener. It goes off automatically when there is an odor or motion."

He looked at me like this was the stupidest thing he'd ever heard in the existence of stupid things. "I hope that wasn't more than a dollar or you were ripped off."

"The sun is going down, so do I have permission to open the windows?" I asked, already walking over to do just that. Between a breeze and the mister, maybe the room would smell less like an old ashtray and more just like stale boy.

"No." Then he grinned when I stopped in my tracks and turned to glare at him. "I'm kidding. Knock yourself out."

"I'd rather knock you out."

"Badass." Riley picked up a slice of pizza and bit off a piece so huge, literally half the slice disappeared in his mouth.

I felt like I instantly gained five pounds on my ass just watching him. So not fair that guys could eat whatever. Hell, Rory could eat whatever she wanted, too, and she never grew tree trunks masquerading as thighs. But I had to fight to stay in shape, with massive amounts of cardio classes and strength training. If you could major in zumba I would because it felt like I spent half my life in the pseudo salsa classes. Sighing, I slid the window open and vowed to only eat one piece of pizza.

There were no plates. Or napkins. Riley was wiping his fingers on his jeans and resting his slice on the closed box. But given the state of the coffee table surface, that was probably the best plan. Dust and cigarette ash probably weren't good seasonings. Lifting the lid carefully so his piece didn't slide off onto the floor, I pulled out my own slice and sat down next to him on the couch. The pizza was loaded with everything, including tiny meatballs, and my mouth started watering.

"Thanks for sharing."

"You're welcome." He finished the slice in one more bite and reached for another one. Something about the movement set off the air freshener again to his left. "Christ." He waved his hand around. "That smells awful."

"You think the air freshener smells worse than this room did?" I was in awe. In my opinion it already smelled better from the ocean breeze mister and the air blowing in through the open window.

"This thing smells like dead old lady."

I laughed. "It's called ocean breeze."

"No ocean I've ever been to smelled like that."

"How many oceans have you been to?"

He grinned. "None."

"Have you smelled dead old lady?"

"Probably."

"No, you haven't. Or if you have, I'm leaving because that makes you a serial killer." Setting my slice of pizza on my knees, I picked a meatball off it and popped it into my mouth. Maybe if I ate slowly, I would fill up and I wouldn't overeat.

"I'm not a serial killer. But I do go gambling and those old women aren't even alive, I swear. They're just propped against the slot machines, abandoned by their families."

There was an image. "I've never been to a casino."

"They're both a lot of fun and massively depressing. Full of saps who think their luck is about to change. I don't believe in luck unless it's bad luck."

"You've never been lucky? You've never won something or had a day where it seems like everything goes right?" I pulled off a mushroom and chewed on it.

Riley gave a laugh. "Look around you, princess. Does it look like anything about my life is lucky? Except for those weeks where if I'm lucky, I can pay all my damn bills."

I wasn't sure what to say to that. He had a point. He didn't sound bitter, not really. Just resigned. Tired. "It sucks that Tyler had to drop out of school."

Tyler had been getting an associate's degree so he could be an EMT, but then he had been arrested for carrying his mother's drugs, and he'd had to drop out. Rory had told me that Riley and

Tyler had been counting on Tyler having a stable job to bring in money, and now that was gone.

"Yeah." Riley stared at my knees. "What the hell are you doing? Are you going to eat that or just pick it to death?"

"I'm not really hungry," I lied.

He shook his head. "I can hear your stomach growling. Are you worried about gaining weight? Christ, you girls drive me crazy."

"Easy for you to say, but we all know everyone hates on the fat chick."

"You're hot. Stop worrying about it."

"Thanks, I guess." I nibbled a pepperoni.

"I'm serious. You have a great body."

I wasn't sure how to react to that. He didn't sound at all like he was flirting with me. He sounded more like a best friend, like Kylie or Rory. None of my guy friends ever bothered to reassure me, and my gay friend Devin just flat-out told me that I could become a heifer if I wasn't careful, that it was in my genes. I carried the predisposed heifer DNA strand apparently.

But while I was trying to come up with a snarky response, he leaned over and crammed his pizza in my mouth. "Bite it."

I started laughing, trying to pull away. I tried to say "Stop it," but it sounded like "Stpack" because of my giggles and the cheese and dough way farther in my mouth than I would put them. Grabbing his wrists, I tried to force a removal, but he was strong, his skin warm, his eyes dancing with laughter.

Finally my options were bite and chew or gag, so I bit and pulled away. As I chewed I said, "You told me once that I have plenty of padding." It hadn't necessarily hurt my feelings because I had taken it that he was just being a jerk, but still, I can't say that I loved hearing it either, even as a joke.

"What?" He looked at me blankly. "When did I say that?"

"When we were sledding. I was afraid to fall off, and you told me not to worry about getting hurt, that I have plenty of padding."

"I don't remember that. But if I said it, I'm sure it was a joke. It's not like I called you fat or anything." He sounded a little defensive.

But I remembered, and he should know that. "I don't doubt for a minute you meant it as a joke, but you wonder why I won't chow down three slices of pizza? It's because practically every day someone says something to me, and to every girl I know, that is a casual joke or careless comment, and after about a thousand of those it's in here"—I tapped my head—"whether you want it to be or not. Every magazine, every TV ad, it's all about skinny and gorgeous, and girls worry they can't measure up."

He was silent for a minute, then he tossed the pizza slice I'd bitten on top of the box. "Sorry. Guess I never thought about it that way."

I shrugged. "It's a societal disease, what can I say? Girls have the pressure to be a size zero just like you guys constantly get called wimp, pussy, fag, girl, all those awful and offensive names to make you feel weak and inadequate. It's stupid."

"You're right. It is very stupid." He turned to me. "But just know that when you're here, you can chow down on three slices of pizza if you want, and I'll never think you're anything less than gorgeous. Even if you chew with your mouth open."

I laughed, appreciating his compliment and the fact that he seemed to get it. "I don't chew with my mouth open!"

"I never said you did. But you can if you want to."

It seemed to be an invitation, so I picked up his piece of pizza and took a healthy bite. God, that was good. It was like a rush of forbidden fat, and my taste buds stood up and did a happy dance.

I chewed and flashed Riley a healthy mouthful, sticking my tongue out to make sure he got a full view.

"Nice," he said in approval. "Fuck this eating like a bird shit. You're hungry, own it. Round it out with a burp and I'll think you're basically the perfect woman."

I hadn't burped out loud since . . . ever. My mother would have melted in mortification, then managed to piece herself back together just to punish me, usually by donating my favorite outfits to charity. My father would have forced me to scrub the kitchen floor. For some reason, that had been his favorite form of discipline, and it hadn't escaped my notice as I grew up that it was a subservient position, on my knees.

Public belching was not a freedom I had embraced since I'd come to college because it wasn't about rebellion to me, it was about doing what I wanted, and frankly, I'd never had the desire to burp out loud. But why not? If I was going to with anyone, Riley seemed the perfect candidate. We weren't exactly friends, and we weren't anything else. So I took a sip of his beer and tried to work one up. I swallowed hard and opened my mouth and held my hands out, but nothing happened.

"What the hell are you doing?" he asked. "You look like you're giving birth."

"Shut up!" I laughed. "I'm concentrating."

"Constipating is more like it."

Gross. It was a good thing I was not trying to impress him. "You're the one who wanted me to burp."

"A burp should be spontaneous, natural." He let one rip. "Like that."

"I just don't have your talent, what can I say?" I tried again and a feeble, forced belch dribbled up. "Ew."

"Yeah, you're going to need some work. But we've got all week."

Why did that actually make me happy? I didn't want to really think about it, but there was something totally different about being with him one on one. I didn't feel as uncomfortable with his snarking as I had before, and there was something actually kind of liberating about not giving a shit what he thought. I could just be myself and it didn't matter. When was I ever actually myself? I wasn't even sure.

My phone rang on the coffee table. I glanced at the screen, and my amusement disappeared. "Oh, shit, that's my mom. I have to answer this." I picked up my phone and gave Riley a pleading look. "Please don't say anything, okay? Just give me five minutes."

His eyebrows went up. "Sure, no problem."

I would have thought he would get up and leave the room, but he didn't. Of course, it was his house and his pizza, so there was no reason for him to move to the kitchen. Heart hammering in my chest, I answered the phone, standing up so I could pace the room. "Hello?"

"Oh, Jessica! I'm surprised I was able to catch you. I was expecting your voice mail."

Somehow my mother always made it sound like an accusation that I had picked up her phone call. Yet if I didn't answer, she was equally annoyed. No way to win, ever.

"Yeah, well, we're on the bus."

"Yes."

"Yes, what?" I asked blankly.

"Yes, not yeah. That is not a word."

Damn it. I clenched my hand into a fist and took a deep breath. "Sorry. Yes, we are on the bus. This may be my last chance for decent reception."

"Oh, okay. Well, I only have a minute. I just wanted to let you know that we got a ticket for you and a guest to the fund-raiser in three weeks for the new wing at Daddy's church. It's important for you to be there."

Ugh. I would rather get a Brazilian wax than spend five minutes at one of those horrible events where everyone sucked up to my dad and he charmed them out of cash. "Mom, I can't go to that. How am I supposed to get back?"

"I'm sure you know someone who can help you out. This is very important, Jessica. We've been working toward this for two years. The congregation essentially pays for your education, so the very least you can do is put on a dress and smile for an hour."

Ah, of course. The Lord giveth, and the Lord taketh away. My parents were giving me financial support, and they could take it away at any minute, and my mother loved to remind me of that on a regular basis.

"I understand that, but if I'm in West Virginia, I can't just buzz up to Troy for the night. People are counting on me." Which was bullshit, and I hated lying, but I hated being manipulated even more.

"Your father will be very disappointed." There was a sniff of disapproval, then she added, "Well, let me know as soon as you can."

I kind of already had let her know. But whatever. "Fine. I'll try to call you next week. By the way, Kylie is bringing my stuff over to the house tomorrow."

"Fine, fine," my mother said, clearly done with the conversation now that she had gotten her guilt trip in. "The housekeeper can let her in. Behave yourself, Jessica."

"I always do." It just depended on your definition of behave. "Bye, Mom."

There was no response. My mother was notorious for just ending the call without a good-bye. Usually she handed the phone to her assistant to tuck back inside her Louis Vuitton purse.

I sighed and crammed my phone in the pocket of my shorts. Riley was eyeing me. "Yes?" I asked defensively, even though I knew what he was thinking.

"You're in West Virginia, huh?" he asked, looking amused. "And what, pray tell, are you doing in West Virginia?"

Biting my nail, I eyed him defiantly, daring him to criticize me. "Building houses for poor people."

Riley let out a choked laugh, and he thumped his fist on his chest, his eyes watering. "Holy shit, are you kidding me?"

"No. It was the only way I could get out of going home for the summer. I know it's an awful lie, but it couldn't be helped."

"So that's why you don't have anywhere to stay."

"Yes." I went over to the coffee table and took another bite of pizza and chewed hard, annoyed. "You don't understand. My parents' house is like prison."

"Somehow I highly doubt that. But maybe we could ask Tyler to compare them."

Shit. I immediately felt bad. "I didn't mean it like that. I'm sure it was awful for Tyler to be in real prison, and there's no comparison, I know. But at home, I can't be me. I have to be what their version of me is." And I just sounded like a whiny, spoiled princess. "Never mind. It's stupid."

But Riley just shook his head. "I'm not judging you, Jess. If you don't want to go home, you don't want to go home. And I give you props for picking the one thing nobody can argue with, though why your parents actually believe you're hanging drywall and grouting tile is beyond me."

"I could do that stuff. If someone showed me." I wasn't completely useless. Just a product of my environment.

He snorted. "I'm sure you could. But forgive me if I don't hand you a nail gun anytime soon."

"Is that for painting your nails?" I asked in a fake Valley Girl voice, tilting my head and blinking my eyelashes. "Like, is it chip-free?"

Riley grinned. "What are you studying in college, acting?"

I flopped down on the couch and took another sip of his beer. "No." Like my parents would pay for that. But I wasn't about to tell him what I was really majoring in.

"There is more beer in the fridge, you know."

"Why get my own when I can drink yours?"

"Thus establishing why I am not in a relationship," he said. "We dudes can't hold our own against the wily ways of women."

Wily ways? I couldn't help it. He did make me laugh. "I feel really sorry for you. Not." Kicking off my flip-flops, I pulled my feet up onto the couch and leaned against Riley's arm, wanting a headrest. "Doesn't it smell better in here already?"

"Christ," he muttered. "I'm going to play video games. You can either play with me or you can go away. It's too hot for you to be touching me."

"You sure know how to flatter a girl."

"I already called you hot and gorgeous tonight. I've met my quota." He nudged me with his bare shoulder so my head flopped a little.

"Stop it."

"Get off me." He nudged me again, lifting his arm to get further momentum.

I caught a whiff of his sweat and deodorant mingling together and I coughed. "You stink."

"Oh, I stink, do I?" He grabbed me in a headlock, catching me off guard. "I'll give you stink."

I squawked and tried to maneuver away, but he had a firm grip on my hair and the back of my neck, and he lifted his arm, burying my face in his hairy and smelly armpit. "Stop, I'm going to pass out!" I said, laughing, trying to scoot backward on the couch.

When he suddenly let me go with a heave I ended up falling on my back, giggling, making a point of coughing and breathing deeply. "You're gross."

But then he leaned over me and my amusement completely died out. He was smiling, but there was something else in his expression. His gaze dropped to my lips, his fingers lacing through mine. I was sure he was going to kiss me and I opened my mouth in anticipation reflexively, and because well, for whatever reason I wanted him to kiss me. It didn't make sense, it wasn't smart, yet I was arching my back and tilting my head and wetting my lips in anticipation . . .

And instead he made the sound of gathering a hocker in the back of his throat. Oh, hell no.

"Don't you dare," I warned him, my finger coming up to point in his face.

He laughed. "This is awesome. I get to fuck with you like the little sister I never had."

Little sister. He just wanted to mess with me like you would a little sister.

I had been expecting, or maybe more accurately, *hoping* for a kiss, and he just wanted to dangle saliva over my face to hear my scream.

I suddenly realized that was why I always hated Riley—without even being conscious of it, I had known that I thought he was hot, while he thought of me as an annoying little sister.

It wasn't a label I was familiar with.

And I didn't exactly like it.

"If you spit in my face, I will knee your nuts," I warned him.

He rubbed my head like I was a dog. "I wasn't going to spit on you. Chill out, princess."

It was the last thing I wanted him to do or say. And maybe I was just tired, or maybe I was lonely, but I heard myself saying in a peevish, snotty, bitch-face voice, "I'm going to take a shower."

"Thanks for the public service announcement," he said, sitting back up and reaching for the TV remote. "Close your mouth in there or you'll drown. Your jaw could use the rest, I'm sure."

For once, I was blank on an appropriately scathing comeback. Was he saying I talked too much or had my jaw open often for a totally different reason?

I decided not to touch it, because truthfully, I didn't want to hear his opinion. Making sure my phone wasn't popping out of my pocket, I just walked past him. The air freshener misted over my thigh as I headed to the kitchen for a drink.

Riley laughed.

# CHAPTER FOUR

I DIDN'T SEE RILEY FOR A FEW DAYS. WHEN I GOT UP THE NEXT morning, he was gone, and I left before he came home. By the time I was back from work, he was in bed. But evidence of our odd cohabitation came in the form of our pissing match over the windows and the air freshener. After work, I would fling open the windows in the living room and kitchen. When I stumbled to the kitchen in the morning for coffee, they'd already be closed. I started to think that Riley was sneaking out of his room like a window ninja minutes after I opened them to close them again because the house always felt stale, a permanent odor that reminded me of the area in front of the airport parking garage elevator. The yuck factor was high.

Maybe if he didn't keep hiding the air freshener the results would have been more positive. But after realizing it was gone I found the stupid thing in the coat closet, and then tucked away in the bathroom vanity, so while he was at work I put it back in the living room, front and center on the coffee table. And he always re-hid it. The second morning I woke up because he opened my door and crept in, mister in hand, unholy grin on his face. Through slitted eyes, I watched him tiptoe barefoot across the room toward me, unaware I had woken up when he turned the doorknob. Closing my eyes quickly, I heard him deposit the air freshener next to my cell phone on the chair next to the bed so that it would clearly spray me when I reached for my phone first thing.

Jerk-off.

An entertaining jerk-off.

It was hard not to smile, but I managed to keep it together until he left. Then I rolled toward the chair and pulled the sheet closer around me, totally amused. Next he'd be tying my shoelaces together or putting itching powder in my T-shirts. Or conducting a panty raid, like we were at sixth grade summer camp. Though speaking of panties, it struck me as ironic that I was well aware that I was only in my panties and a tank top as he had crept into my room, and he could clearly care less. He hadn't even looked at me. In my experience, if you flirted, it wasn't exactly hard to get a guy to want to at least hook up with you, but Riley didn't seem to find me attractive. Sure, he'd complimented me, said I was hot, had a good bod. But he'd said it in the way you say your sister is pretty, not in the way you talk about a girl you want to bang.

It had been a long time since I'd felt unbangable.

Maybe that was a good thing.

Maybe, for the first time ever in the history of my post-puberty life, I could actually be friends with a guy.

Doubtful. But hey, stranger things had happened.

It wasn't like my brother and I were friends—totally the opposite. Paxton had practically made it his life's work to get me in trouble. If I was my mother's disappointment, the daughter who could never quite be the perfect (in her opinion, anyway) woman she was, my brother was her precious perfect son. It was what it was, but it totally didn't give us the kind of sibling relationship you saw on TV. I avoided him, and he posted asshole comments on my Facebook page. That was the extent of our interaction.

So I was going to try to enjoy the weird dynamic with Riley and stop analyzing it.

I didn't have to work, so I read outside on the back deck, and after an hour of glancing up from my book to the ashtray posing as a yard I couldn't take it any more. I didn't think of myself as OCD or anything, but that was just seriously gross. Going into the garage, which was even hotter than outside and smelled like motor oil, I found a pathetic old broom and a dustpan. Sweeping like it was my job, I managed to collect about a hundred cigarette butts into a pile and push them on the dustpan. Then I tossed them into the garbage can, feeling a whole lot better about my view. There were still random butts scattered here and there but short of a fire hose or picking them up by hand, there was no way to get them all. Hey, it was an improvement.

Then, because I was nosy, I decided I was too hot to sit in the sun anymore, and I went into the house and started opening kitchen cabinets. There was an assortment of plastic tableware, gas station soft drink tumblers, and chipped coffee mugs. I had already discovered that the flatware was in a drawer next to the sink and that the spoons I used to eat my yogurt would bend if you were even at all aggressive with your scooping. I figured this was definitely an education in how to live on the cheap, and I might actually need the knowledge someday.

Welcome to the real word, Jessica Sweet.

Though I couldn't claim that seeing how real people make ends meet had anything to do with my going down the hall and peeking into Riley's bedroom. That was just pure curiosity. I'm not sure what I was expecting. Porn scattered all around? Some sort of visual insight into Riley Mann? All I saw was a dark room with a towel draped over the window, the bed frame an eighties black lacquer monstrosity that looked like all the members of a hair band should be sprawled on it in leather pants making metal horns. It so didn't look like anything that Riley would actually buy, and it was borderline creepy. But then I spotted the framed picture on the dresser, an eighties prom portrait, the aqua-blue dress with poofy sleeves swallowing the petite brunette with the balloon arch behind her, and I realized this must have been Riley's mom's room.

Feeling guilty for spying, I retreated, heart pounding in fear that I would get caught and something else I couldn't quite interpret.

There were lighter squares on the paint down the hallway, showing that at one time pictures had hung on the walls, and I wondered what it had been like in the house twenty-some years ago, when Riley's parents had been young and in love, wanting a place to raise their family. What had happened? Or were they ever in love? Were my parents in love? Did love even exist?

I wasn't sure. It just seemed like lust led to love, which led to unhappiness.

Unable to be alone anymore in a space that wasn't my own, I texted Bill.

What are you doing?

Then I immediately hated myself for poking. What was so hard about being in my own thoughts? And why did I need reassurance that Bill still liked me even though he didn't want me to stay in his apartment?

It also reminded me that Riley was actually being pretty damn nice to let me stay with him.

I decided I needed to do something to say thanks. There wasn't a lot I could offer him that he would accept. If I offered money, he would say no. He was too proud for that. If I offered him payment in beer, he might say yes, but that was a guy gift. I wanted to do something that was girly, that he would remember had come from me. And okay, maybe it was just a compulsion to improve the grossness of the house, but I wanted to de-gross it. Or at least one room. The living room looked a little overwhelming since there was no way I could replace the dirty furniture or the carpet. But a peek under the corner of the carpet showed hardwood floors under there. The kitchen seemed easier to tackle. It basically just needed some paint and accessories. A nice masculine update. Fresh paint alone would kill some of the smoke smell.

The kitchen table was an old oak rectangle, and I had noticed on day one that at some point, the boys had started writing on it with a Sharpie. There were random notes to one another like "Buy milk," and brotherly slurs such as "Tyler sucks dick." There were doodles of faces and animals, and there was even a recipe for cheesecake, written in Rory's handwriting. I envied her for belonging here with them, a weird little camaraderie, and I envied them for having the freedom to write on a piece of furniture in permanent marker if they wanted to. Not that they hadn't paid the price for it—I knew that. But there was something about their brotherhood that made me feel left out.

Made me want to put a big old "Jessica was here" across the room.

I texted my friend Robin, the only one of our girlfriends who

was spending the summer in Cincy. Want to go to the hardware store
with me?

Is that a new club?

I snorted. No. I mean for real hardware store. For paint and stuff.

Oh. Sure I guess.

An hour later we were strolling down the aisles of the hardware
store, looking very out of place among the shuffling elderly couples
and workmen dressed in grubby clothes eyeing us with naked curiosity. It might have been Robin's skintight bright-blue tube dress.
It didn't exactly scream home improvement. Personally I felt like I
should be wearing steel-toed boots instead of flip-flops, but I was
going to make the best of it. I just wanted paint samples for the
kitchen and a brush to test them on the wall.

"So why are you doing this exactly?" Robin asked, her earrings
jingling as she leaned over to pull a hot-pink paint chip card out
of the shelf.

"I just want to do something nice for Riley since he's letting me
stay there."

"You could have sex with him. It would be easier and more fun."

I had no doubt of that. "It would also put me right on the edge
of being a whore. Sex should never be as a favor or a thank-you. I
have to draw the line somewhere."

"That's a shame," she teased, going for another paint chip.
"Look, this one matches my nails. You're picking all the boring
colors."

I was staying in the steel-gray and blue-gray family, wanting to
do something modern and chic and masculine without veering into
man-cave territory. "It's a house of four guys. I can't do a lemon-
yellow kitchen."

"I don't see why not. Yellow is a happy color. Are you going to put this in your design portfolio?"

"I probably should." I hadn't thought about it, but it was the perfect before-and-after design on a dime. "But I'm not planning to spend more than like seventy-five bucks so I'm not sure how much impact it will have."

"Think of it as a design challenge. Let me know if you want some art. I can do something for you." Robin was also in the design school with me, though she was focusing on visual arts. Her love was painting, but she was being practical by getting a dual degree in graphic design and art.

Nothing about my double major was practical unless you asked my mother. I was getting degrees in both religious studies and interior design. So basically I was majoring in future preacher's wife. Their vision for me was that after graduation, I could stencil Scripture passages on the wall of my husband's dining room for fund-raising dinner parties. But agreeing to their course of study was the only way they had been willing to let me attend a state school instead of a private Christian college.

I did love design, both interior and fashion. But it made me feel guilty because it seemed so freaking frivolous. Kylie wanted to teach grade school. Rory wanted to be a doctor. And there was me, wanting to rid the world of shit-brown carpet and spandex. Not exactly life changing. Then again, in some cases it arguably could be.

"That would be awesome," I told her. "Something with typography. Maybe food related . . . just like a big piece that says 'EAT,' or 'YUM YUM,' that sort of thing."

"You want me to paint YUM YUM for the kitchen wall of the Mann brothers? Now that is singularly amazing."

I laughed. That did seem a little creeper. "Maybe EAT is a safer bet."

"Oh, hell no. Where is the fun in that? Just let me know what colors you want and I can do it in like an hour."

"Cool. Okay, I'm going to get these samples and then we can go."

THE REACTION WHEN RILEY CAME HOME WAS NOT WHAT I WAS expecting. I had painted four squares on the blank kitchen wall and was studying them as they dried, trying to decide which I liked best. Frankly, any would be better than the yellowed and dingy white walls with dozens of scuffs and stains on them.

"What the fuck are you doing?" Riley asked me, by way of greeting.

He looked sweaty and hot and tired, his nose sunburned. He was wearing a white T-shirt that was about as filthy as the kitchen walls, his tool belt in his hand. I'd never seen myself as a girl who dug a man with power tools, but there was some kind of just automatic response my body was having to the belt and the work boots. It was like an animal instinct that I knew in a zombie apocalypse I would have a better chance of survival with Riley than a marketing major.

"I'm choosing a paint color. Which one do you like best?"

"They all look the same to me. But there is no way you're painting this kitchen. It's fucking pointless." He dropped his belt on the table and went to the fridge, dried mud crumbling off his boots as he walked.

"Why? It's a very cheap way to refresh a room."

"Thanks, Martha Stewart, but I'm not spending a dime on this house. Another six months the bank will be kicking us out. It's a waste of money." He pulled a beer out and popped the tab.

"Oh, and you never waste money?" I asked, looking pointedly at the beer in his hand.

His eyes narrowed before he took a long swallow. He let out a lip-smacking sound of satisfaction. "Ah, that tastes awesome. And did we get married when I wasn't looking? Because you sound a hell of a lot like the nagging wife I swore never to have."

He might have a point. But so did I. "Look, it's simple psychology. Our environment affects our mood. This is a depressing environment. An investment of seventy-five dollars spread out over the six months you may still be living here is barely three dollars a week and it can have a huge impact on attitude."

"Are you for real right now?" He shook his head. "If this is such a depressing environment you don't have to stay here, you know. You can go climb on Nerd Boy and talk him into putting up with you."

That stung. Wounded, I lashed back at him. "Don't be an asshole. I'm trying to do something nice. And for the record, I wasn't expecting you to pay for the paint, it was supposed to be a gift."

"I don't need your damn charity and I don't need this kitchen painted." Riley put down his beer, and he went over to the one blank wall where my fresh paint squares were drying. I jumped when he kicked the wall with his heel, denting the drywall. "This house should be burned to the ground. It's a fucking cesspool, and before the bank kicks us out I'm taking a sledgehammer to everything in it." He kicked twice more, finally succeeding in putting his heel into the wall. "This is me not giving a shit about this house."

"Fine," I retorted. "Do that in six months. But maybe in the meantime everyone else who lives here would like to enjoy their surroundings."

"You don't live here," he said.

Like I needed reminding. Like I wanted to. "I meant Tyler, Jayden, and Easton."

"You're really annoying."

"And you're stupidly stubborn. It's like you're determined to be miserable."

"What do you know about miserable, princess? What do you know about having your mother stoned out of her mind nailing you in the head with a frying pan, huh? What do you know about walking in and seeing your eight-year-old brother eating moldy bread and drinking spoiled milk?"

"Nothing," I said, frustrated with him. Frustrated that he didn't respond to me the way other guys did. Why couldn't he just accept that I was trying to be nice? Why did no one think I was capable of being nice and then when I was it was rejected? "But when Rory comes over here and bakes cookies, does it make you mad?"

"No."

"Do the boys like it?"

He bit his fingernail and looked at the floor. "Of course they like it. They're cookies."

"So what's the big deal about a little home improvement? I promise it won't be girly. It will look like four dudes live here."

There was an enormous pause, and I waited in anxious anticipation. This was important to me, for whatever reason.

"Fine. For the boys." His jaw worked, but he even managed to say, "Thanks."

I grinned, relieved that he had given in. "Don't thank me yet.

I'm going to need your help. I have no freaking clue how to paint a room."

He snorted. "So your gift is causing work for me?"

Oopsie. It was a bit of a Kylie move. "It will be worth it," I promised. "I just need some advice, not actual man power. Though I'm determined to spend as little as possible, so I might need some minor construction help now that I think about it." I gave him a pleading look. "Please?"

Riley shook his head. "Unbelievable. I swear, you'd test the patience of a saint."

"If not a saint, definitely I test the patience of a preacher. Just ask my dad."

"Your father is a preacher?"

"Yes." It had to come out sooner or later, so I figured I should just get it over with. Let the jokes begin.

But Riley just nodded. "I guess that makes sense."

"What's that supposed to mean?"

"Just that I can see now why you might not want to go home for the summer. It's probably tough to deal with all those expectations. You have to be a good girl, right?"

Suspicious, I nodded. This wasn't the normal reaction I got. Usually guys made cracks about preachers' daughters being the most fun and how if you had sex with one it made you closer to God. The usual crude and stupid comments.

"You don't think I'm a good girl, do you?" I asked, already knowing the answer. No one really thought I was a good girl, even though I didn't think I was a bad girl. Where was the label for the morally ambiguous? Nothing I ever did hurt anyone else, but I can't say I was contributing a whole lot to the greater good of mankind. But I figured that could wait until I was on my own, when I wasn't walking this fine line of pleasing my parents while still having enough space to breathe.

Riley handed me his half-finished beer, confusing me. But before I could ask why, he looked me in the eye and said, "Jess, I've got no business judging anyone. But I can offer you some advice if you don't mind."

"Sure." Though my palms started to sweat anticipating what he might say.

"Never ask someone to tell you who you are. You tell them."

The irony was, I had thought I was doing that when I'd come to college, but I realized Riley was right. My message of who I was wasn't clear to anyone, not even to me. A hot taste of dissatisfaction filled my mouth. "Yeah, I get that. But it's not so easy with my dad."

"I'm sure it's not. But you're on your own now, right?"

I nodded and took a sip of the beer. "I'm drinking this."

"That's why I gave it to you. And if you want to offer me advice right back, here's your chance. I opened the door."

He leaned on the kitchen counter, crossing his ankles and his arms, a sly smile on his face. I wondered what he thought I would say. He certainly looked like he thought I was predictable. It was hard to study him, because I didn't understand my reaction to him. Annoyance was still there, simmering under the surface, wanting to smack his arrogance off his face, but there were more complex feelings there now as well. An odd sort of kinship, attraction, definitely, and maybe something that if the thought didn't make me want to throw up a little, tender.

It was that last one that prompted me to say, "Yes. I do have some advice. Use sunscreen on your face tomorrow. You don't want to end up losing half your nose at forty from melanoma."

First his eyes widened in surprise, then he laughed, even as his finger came up to stroke over the red skin on his nose. "I didn't see that one coming. Thanks, Mom. I'm going to go take a shower." On his way out of the kitchen, he casually tapped the paint sample on the far left. "I like this one the best."

That simple gesture made me feel a little gooey inside. So after he went to bed, I put my odor-free sunscreen bottle on the counter in the bathroom with a note that said *Safety First <3*.

# CHAPTER FIVE

A SMALL PART OF ME EXPECTED A SMART-ASS COMMENT BACK in response to my note, but I didn't get one. Was I disappointed? Yeah, I'm not going to lie. If Riley couldn't predict me, I couldn't predict him either.

But I had enough to keep me busy. I searched online for step-by-step instructions on how to paint a room, and I made a supply list. I decided to take the bus back to the hardware store, which made me a little—okay, a lot—nervous, but I couldn't ask Robin to drive me again, and Riley had taken his car to work. I didn't want to wait to get started because now that I had a green light from Riley, I was excited about the Mann kitchen makeover. I wanted to do it immediately, if not sooner.

So putting my wallet in my backpack, I slung it over my shoulders, stowing the change for the bus in one pocket, my phone with the bus routes pulled up on it in the other. Keeping an eye out for gangbanging tweens, I walked down the street to catch the 10:55 bus. It was sweaty-balls hot again. My T-shirt was already sticking to my ribs. By the time I climbed on the bus, the back of my neck was wet and I was thinking maybe it was time to buy myself a crappy car. This was a suckfest.

But once I got to the store, ignoring the stares of two scruffy guys in the parking lot and one belligerent and overweight store greeter, I actually enjoyed myself. It was challenging to figure out what to buy all by myself instead of just having things miraculously appear they way they did back home. If my mother wanted the house redecorated, she hired someone. If my father needed his suits dry-cleaned, he put them on the front step and someone came and picked them up and then two days later they reappeared. Our housekeeper did all the grocery shopping, and the lawn service mowed the grass.

This was me studying labels and prices and finding the best deal on paint brushes, and it was stupidly liberating. My whole life my mother had been complimenting me for being pretty, but having decent genetics was no compliment to me—it was a pat on her own back for birthing what she considered a beautiful child. I wanted to get credit for something I had done, something I had control over, an achievement, not for being born with blond hair.

"What's the difference between regular brushes and foam brushes?" I asked a clerk, a man in his fifties who looked friendly and helpful but not creepy. He didn't smile too big or stare at my chest, so I felt comfortable approaching him.

"What are you painting?" he asked. "Foam tends to be for small areas, for stenciling, or for picture frames and things like that."

"Oh. I'm painting a whole kitchen. Well, I'm going to attempt to paint a whole kitchen."

"You'll be fine," he assured me. "But go with a brush to cut in the edges and a roller for the rest." He walked me to the shelf and pointed out each item.

Feeling ridiculously proud of myself, I trudged back to Riley's with a gallon of gray paint in my hands, the rest of the supplies in my backpack. Going in through the kitchen door, I spread out everything on the table like I had been jewelry and makeup shopping. I wanted to see it all. Hugging myself in anticipation of a twenty-four-hour transformation to awesome, I planned out the next day's shopping trip. I would knock out the painting today, then first thing tomorrow I would be able to accessory shop, which would be the real fun.

Three hours later, when I had to quit and take a shower for work, I realized I was an idiot. This was going to take me a week, not one afternoon. After wiping down all the baseboards per Internet instructions, I had only managed to tape off half the room. I hadn't even cracked open the can of paint yet.

Going into the bathroom, I stripped to shower the smell of loser off of me, feeling defeated. I had a text from Bill on my phone, a much-delayed response to the text I had sent yesterday.

Want to hang out tonight?

Did I? The answer was not really. But what else was I going to do? Come back here and search for the air freshener while Riley slept?

Sure.

Then I put my phone down on the counter, suddenly feeling weird that I was texting Bill while I was naked in Riley's bathroom. Which made no sense whatsoever.

But after only grabbing a late-night coffee with Bill and listening to an acoustic guitar player at a local coffee shop for an hour,

I yawned and begged off, claiming I had to work early the next day. I had no idea why I did it. But sitting there, my leg bouncing, my work shirt still smelling faintly of barbecue sauce, the front door to the shop propped open to let in the night breeze, I just wanted to go back to Riley's. I wanted to measure the wall space and look up the best stores to buy cheap glassware and ashtrays. If smoking had to happen, it should be done in style. I had told Robin I wanted the art piece in yellow and royal blue, and I texted her a link to the font I liked.

"Are you okay?" Bill asked as he drove me back, being a good sport about leaving at midnight. "You seem . . . edgy."

"I'm fine."

"Is it because of what I said the other day? I'm sorry, I was just stressed about exams and I shouldn't have just blurted all that shit out like that." As he pulled up in front of the house, he put the car in park and gave me an earnest look, pushing his glasses up his nose.

Sighing, and not sure why, I hated this sudden moodiness that had taken me over. "No, it's cool. It was a lot for me to ask." Funny, though, how I had never expected him to say no. I didn't want to think that I used sex to control, but there it was in black and white. I had expected that the enticement of nightly sex for a week would have had Bill agreeing without hesitation, his tongue hanging out.

It made me feel like shit.

"This doesn't look like a very good neighborhood," Bill said, glancing around. "Are you sure you're okay here?"

Bill and Nathan's apartment wasn't exactly in a glam zip code but I didn't bother to point that out. "Yes. Riley's here. Thanks for the ride. I'll talk to you soon."

I started to open the door, but Bill touched my shoulder. "Jess."

"Yes?" Somehow I had a feeling I wasn't going to want to hear what he had to say.

But he just shook his head. "Never mind."

My first reaction was to press, but then I decided I had been given a free pass. Whatever he was thinking I wasn't going to like it. So I got out before he could change his mind and walked up the gravel drive, deciding to try the front door since the lights were clearly still on in the house. I wondered why Riley was still awake.

The answer was obvious immediately. When I pushed open the front door, the smell of fresh paint overwhelmed me. Amazed, I went into the kitchen, which was ablaze with light and the sound of metal music cranking loud from Riley's phone. He had painted three of the four walls already. The hard ones. The ones with the cabinets and the one with the back door and the window, the ones that required all that taping, which I had saved for last. Only he hadn't used tape. He had obviously just freehand painted the edges. It was impressive. The only wall remaining was the completely blank one and he was already tackling it with the roller, gray spreading in front of my eyes as I moved into the room.

The color looked amazing, but not quite as amazing as him.

"What are you doing?" I asked, stunned. "You didn't have to do this. This was my idea. I didn't really mean you had to do the painting, too. I just wanted some help hanging some art."

But he shrugged, the muscles in his arm bulging as he rolled efficiently. "Couldn't sleep. And I have this thing where I can't sit on my ass and watch a girl laboring on my behalf. It makes me feel like a dick."

Touched beyond anything that was smart or emotionally healthy, I said, "The color looks great, don't you think?"

"It doesn't look like ass," was his assessment.

I frowned, and he glanced back at me and grinned. "Fine. It looks nice. But that's as gushy as I get, princess."

Impulsively, I wrapped my arms around his waist from behind and hugged him, my breasts pressing into his back. "Thank you."

He stiffened, then said, "All right, calm down or I'm going to drop this roller."

Letting go quickly, because I liked the way my body felt against his too much, I said, "Can I help?"

"Take the brush and paint that last corner. Just go up and down the seam. You don't need a lot of paint."

"Okay." I took the brush that was laying in the paint tray, and I dipped and carefully lifted it. It dripped on the floor. "Shit." I wiped the floor with my finger.

"Use a hand towel. They're basically rags anyway."

They were. Replacing them was already in my mental budget. I grabbed a dingy towel off the counter and cleaned my finger. Then I bit my lip as I jammed the brush in the corner and dragged it up and down, feeling an absurd amount of pleasure from covering the filthy white.

"I'm not as helpless as I look," I told him, because I wanted him to understand I was capable, just, well, sheltered. "I just don't have a lot of practical life experience."

"Now there's something I never would have guessed."

"Ha ha." I dipped the brush again, being more careful not to overload it and let it drip this time. "I think the only times I've had to do anything that could be considered manual labor were when I was being punished."

"You get punished a lot?"

"Of course. It's impossible to be perfect." I carefully went up on my tiptoes to reach as far as I could. "And despite the Christian concept that God makes no mistakes in our creation, my father has very specific guidelines for what makes a good person."

I pulled a kitchen chair across the floor to stand on. I couldn't quite reach the corner.

"You the rebel daughter?"

"No. I tried really hard to please him, actually. I'm not even sarcastic with him."

Riley laughed. "Now that I find hard to believe."

"It's true." I finished my corner and shifted the chair back out of the way. "But it's like walking on eggshells, you know?"

"Trust me, I know that feeling." Riley was moving closer and closer to me as he brought the roller to meet the corner I had just painted and finish off the wall. "My mother usually ignored us, which were the best days. Other days she cried and needed reassurance, or she was sick from the drugs. The worst days were the ones where she was violent or strung out. It was like holding your breath all the time, waiting for the next big explosion."

His eyes shifted from the wall to me as he covered the last bit of white, his right arm paused. I felt trapped in the corner, his body warm, the light harsh, paint fumes intense. But all I could think about was him. The way his lips moved when he spoke, the rich coffee color of his eyes, and the shadow of his beard.

"That sounds like a terrible way to grow up," I said quietly. "I wasn't trying to compare." I felt whiny in comparison, even though I had just been trying to explain why I didn't know how to do anything particularly useful.

"I know. Don't be so fucking sensitive." He switched the roller to his left hand and nudged me with his right shoulder. "We're just sharing, Jess. Talking about our feelings. Getting to know each other now that we're roomies and painting pals."

The stupid way he was looking at me, his goofy expression as unlike him as his words, made me laugh. "Dumbass."

I stepped back and surveyed the room. "Awesome paint job, though. I can't believe how fast you did this. You know, they sell gallons of mess-up paint that someone asked for but then didn't want for like eight dollars a gallon. We could totally paint the living room, too."

"No."

"Why not?" I asked, smiling at him with what I hoped was charming enthusiasm. I wasn't surprised he'd said no. I was expecting it, and mostly I just said it to annoy him.

"I don't need a reason. Just no. And clean this paint tray and the brush in the basement sink."

Blech. That sounded unfortunate. "Clean them how?"

"With *water*," he said slowly and clearly, like he was speaking to a moron, making a mock scrubbing gesture. He shook his head. "God help us."

I stuck my tongue out at him.

Moving with a dexterity I didn't know was possible, his hand shot out and he actually caught my tongue between his fingers.

"Heth!" I said, trying to say *hey*, but without a freely movable tongue it came out garbled. Laughing, I swatted at his arm and tried to pull back.

"Shit, watch out!" he said, eyes going wide in amusement, his hand whipping behind my head.

"What?" I spun around and saw that his hand was the only thing preventing the entire back of my head from touching wet paint. "Oh, crap!" I hadn't realized how close to the wall I was.

When I stepped forward, he pulled his hand back and showed me that his knuckles were covered in gray paint. "Way to go."

"Sorry." Then I ruined the apology by giggling.

"Think it's funny?"

I nodded. "Just a little."

Riley took his wet knuckle and reached out toward me, a gleam in his eye. I couldn't back up and when I tried to dart to the side, he blocked me. Then before I realized what he was doing, he had smeared wet paint on my upper lip like a mustache. I sputtered. He laughed.

"Damn, now *that* is funny."

I could only imagine how not sexy I looked. Still holding the brush in my hand I brought it up to his chest and painted an X on it. In the middle of my action, he realized what I was doing and grabbed my wrist so that the second line squiggled awkwardly off the side of his shirt. I laughed. "You made it worse."

"I like this shirt!" he protested, glancing down at it.

"Are you joking? That shirt is a white undershirt from Walmart. Or actually, it was white at one time. Now it's the color of a tea bag."

"You're exaggerating." He looked up and studied me, very serious. "Jessica?"

"Yes?"

"I mustache you a question."

My lip twitched. "Let me mullet over."

We both lost it. He pulled out his phone. "We need a picture of this."

Did I want to preserve a picture of me with a painted gray mustache? Not necessarily. But I did want a picture of me with Riley, and I did want to see what I looked like. There were certainly more embarrassing pics of me floating around the Internet—hello, why do all friends insist on posting pictures with your eyes closed?

"You can't tag me," I told him.

"You don't look that bad."

"It's not that. I'm supposed to be in West Virginia, remember?"

He grinned. "Oh, yeah, that's right. Come here, sinner. Wait, give me a matching 'stache first."

Riley stood stock-still while I artistically swooped the paintbrush over his face. "This is hard, because you have legit stubble." I was also aware of just how close to me he was standing. How close my mouth was to his.

He looked unaffected, though. "Your life is so hard."

Just for that, I gave him a handlebar mustache, painting curls at the ends with a flourish. "You look amazing."

"All right, pose with me. No duck face. I hate duck face. I will pop your lips with a pin if you do duck face."

"Tell me how you really feel."

Riley threw his arm around me and held up the phone with the other. I leaned against his shoulder, and gave a serious Hercule Poirot stare, one eyebrow raised, a finger pretending to twirl my paint mustache. Riley snapped and we looked at it. I looked evil. He looked adorably cute, grinning with his dimples flashing, looking every inch of a guy despite the gray paint.

Seeing us together did something weird to me. I sucked in a breath, heart pounding, and I tried to laugh, but it came out sounding louder than I intended.

"I'm Riley Mann, and I approve this message," he said. He didn't seem to notice I was acting like a freak.

"That's because you look good and I look scary," I told him.

"Yep."

Of course. I had totally walked into that one. I shoved him. "Send that to me, jerk."

"Send you the picture you don't like?"

SWEET 69

"I didn't say I don't like it. Just that I resent that you look better than me."

"Get used to it. Now you'd better wash that off your face before I have to scrub you with turpentine."

"Sounds hot." I hadn't thought about the fact that the paint was drying. Rushing to the bathroom, I took to my face with exfoliant. I ended up beet red with raw skin, but the paint came off.

Riley stood behind me waiting his turn. I was so determined to get the paint off quickly I didn't even protest that he was just lingering in the doorway watching me. It occurred to me at one point that he seemed to be looking at my butt, but given that his expression never changed, it didn't seem to have much impact on him.

I turned to him. "The sink is yours." I looked like I'd been slapped with a wet noodle, my skin stinging, but I was paint-free.

"Can I use that stuff?"

"You want to exfoliate?"

"I want the paint off." He picked the tube off the counter. "How do I use this?"

"You rub it on," I said dryly. "Then wash it off."

"Can you do it for me?" He held the tube out to me.

If it was any other guy, I'd think this was some sort of awkward come-on. But this was Riley. He might as well be asking me to pop his pimple or dig out a splinter for him. There was nothing even remotely sexual in his expression.

Maybe he didn't like blondes.

Maybe he liked exotic brunettes.

I wondered what I would look like with dark hair.

Then I mentally grimaced. Stupid. That's what I would look like with dark hair. Like a desperate chick trying too hard. What the hell was wrong with me?

Slapping scrub on his face, I rubbed it vigorously into his skin, trying not to make eye contact or think about the fact that I was thinking about what kind of girl he thought was hot.

"I'm not going to suggest nursing as a career for you," he commented. "You don't exactly have a gentle touch."

Lifting a washcloth—one of mine, I might add—I rubbed off the lotion. Hard. "Do it yourself if you don't like the way I do it." Or maybe get a brunette to do it.

Ugh. Why was I being a crazy bitch? I threw down the washcloth and nudged past him. "*Excuse* me."

"Sure." He held up his hands. "Wasn't trying to block you. You going to bed?"

"Yes, if that's okay with you." Bitch just kept right on rolling out of my mouth, and I couldn't seem to stop it.

"I have no opinion on it one way or the other."

Which was exactly why I was so annoyed. I wanted him to have an opinion about me. About bed. About me in bed.

"Good night." I paused in the doorway and forced myself to be rational. "Thanks for painting the kitchen."

"Gee, it was my pleasure," he said, eyeballing me in the mirror.

Yeah. That was the most obvious sarcasm yet. Because I knew I was being a dick, I just retreated to my temporary room. Where I did something really ridiculous. I opened the picture that Riley had sent me and I stared at the two of us as I lay on the bed, fully dressed, lights off. Over the drone of the air-conditioning I murmured to myself, "Riley Mann," and then felt like the biggest middle school dork that had ever existed. I didn't crush on guys. They crushed on me.

So what the hell was wrong with me? I checked my menstruation app on my phone to see if I could blame the sap attack on hormones, but no such luck. It was a whole week until my period.

Rolling on my side, I did something equally as bizarre. I forwarded the picture to Rory with the label "Roomies."

She texted back a minute later. LOL. Tyler wants to know what dope you two are smoking. U look like you like each other.

No drugs. Just paint fumes.

Did you paint the kitchen???

Yep.

Wow. Awesome.

Yeah. That was me. Feeling awesomely stupid.

I deleted the text from Riley with the mustache picture in a moment of owning my power.

Which was lame because I knew that it was still there in the text I'd sent Rory.

It wasn't hot in the room, but my body felt like it was heating from the inside out. There was no way I could get undressed without risk of extreme arousal. I lay there, phone on my chest, legs crossed, reciting Bible passages about death and destruction to myself until I finally fell asleep.

I dreamed that a swarm of locusts had Riley's face.

Which was perhaps the most deeply disturbing image I'd ever encountered in my life.

# CHAPTER SIX

THERE IS AN INHERENT PROBLEM WITH LYING ABOUT YOUR location. You either have to invite everyone around you into the secret or you look like a psycho. Given that I didn't want to admit to everyone I knew that I was supposed to be sweating with a nail gun in the backwater, I was just coming off as a raging bitch.

So not only was I not giving of my time freely to help others, I was being nasty to my friends.

Yay, Jessica.

"Don't check in!" I snapped at Robin as we settled down into our lounge chairs at the water park.

"Why the hell not? Maybe someone can meet us here."

"I don't feel like dealing with people today." I slapped sunscreen on my arms and tried to think of a better reason, but my brain wasn't firing at full capacity after my stupid, ridiculous night of crap sleep, where Riley buzzed me in an erotic biblically inspired flyby. Effing disturbing. It was like I'd fallen into a B horror movie.

I had half expected to wake up and find WHORE OF BABYLON scratched into my skin with a needle.

"Are you hungover? Because you're acting like a whole lot of biotch."

I sighed. "I'm sorry. I'm exhausted. I think I'm getting a cold." Lie. Yet another lie on top of the already existing lie. Robin was my friend, and frankly I didn't have that many tight friends. With Rory and Kylie gone for the summer, I was going to be lonely if I didn't treat Robin just a little bit better.

As Robin tied up her dark hair into a bun and readjusted her sunglasses, I squirted more sunscreen on my knees. "Okay, the truth is I totally lied to my parents about staying here this summer. They think I'm building houses with a mission group in West Virginia."

Her eyes widened. "Are you shitting me?"

"No. Unfortunately. I just couldn't go home, but I didn't really think about how hard it is to hide your whereabouts with social media. My parents aren't exactly checking my Facebook page, but my brother does. I tried blocking him, but he told my mother and she made me re-friend him."

"You tried to block your brother?" Robin looked amused by the very thought. "I should have thought of that. My brothers like to post pictures of obese hairy men on my page and tell me that's what I'm going to look like at forty." She studied her arms ruefully. "It's the Latin genes. I spend half my life waxing hair off my body."

Relieved that she didn't seem horrified by me, I said, "So you won't tell? And you don't think I'm an evil human being?"

She shrugged. "No. I mean, who hasn't wanted to avoid their parents at one point or another? And I was raised in a huge Latino

Catholic family, and everyone is always up in your business. It must be nice to turn that off for a few weeks. I'm kinda jealous of you."

"I guess everyone has their family drama." I adjusted the yellow bikini top I was wearing, slipping the straps off and tucking them into the cups so I wouldn't get weird tan lines.

"Yep. My grandmother is furious that I got a D in Spanish. She doesn't seem to get that listening to her speak it and being able to understand it for the most part is totally different than writing it grammatically correct. I actually feel like I have a disadvantage because I had all this quasi background info. But to her, it means I'm spitting on my heritage." She sipped her water bottle. "It gives me a headache."

"That does suck." We were at the edge of the wave pool, and a million kids were tearing by, moms hollering at them to slow down. I picked up my fashion magazine and flipped idly through it, trying to find an article that grabbed my attention.

"Hotties, eleven o'clock," Robin murmured.

I glanced up. I saw a lot of hair gel and mirrored sunglasses. There were three of them and they were checking us out. It was hard to distinguish one from the other with their bulky muscles and giant floral swim trunks. "I'll let you take this," I told Robin. "I'm not in the mood."

"You're not in the mood to flirt?" She sounded scandalized.

I had to admit, it was a rare occurrence that I didn't want to meet new people. I liked hanging out, moving through a crowd, demanding that I be entertained. But today I just wanted to hide behind my sunglasses and scowl. "No. I'm not. Hey, when can you get me the typography piece?"

"Tomorrow. It will only take me an hour, then it has to dry for another hour or two."

"Cool. Thanks."

"Sure. Oh, here they come." Robin sat up a little straighter, her red bandeau bikini top standing at attention.

"Hey, wassup?" Douche #1 said.

"Ladies," Douche #2 said.

"This chair taken?" from Douche #3.

Yeah, so not in the mood. Which is why when Douche #1 said, "Want a beer?" I nodded.

So I was risking getting busted for open container. This was the only way I was going to get through the day without being consumed by thoughts of Riley Mann, the swarming bastard. I had a terrible feeling that for the first time in well, ever, I was suffering from the insanity of an unrequited crush. It sucked. Hard.

Fortunately the Douche Trio was smart enough to have their beer disguised in travel mugs. While Douche #2 assured me they were twenty-one, they didn't want to get kicked out.

"I'm not even twenty-one," I told him. "So you're really flirting with danger here."

"Is that your name?" he asked with a wink. "Danger?"

Oh, God. "Yes. Jessica Danger." Hell, it kind of suited me. Much more appropriate than Jessica Sweet. We all knew that was an ironic name for me.

Six hours and I'm not sure how many beers later, I let him give me a groping, wet-tongued kiss in the parking lot and I hated myself for it. But I was tired, drunk, confused by my own feelings toward Riley, and it seemed easier to just allow it than to work up a protest. But I did shove him off when he got too enthusiastic.

I felt nothing. I looked at him and I felt absolutely nothing. No attraction. No memory of what his name was or a single word he had spoken to me throughout the day.

"Can I get your digits?" he asked, holding his phone out for me.

"No," I said shortly, climbing into Robin's car and slamming the door shut. I locked it and shut my eyes, hot tears behind my lids. What was I doing? And I didn't cry. I never cried.

He knocked on the window, looking pissed, but I ignored him and he wandered away, probably calculating how many beers he had wasted on a girl who wasn't going to blow him. My heart wasn't exactly bleeding for him. I had given zero encouragement and half-assed conversation all day.

Robin got in a second later and threw her beach bag in the backseat. I was wearing denim shorts over my bikini bottoms, but Robin hadn't even bothered with that. When she turned the car on and the AC cranked on, she flicked it off with a shiver. "Are you okay?" she asked. "You seem totally upset."

I sniffled, annoyed. God, crying stung my eyes. How did chicks do this all the time? "I'm hungry," I told her. "Can we go to the gas station? I want a candy bar."

"Sure."

Too much sun. Too much beer. Too much time with douchey guys that I wasn't interested in while I snuck glances on my phone of the picture of the guy I *was* interested in. Altogether a fail of a day. "I think I owe every girl I've ever rolled my eyes at for liking the wrong guy an apology."

"You didn't actually like that guy, did you?" Robin asked, startled, pulling out of the water park. "I thought you just drank too much beer."

"I did. By the way, should you be driving?"

"I only had two beers and the last one was like three hours ago. You dusted me with the drinking."

"Oh, okay. And no, I did not actually like that guy. I don't even remember his name. I'm not sure I ever heard him when he told me, that is how little I gave a crap."

"I think it was Rico."

I snorted.

"Then who do you like if it isn't Rico?"

If I hadn't been buzzed, I never would have admitted it. But I was, so I said glumly, "Riley."

Robin made a choking sound of horror. "Oh, shit. That's probably not good."

"No." I nodded in agreement as we pulled into the gas station. "It's idiotic. He treats me like an annoying little sister and I should be glad, really. If I have sex with him, I think my vag would explode."

Laughing, Robin parked and got out of the car. "I want a drink. And if I were you, I would risk my vagina exploding for one night with that hunk of man meat. Riley is fucking hot. He was tagged in a picture with Rory and Tyler and I felt I needed a bib."

Tell me about it.

Twenty minutes later Robin dropped me off and I struggled with all the bags. Before we'd hit the water park I had asked her to stop off at a discount home goods store and I had gone accessory shopping for the kitchen, so I had three bags over my right arm, plus a bag full of candy and energy drinks from the gas station and a fast food bag with the remnants of a chicken tender meal from the drive-thru. Having stuffed my face, I was decidedly less drunk, but I wouldn't have classified myself as sober, which was obvious when I clipped my shin on the coffee table in the dark and ricocheted off the hall wall twice.

"Damn it." I made it to my room and flicked on the light. I was freezing from still wearing a wet bathing suit so I pulled off my bottoms and slipped into panties and pajama pants. Then yanking my hoodie off the window, I peeled the duct tape off the cuffs and pulled it on over my yellow bikini top, leaving it unzipped. I wanted to snuggle in the warm fabric, to get a hoodie hug. It was old and had been washed a hundred times, a Christmas gift my sophomore year in high school. My mother had threatened to burn it when I had been home on Christmas break, saying it was so faded and threadbare that she wouldn't even dream of donating it to the homeless shelter. But I loved it and right now, it felt like just what I needed.

Heading back to the kitchen to finish eating, because I didn't want my room to smell like old fries in the morning, I flicked on the kitchen light and screamed.

"Holy shit!"

Riley was sitting in the kitchen, in what had been the dark until I had turned on the light.

"Oh my God, what are you doing?" I breathed out in relief. "You scared the shit out of me."

But despite my own alcohol remnants, I could see immediately what he was doing. There was an ashtray on the table with a burning cigarette resting in it, a half-empty glass next to it, and a mostly empty bottle of Jack Daniel's rounding out the trio. Riley was sitting slack in the chair, his eyes dull, wearing nothing but his black boxer briefs. I wasn't sure what was more distracting to me—the mostly empty bottle of liquor or the view of his muscular chest and thighs, his metal-studded bracelet and iron cross still on against his bare skin. The table was partially blocking the view of his briefs, and I decided that was a good thing.

I was in way too weird of a place for anything good to come out of me checking out his junk.

"Sorry," he said. "Didn't mean to scare you."

"Why are you drinking alone in the dark?" I set the bags down on the table and pulled out a sports drink. After taking a sip I held it out to him. "Want some? You look like you need it."

I thought he would actually reject it, but he did take the bottle and gulped some of the drink before eyeing my other bags. "What's in there?"

"Chicken nuggets. Fries. Three chocolate bars and a bag of chips."

"What, do you have PMS or something?" he asked, making a minimal effort to reach out and hook the bag with one finger and drag it toward him. He dug in for a French fry and ate it half-heartedly.

More like all self-control disappeared entirely with a six-pack. "No. Maybe I'm just a pig."

He finally looked over at me, eyeing my outfit. "Is that your bra?"

If he wasn't clearly loaded I would have been annoyed. "No. It's my bikini top. I went to the water park today."

"Oh." His eyes narrowed at my chest. "Yellow."

Thanks, Captain Obvious. I fought the urge to roll my eyes. "So any particular reason you're having a party for one?"

He lifted his cigarette to his mouth and took a deep drag. As he blew out smoke, he gestured to some papers on the table. "That."

My heart dropped. "We're being kicked out by the bank?" As I reached for the papers, I wondered at my use of the word "we."

"No. That will be a while still. This is about Easton. The social worker is coming next week to do a home inspection."

Oh, no. He was worried about Easton, which was worse. Way worse. I knew that Riley had filed for custody of Easton when their mom died. Jayden was eighteen and considered an adult, but Easton was only eleven.

Riley picked up the bottle and drank directly from it. "They're going to take him from me, I know it." His voice cracked at the end of his sentence, and suddenly there were tears welling in his eyes.

I didn't know what to say or to do. Seeing him so vulnerable, so clearly in pain, stunned me. I wasn't the girl you went to for a hug. I wasn't the friend who knew the right thing to say. I couldn't soothe and comfort and make it all okay. I was just Jessica, sarcasm my only superpower.

But my heart ached for him, and I felt right then that I would do anything to make it okay for him, that I had to pull my head out of the Bud Light can and be a true, honest-to-God friend to him.

"What makes you think they'll take him away?" I asked. "You're his brother, and you have a steady job. He's lived with you almost his whole life. This is his home. I would think stability counts for something, right? And no one else is contesting custody, are they?"

He shook his head, lifting his cigarette to his mouth again. "No. My aunt Jackie disappeared a month ago, probably shacked up with her drug dealer. Her son is in jail, and they're my only family, besides good ol' Dad, who isn't eligible for parole for another ten years. But look around you, Jess. I mean, you clearly know it—this place is a dump. It reeks in here, and that social worker is going to take one look around and think that my brother belongs in some fucking foster home with people who don't give a shit about him."

Without warning, Riley took the whiskey bottle and hurtled it at the back door, where it smashed, amber liquid trailing down the wood.

I jumped.

"Seven years," he said passionately. "Seven fucking years I have been working for the goal of making sure that kid doesn't end up in the system and now I'm going to fail and he's going to pay the price for me not being man enough to save him."

"Hey," I said gently, shocked by the self-loathing, by the burden that he clearly had been carrying for way longer than a twenty-five-year-old should have to. "You haven't failed. We have a few days. A couple of cans of paint, we'll pull the carpet up to get rid of the smell, no big deal. No one expects you to provide anything more than a clean and safe environment for Easton, and you're doing that."

He didn't say anything.

"I think Easton is very lucky to have you. He may have drawn a shitty card when it came to your parents, but he has you and that's going to save him, Riley. He's going to be fine, and you can be proud of yourself for everything you've done and sacrificed." I meant that. So many guys would have bolted, but Riley was in for the long haul.

"Tyler is better at the surrogate parent thing than me." He took the last drag of his cigarette and stubbed it out. "I'm not good at the whole homework and shower and take-him-to-the-doctor thing. I seem to be missing the nurturing gene."

"You and me both," I told him. "I'm not sure I'm cut out to be a parent." I had never admitted that to anyone. It made me feel like such a jerk. But I wasn't sure I would be a good mother. I couldn't imagine singing lullabies or cleaning up snot.

"I don't want kids." He dug into my shopping bag and pulled out a pack of peanut butter cups. "Can I eat these?"

"Sure."

"I figure having kids is like the biggest gamble ever, and if you fuck it up, you're not just messing your own life up but another human being's. That's too much responsibility."

"That's because you've been raising your brothers for years.

Maybe you'll change your mind someday." I gave him a soft smile. "When you meet the right girl." Isn't that what they always said? You met The One and suddenly you were envisioning picket fences and baby strollers? It was hard to picture that for myself since I had never once come even remotely close to being in love.

Riley was the first guy I'd actually been genuinely interested in in about forever and a day and yet, he just might be the first legitimate friendship with a guy I'd ever had. Where you had real conversations and shared genuine thoughts and emotions. I didn't want to screw that up.

"Nah, I doubt it. But yeah, it's been hard. But I don't resent taking care of Easton, I don't mean that. I would do anything for that kid, and Jayden, too. They're awesome kids, despite all of my mom's shit, and I work hard to make sure they have food and a roof over their heads." He flashed a quick grin, but his eyes were troubled. "For now, anyway. But they deserve better than I can give them, and that makes me angry."

"Stop beating yourself up. Your dad is in jail. Your mother was a drug addict. It's a miracle none of you are serial killers or junkies yourselves. I think if you can get Easton to eighteen and he is a decent guy, then you've done a damn good job. And if he ends up in an alley with a needle in his arm, it's not your fault."

Maybe that wasn't exactly the right thing to say.

Riley stopped cramming chocolate into his mouth long enough to cock his head and say, "Now there's an image. Thanks for that."

I flushed. "Sorry. This is why I can't be a mother. I give terrible advice."

But Riley laughed. "No, you're fine. I appreciate the effort. Most girls would have hidden in their rooms, or told me to suck it up, or tried to distract me with sex."

Well, it wasn't like that last one hadn't entered my head. He was practically naked and we were both buzzed and I was oh, maybe falling completely head over ass for him.

I ignored that. "I'll help you with cleaning up the house. I'm happy to help. We have all weekend. This place will shine like the top of the Chrysler Building."

He gave me a lopsided smile. "Come here."

"Come here where?" I asked, suspicious.

"Here." He held out his hand.

"Are you going to give me a wet willie or something?" I asked, reluctantly standing up and going over to him. I took the remaining half of the peanut butter cup out of his hand and ate it. "Yum."

"Sit down." He gestured to his lap.

Oh, no freaking way. No, no, and no. I was not going to sit on his lap when he was in nothing but boxer briefs, eyes still glassy from alcohol. I wasn't known for resisting temptation. As a kid, if you waved candy in front of me, I would have traded my family for a bag of Jolly Ranchers. I had to admit that I wasn't sure I could control my feelings when he was so tantalizingly close to my touch.

"Absolutely not," I told him, unscrewing the cap on the energy drink to hide my expression from his eyes.

But while I was sipping, he grabbed me and pulled me down onto him.

"Riley!" I tried to maneuver away, but it was too late. I fell with a *thunk* on his thighs, and I realized wiggling around was worse than sitting still. "What?"

"You're really going to help me clean this dump up?" he asked, suddenly looking earnest.

I studied him for a second, my heart squeezing. "Yes. I already was, but this is just a little more large scale, but still no big deal.

We'll have this place looking amazing and they'll give you custody of Easton. I promise." Of course, I couldn't promise any such thing, but I didn't want to see him like that.

He smiled. "Thank you. You're a good person, you know that?"

I shook my head. "I'm not, not really. I'm not awful, but I'm not so nice, truthfully."

"You are, too. You're helping me, aren't you?"

"That's what friends do." I put my arms on his shoulders because I was losing my balance. "And we're friends, right?"

"Yeah." His hand was warm on my back. "We're definitely friends, Jess. Though I just realized I don't know your last name."

"It's Sweet." I fingered his necklace, enjoying being this close to him. It might never happen again, so I was going to take advantage of the opportunity. Heat radiated off him, and I could smell the whiskey on his breath. "Ironic, huh?"

"Seriously, that's your last name?"

I nodded, cheeks burning for some reason. I didn't blush any more than I cried. So annoying.

"I think it's appropriate. You are, actually, very sweet." Riley's hand shifted underneath my hoodie onto my bare skin, and I shivered. "That's what I think."

"I think you're drunk." Why did he have to touch me like that? His hand was just resting on the small of my back, his thumb brushing back and forth lazily.

We were in a dangerous position, and he didn't seem to have a clue. For a long minute, he studied me, his eyes dark in the harsh light of the kitchen, and I held my breath, wondering what he was thinking, wanting him to say something . . . important.

"Maybe." His gaze dropped. "I never realized how big your tits are. Damn, all this yellow is really distracting."

Yeah. That wasn't it.

Disgusted, I jumped up off his lap. "On that note, I'm going to bed. And you should, too. Nine a.m., buddy, you need to be in the living room ready to work."

He saluted me and reached for his cigarettes.

"And no smoking in here!" I zipped up my hoodie all the way. "We just painted this kitchen!" With a sound of exasperation, I threw up my hands and left the room.

Then I had a thought. Rounding on him, I added, "Don't try to clean up that glass tonight. You're too drunk and you'll cut yourself. We can get it tomorrow."

The corner of his mouth lifted. "And you don't think you're good mom material. I think it's there, you just hide it under all that blond."

As if that didn't have me speechless, he chose that moment to stand up. Riley sitting in underwear was bad enough. But when he rose in an unfurling of naked hotness, standing in front of me like every girl's fantasy, my mouth went dry. I half expected water to suddenly drop from the ceiling and land on him for a perfect package of gorgeous wet skin and finish me off completely.

The Wicked Witch had nothing on me when it came to melting.

"Put some pants on," I told him.

He pointed an unlit cigarette at me and grinned. "See? Right there. Mom. That was perfect."

First he said I was like his little sister.

Now like a mother?

It was going from bad to worse.

## CHAPTER SEVEN

I DIDN'T EXPECT RILEY TO GET OUT OF BED BEFORE NOON, BUT there he was, in the kitchen at nine on the nose, brewing coffee and looking sexy in all his hungover scruff. He had a beard growing and dark circles under his eyes, his hair spiked out in all directions, as he shuffled barefoot in a pair of ratty jeans. No shirt of course. I was starting to think I was going to have to buy him a pack of T-shirts for my own sanity.

"What's up?" he said, his voice sounding like he'd spent the night swallowing rocks. He gave a wet cough that made my stomach turn.

I wasn't feeling all that fabulous, and the phlegmy sounds he was making weren't helping. "Hey." Flopping in a chair, I debated what to eat.

"Want some coffee?"

"No, it's too hot for coffee."

"It's good for a hangover, though, which I have." He leaned with his elbows on the counter and rubbed his forehead aggressively. "Did I really kill a fifth of Jack?"

"Except for what you threw against the door, which wasn't that much. So yeah, basically." I stood back up, deciding I needed to eat something sooner rather than later. Fishing a yogurt out of the fridge, I asked, "So you don't remember anything?" I was disappointed by that. It felt like we'd shared some kind of moment of bonding, and as stupid and lame as it sounded, I didn't want that to be gone.

"I remember everything. I was just trying to convince myself that I really wasn't stupid enough to drink that much."

"Oh. Hey, it happens."

Riley poured himself a cup of coffee and basically drank it all in one gulp. "Shit, that's good." He shoved himself up off the counter. "So what are we doing today? You're the brains behind this, I'm the brawn. Just tell me what to do."

I wished.

But practically speaking, in terms of the house, I did have a plan. "I'm going to finish cleaning up the kitchen. I bought new knobs for the cabinets, and I have some things to hang. You're going to hang them, because I have no clue how to do that. Then we'll tear up the carpet in the living room."

"All right." He closed his eyes for a second, like he was calling up fortification. Then he snapped them back open and slapped his hand on the counter. "Let's do this. You get what you need, I'll get my drill and a knife to cut the carpet."

Apparently he kept his drill and a knife in his bedroom. That struck me as more than a little weird, but maybe it was a safety issue with Easton and Jayden around. "Why don't you keep that in the garage?" I asked as I came out of my room with the bags from the store.

"Are you kidding me? It would be stolen in ten minutes. Have you been in the garage? The only thing in there is a lawn mower that doesn't run because someone stole the starter off it, and those old busted plastic sleds."

"There's a broom in there, too." I started opening the individual plastic bags with the new brushed-nickel knobs. The eighties colonial pulls were gross and needed to go. "I found it the other day."

"I'm sure it was happy to see the light of day since no one has used that in about a decade." Riley was cleaning up the glass from the broken bottle with his bare hands, squatting down in a way that made his jeans drag down.

I balled up the receipt from buying the knobs and threw it at him. My aim was surprisingly good, and it landed in his butt crack before bouncing back off. "Score," I told him, amused. No matter how sexy the guy, plumber's crack has a way of killing the heat level.

"Hey, are you objectifying my body?" he asked, not bothering to pull up his pants.

"Yes." I started untwisting the existing knobs, surprised at how firmly they were on there. It took me five solid minutes to get one off.

"Try this," Riley said, opening a cabinet and showing me the back of the screw. He held the drill up and pushed something and bam, like that, the screw retreated and the knob fell off the front of the cabinet.

"Tricky," I told him. But when he handed me the drill I could barely hold it up, let alone line the tip up to the screw. When I finally got it, I pushed the button and the kickback startled me so that I jerked back, and nothing happened. "Hm."

Riley just watched me attempt a second time, his eyebrows raised.

"Don't judge me," I said when the drill fell away again with zero effect on the screw. "I've never held a power tool in my life."

"It's not a table saw. It's a hand drill." But he took the drill back from me. "You do something else. I'll take these off or we'll still be here two hours from now."

I started to stick my tongue out at him, then remembered what had happened the last time I'd done that. So while he made fast work of knob removal, I pulled out the Sharpie I'd bought, and I went to work on the kitchen table, covering up the swear words with paislies and curlicues. I didn't want to destroy their odd message board of sorts, but I didn't think the social worker wanted to read about dick sucking on the table where an eleven-year-old was eating his Cheerios. Then when I was done, I put a cookie jar in the shape of the Mystery Machine from *Scooby Doo* in the center of the table. Then I filled it with store-bought cookies.

Riley tossed the old knobs in the trash and lifted the lid, swiping a cookie. "Seriously? A cookie jar? This is the tits, Jess."

"I guess that's a positive thing?" I asked. "By the way, when these cookies run out, make Rory bake some more. I don't do that."

"So you've said." He kissed the top of my head, getting crumbs in my hair. "We all have our role, babe."

Mine, apparently, was to be his sister/mother. How in the hell did I get myself into that position? It was about as foreign to me as celibacy.

Since the kitchen was now gray, I wanted blue and yellow accents, so I had bought yellow canisters to hold flour and sugar and coffee, and after clearing every random thing that was cluttering the counter off it and shoving them in a cabinet, I arranged the containers. Then I set a pump with soap next to the sink and hung the blue and yellow towels on silver hooks that I made Riley drill into the wall. I set up a little coffee station with blue mugs and a yellow sugar bowl. Just getting rid of the weird stuff they had laying around—I mean, who needs a phone book and seventeen lighters?—it already looked better. With my accessories, it looked like while the kitchen was old, someone who gave a shit used it.

"Over a little. To the right. The right, Riley," I said in exasperation as he shifted the art I'd bought to the left, not the right. "Show me which hand is your right."

"Fuck you," was his opinion. But he did shift the piece to the right. He had already given his thoughts on the peace sign made out of license plates by calling it "weirdo hippie shit" but I actually thought it gave a cool pop of color to the room. Pop of color was to design what protein was to food—it was one of the basic food groups.

It was actually mine, something I'd bought at an art festival when I was thirteen and feeling the peace symbol. My mother had thought it was a hideous piece of trash, so I had boldly displayed it in my room all through high school and had brought it to school with me knowing if I left it behind, she would toss it in the trash. I didn't want to hang it in my dorm room, but I wanted to keep it for sentimental reasons. When I looked at it, I felt thirteen again, in love with rainbow colors and glitter and patriotism. I had a plan then to visit all fifty states with my peace symbol and blog about it.

What happened to that kid? I wondered. When did I get cynical?

But then again, maybe I hadn't, because here I was, hanging that peace sign on the wall of a house that was Easton's safe haven.

"This is mine, you know," I told him. "I bought this at an art festival for twenty bucks when I was thirteen. I'm letting you borrow it, gallery style. Someday I might want to take it back."

"Mark where you want it hung," he said. "My arms are killing me."

Exasperated, I took a pencil and made a mark at the top where I wanted it hung. I was sorry I'd told him anything personal. "Fine. Here."

"Jesus, thank you," he sighed. He set it on the floor and reached for his drill. "You have good taste, you know. It looks awesome in here, I'm not going to lie."

"What was that?" I asked, cupping my hand to my ear, pleased with the compliment. "I didn't hear you over the sound of the drill and your large ego."

He efficiently drilled a screw into the wall and hung the peace sign. "I said, you have good taste. See, I can admit it. No one would guess this is the same kitchen."

"Thank you." I was preening. I could feel it. I couldn't help it. I was craving his appreciation. How completely pathetic was that?

He turned and hit the button on the drill in my direction.

I shrieked. Which of course made him grin and step even closer to me.

"Stop it," I said, unnerved by the sound and that spiraling tip pointing at me. I could lose an eye or something.

"What?" He shoved it toward my face. "What's the matter?"

I darted away, laughing, and tripped over the garbage can. I bumped against the wall and the peace sign fell. Riley caught it and hung it back up.

"Way to go, Jess. You almost killed peace."

Before I could retort something nasty, there was a knock on the back door. Riley went and opened it, and I saw Robin was standing there, wearing short shorts and a sparkly blue tank top. I had texted her and she was there to deliver the art piece.

"Hey," Riley said, in a voice of surprise and intrigue. "Can I help you?"

I realized that he had never met Robin. I also realized that Robin was an exotic brunette. Which made me realize that asking her to come over was a very stupid and idiotic idea.

To her credit she didn't drool over Riley's chest the way he was drooling over hers. She just said, "Hi, I'm Robin. Is Jessica here?"

"It's for you," he said over his shoulder. But without moving out of the way, he held out his hand. "I'm Riley. It's really nice to meet you."

Gross. I nudged him out of the way. "Hey, Robin. Come in. Riley, move your ass."

Robin skirted him, looking curiously at me, the canvas in her hands. "I can't stay, but here it is."

I took the canvas and turned it around. It said YUM YUM, spelled out in candy wrappers on a gray background. It was perfect.

"I decided just paint was boring." She gave a shrug. "It may be too cute for a house of guys, but I couldn't resist."

"It's awesome," I told her. "It goes perfectly next to the peace sign because they're using similar mediums in similar colors. Don't you think so, Riley?"

"Sure." He nodded. "Though I can't guarantee Jayden won't pull those wrappers off hoping there is still a speck of chocolate in them."

I scoffed. "He wouldn't do that."

"You haven't seen him around sugar. He inhales it like an anteater."

While I played around with placement on the wall, Riley put his old coffee in the microwave and heated it up. "Thanks for making that, Robin," he said. "That was really nice. And Jess and I are just going to get some lunch."

We were?

"Do you want to come with us?"

*No. Say no*, I tried to mentally project to Robin. I probably would have a classic college girl meltdown if the first guy I'd been genuinely attracted to in three years hit on one of my best friends.

Fortunately, I had told Robin in my beer buzz the night before that I liked Riley. And she knew the girl code. She shook her head. "Oh, no thanks. I have to work today and I have a ton of stuff to do before that."

Yay, Robin. I owed her a beer for that. Hell, a case of beer. "Oh, that sucks." I paused for a beat. "But thanks, you're awesome. I'll text you later." So get the F out.

She grinned at me. "You're welcome." She reached over and gave me a hug, which was weird, because I didn't do hugs and she knew that. But it was a ploy to whisper in my ear. "Holy hotness. Total vag explosion."

"Tell me about it."

"Are you two going to make out?" Riley asked, sounding hopeful.

I looked around for something to throw at him but came up short. The room was too clean to be risking breaking anything, anyway.

"Let me walk you out," Riley said to Robin when she moved toward the door. "I don't want any of the neighbors getting any ideas."

Funny how he didn't seem to have a problem with me coming and going on my own. But there wasn't anything I could say that wouldn't sound insane and I couldn't exactly follow them either. So I just stayed in the kitchen and felt bitchy. The room looked amazing, like a hundred and ten percent improvement with the new cabinet knobs and all the other touches, and yet I was discontent. Maybe my mother was right—I was never grateful.

He was gone a long time. "Do you really want lunch?" I asked when he finally came back in, smelling like smoke. "Or was that just a way to try and get Robin to hang out longer?"

"Yes, I want lunch. I'm starving. The whiskey burned a hole in my gut and I need to fill it." He started down the hallway to his bedroom. "Your friend is cute."

"I know," I yelled bitterly from the doorway of the kitchen. "And she's single," I added, just because I was a masochist and I wanted to see his reaction to that information. And maybe because if he was going to hit on her, I just wanted to get it over with.

"That's a shame, I guess. Unless she wants to be single, then that's good." He reemerged from his room, wearing an AC/DC shirt.

"I have no idea what she wants," I said, trying for dignified but sounding more like I had a stick up my ass.

"Are you okay?" he asked, sounding dubious. "I think you must be hungry, too. You sound like Jayden when he's forgotten to eat."

I couldn't really argue with that. "I'm fine. Why wouldn't I be fine? And if you want to hook up with Robin, go for it, she has a great body."

Now why the hell did I say that last part? It was a rookie mistake I saw girl after girl make, and I had always rolled my eyes at their naiveté. Never let your emotion dictate what comes out of your mouth. It was a lesson straight out of Guy 101. The minute you did that, you handed control over to them.

Damn it.

His eyebrows shot up. "You want me to hook up with your friend? That's very generous of you. I appreciate you looking for a landing spot for my dick."

"Don't be crude," I chastised.

"You're the one who is suggesting I hook up with her five minutes after I met her."

"Never mind." I went to my room to get my purse and threw it over my head so that it dangled on my hip. I was wearing an old shirt with peanut butter and jelly high-fiving each other and basketball shorts I worked out in, but I didn't give a shit. It wasn't like putting on cuter clothes was going to change the outcome of this day.

"Are you jealous of your friend? Because that seems like a bad foundation for a friendship."

"Why would I be jealous of her? And what do you know about friendship?" Verbal vomit officially commencing. I grabbed a cookie out of the Mystery Machine and crammed it in my mouth just to shut myself up.

"Apparently nothing."

We went and got sub sandwiches, and Riley ate his footlong and half of my six-inch, along with two bags of chips and a soft drink that was roughly the size of my dorm room wastebasket.

"Do you have any pictures of your family on your phone?" I asked, an idea for the long hallway to the bedrooms popping into my head.

"What do you mean?"

"You know, like snapshots of the boys. Ones where no one is flipping off the camera."

He grinned. "That may be a tall order." But he dutifully pulled out his phone and started scrolling through pictures. "Here's one of Easton on his birthday. I got him a giant cupcake." He held it out to me.

Easton was smiling, his dark eyes shining, as he held his giant cupcake up to his mouth, about to take a bite. "That's perfect."

"Here's Jayden with Rory."

Jayden had his arm slung over Rory's shoulder, and they both were smiling. Again, I felt a twinge of envy. "That's cute."

Then Riley's smile fell off his face as he flipped through more pictures.

"What?" I asked.

"It's my mom." He studied the screen of his phone. "I know it sounds weird, but I do miss her in a way." He turned the phone to me. "Maybe it's because I remember her before the drugs, but she wasn't a bad person. Not like my dad. He's just a dick. But my mom was just, well, an addict."

I thought of the picture of her in his bedroom at her prom, and I looked at the picture he was showing me. She looked shrunken, fragile, hardly any bigger than Easton, as she pulled him against her in a hug. He was making a funny face, but she was smiling, like she'd been caught in a laugh, her mouth open to show missing bottom teeth, her skin sallow. But there was genuine happiness there in her eyes.

"I understand," I told him. "She's your mom. I'm sure she loved all of you."

"She did. She just couldn't stay away from the smack. And it killed her." He swiped past the picture. "So why did you ask, anyway?" he said, brisk, shaking more chips onto his sub wrapper.

"We can print some of those out at Walmart and hang them in the hallway. It will look great, and personal. You know, let the social worker see that you're a real family." I had a thought. "Let me take a close-up shot of your tattoo and we can use that one, too. It's a tattoo that says you love one another."

He made a face. "You make it sound so dorky."

I laughed. "Sorry. I mean, it's a very tough symbol indicating that you'll kick anyone's ass who messes with your brother. Is that better?"

"Definitely."

By the time we got back to the house with more supplies I was already exhausted. Then we started tearing up the carpet, and I decided that I needed to find a career where I could just look pretty, because this shit was hard work.

"Oh my God," I gasped, yanking on the piece Riley had cut that I was supposed to be rolling back. Sweat was dripping down my back, and the work gloves he'd given me kept slipping as I jerked the carpet.

"This was your idea," he reminded me, using his boot to hold down one section while he tugged where he'd sliced with the knife.

"I was a fool." An exhausted fool. I lay down on the filthy carpet to catch my breath.

"Man up."

"I'm not a man."

"I noticed."

Well, that was something. I rolled onto my side and wished an ice-cold lemonade would appear in my hand.

"Men don't whine as much as you do."

Lovely. "You haven't met my brother," I told him.

"By the way, this is a perfect photo op," Riley said. "You're supposed to be rehabbing houses, right? Here you go. This way you can prove it. It might not be the exact same situation as what you told your parents, but it's something."

"Good call." I dug my phone out of my bra. "Take my picture."

"You keep your phone in your bra?" He took it from me. "Wow, this is sticky." He wiped it on his jeans. "You might want to get off the floor if you want to look like you're working hard."

"Slave driver." I peeled myself off the floor and then went back to rolling old carpet on my knees while Riley took a picture.

An hour later all the carpet was out on the front lawn for garbage pickup and we were in the midst of a dusty hell. Coughing and waving my hands in front of me, I threw open the windows, risking Riley's wrath. I went over the floor with the broom to collect the piles of disintegrating carpet backing that had been left behind while Riley ripped out the boards that lined the edges of the wall, spiky nails sticking out of them. Another hour and we had mopped the floor and put the furniture back and it actually looked pretty damn good. The floor wasn't perfect. It had grooves and scuffs in it, but it was a huge improvement over the nasty carpet, and it smelled clean and fresh.

I flopped on the couch. "I have to leave for work in thirty minutes. This is going to be a hellish night."

"Sorry, kid." He did look like he felt bad for me. "I can drive you to work."

"Thanks. You're going to take a nap when you get back, aren't you?" I asked, feeling very envious.

"Probably not." Then he grinned. "Okay, yeah, totally."

But not only did he drop me off, he picked me up at eleven, when I was dragging ass. I laid my head on his shoulder and yawned while he drove.

"Poor princess," he said, and it actually sounded sincere.

I fell asleep before we even got back to the house and didn't wake up until he lifted me into his arms.

Whoa. For real? That woke me right up. "You don't have to carry me," I said. "I'm awake." But I snuggled in closer to his chest. There might never be another moment like this to feel his body that close to mine.

"Babe, if someone is offering you a free ride, take it."

He had a point.

"I'm too heavy," I said, because that's what we say as girls. We love the thought that a guy can carry us, but then we worry that he'll start thinking with each step that you were way heavier than he expected and that maybe you should lay off the ice cream. It's also maybe a slightly passive-aggressive way of seeking the reassurance we need. Toxic, sure, but it slipped out before I could stop myself.

But Riley didn't play the game. There was no reassurance. He just said, "Shut up, Jessica."

The words were harsh, but his voice wasn't. In fact, when I looked up at him, I saw something that took my breath away.

When he set me down on the front step to open the door, I tugged down my shirt, which had ridden up, all sleepiness gone because I knew what he was considering. He wanted to kiss me.

I knew that look. It was unmistakable.

And I wanted him to kiss me more than I had any other guy who had given me that look.

"Don't be mean," I murmured.

He cupped my cheek with his hand and said, "The last thing I feel right now is mean."

And despite the warm night air, I shivered in the dark, the feeble porch light glowing over us, bugs knocking into it.

"Good," I said, and I smiled up at him.

# CHAPTER EIGHT

FOR A FEW SECONDS, HE JUST STUDIED ME, UNTIL I STARTED
to get nervous. What was he thinking?

I said, "What are you doing? Are we going in or just going to
stand here all night?" If he wasn't feeling mean what was he feeling?
Riley wasn't as easy to figure out as other guys.

"I'm wondering if I kiss you if somehow your father will know
and smite me. That's the word, right? Smite? Smited? Smitten?"

Smitten? No, that had not just come out of his mouth.

But my body started to tingle in anticipation, relief surging
through me. He was asking for encouragement. I could do that, no
problem, because I most definitely wanted him to kiss me.

"Are you *going* to kiss me?" I asked, completely confident he
would now, with a little coaxing. "And no, you won't be smote.
My dad is a preacher, not God."

"So what if I am going to kiss you? Are you down with that?"

"I'm good with it, but I thought you hated me," I teased him,
leaning on the door frame out of his touch, amused that he was

asking for permission. It made me feel more confident, less at a disadvantage in that I probably liked him more than he liked me. "You said I'm like a little sister to you." I wanted him to kiss me, but I also wanted to hear him say out loud that he was attracted to me. Hey, guys aren't the only ones who need their egos stroked.

"Hate is such a strong word," he said, reaching out and fingering the cross I wore around my neck, the one that had been a gift from my father for my sixteenth birthday. Pure gold. "I never said I hated you."

Desire started to simmer as he leaned in close to me, as I anticipated the kiss I had somehow known we'd been heading toward all week, or at least hoping for. I opened my mouth and crossed my ankles, the tight ache between my thighs distracting.

Then he ruined it.

"I mean, I find you annoying and bratty, but I don't hate you."

Really? I tried to pull away, but he put his hands on the wall on either side of me, trapping my body against the house as he grinned at me.

"You're an ass," I said.

"I'm just being honest. Because you *are* bratty, even you have to admit that, but I also find you intelligent, sexy as hell, and strong. I like that you'll take the public bus even though you have no clue what you're doing and you're scared. I like that you're staying in this dump when you could probably call up Daddy and get money for a hotel, even if he doesn't know where you really are."

The last bit wasn't even close to the truth, but I was too busy enjoying his compliments to correct him. Because Riley was right— I was all those things. I could be annoying and bratty, yet I liked to think I was somewhat smart, and I knew I was strong, tenacious.

That he saw me for who I was did weird things to my insides that had nothing to do with sex.

"I admire that you're willing to pitch in and pull up nasty carpet to help me keep my brother."

"It's no big deal." But it was a big deal. All of it. All of this.

His lips barely brushed mine in the most innocent kiss I'd shared since middle school. It made me shiver again.

"Now you can tell me what you like about me," he prompted, while I stood there struck silent.

It was hard to think with his arms engulfing me like they were, his mouth so close to mine. I wanted to run my fingers through the stubble of his beard and bite his bottom lip. But I managed to focus long enough to say, "You are definitely an asshole, but what I like is that you are so responsible, you take care of your brothers, you do what you have to do, and yet you still laugh. You have a sense of humor, and you don't take yourself too seriously."

"I guess we're pretty fucking awesome, aren't we?" he asked.

I nodded.

Then, without any clear signal from each other, we both went for the kiss, and it was a hot collision of mouth and teeth. It was hot and wet and perfect. Wow. And then wow some more. His stubble was rough on my skin, his hands gripped me tightly, and his mouth fought to dominate mine. It was a sexy, skilled kiss, and I was breathing hard and wanting more when we paused.

"I've been wanting to do this all week," he muttered.

"Oh, yeah?" I hadn't really known that. I wanted that, but I hadn't been sure. At all. He had kept making it seem like we were friends and nothing more, and I had believed him. I had never been more glad to be totally wrong in my life. Feeling a little smug, I ran my tongue across his bottom lip. He gave a soft groan.

"Yeah. Every night I've been beating my dick like it owes me money."

Really? I snorted. "Shut up and just kiss me. You're better at that than talking." But the truth was, I didn't care what he said. I was excited, relieved, ready to take what he was offering and give him whatever he wanted, because I had managed to fall hard for him, fast, in a way that I never did.

He laughed.

As Riley pressed me against the house, hungrily kissing me, I clutched at his T-shirt, enjoying the feel of his hard chest. I had always been a girl who liked a muscular guy—not the juiced-up gym hardbodies—but a body like Riley's, earned from lifting heavy materials and sweating through a day of manual labor. Going lower, I slipped my hands under his shirt, groaning a little into his kiss as my fingers touched that smooth, hot skin of his abs.

"Feel free to keep going lower," he murmured, pulling his lips from mine.

Amused, I said, "That's so nice of you."

"I'm a giver." But then he pulled his head back. "But maybe we should go in the house before the neighbors get jealous."

He had a point. He took my hand and pulled me inside, the door closing softly behind him. I let him push me back against the door, fingers entwined with mine, his mouth doing delicious things to my insides as he kissed me again and again.

Not every guy can kiss, and not every guy knew how to use his tongue, but Riley and I seemed to be a perfect fit, our tongues teasing in a perfect give-and-take.

I let my hand wander down and I found his erection, hard and thick in his jeans. "Hm, what's this?" Stroking him, I felt the tug of desire and wondered if we were really going to do this, take it further than just a kiss. I wanted to physically, there was no doubt, but there seemed to be a lack of urgency on his part.

But that was Riley. He did everything with that swagger and that smile, and why should this be any different? Yet I'd seen him burst out in anger, and I'd thought, somehow, that he would attack me with passion. Or maybe that was just my fantasy—that he wanted me so badly he had to have me *now*.

Instead he was now lazily nuzzling my neck and keeping his hands just above my ass.

Yet I was the one stroking his penis. Suddenly doubting myself, I wondered what he really wanted, how he really felt about me. So he didn't hate me. And he liked certain things about me. But was that it? I was afraid to ask, so I went with what I knew would almost guarantee a positive response.

I popped the button on his jeans, hoping for a more aggressive reaction. "What's in here?"

"I don't think you'll be disappointed."

That's what every guy said. I was sure in his case it was true, given what I could feel beneath my palm, but I wanted something more from him, and I wasn't sure what it was, exactly. So I kept fishing. "Are you pierced like Tyler?"

I meant it as a sexy tease, but his lips stilled on my neck and he pulled back. "Tyler has his junk pierced?"

"Yes," I said, surprised. "You don't know that?"

"Why would I know what my brother does with his dick?" Riley looked repulsed by the very thought. "And by the way, how do you know?"

Uh-oh. He didn't know I had hooked up with Tyler. How could he not know? "Well . . ."

"I can't believe the shit you girls talk about. I wonder if Tyler knows Rory is spilling about their sex life. And no, I am not pierced. I have no desire to have a needle shoved through my dick."

I wasn't sure what to do. I had to tell him the truth, or it would come out later and bite me on the ass hard, but how exactly did I say that? Then again, it wasn't a big deal. It shouldn't be a big deal. It was all pre–Riley and me, so who cared, right?

So I told him, "Rory didn't tell me."

Now his expression turned puzzled. "So then how do you . . ." And then he got it. He recoiled from me. "*Oh my fucking God! Are you telling me you've had sex with my brother?*"

"Yes," I said, because I wasn't a liar and I wasn't ashamed. "I thought you knew."

"Why would I know that?" he asked, his hands going up to push through his hair. "I don't get detailed sex logs from Tyler. God! I can't believe you were going to let me do this without knowing."

"I thought you knew!" I said, starting to get pissed off. There was no deception or cover-up. Nathan and Kylie and Rory all knew, so I just assumed Riley did, too. I was still against the door and I moved forward, but he took two steps back, hands coming out in a defensive posture, like I might attack him or something.

"What's the big deal?" I asked, upset that I had opened my mouth and said anything, upset that instead of having him look at me like I was amazing, like he had been ten minutes earlier, he was eyeing me like I was a circus freak. World's Sluttiest Girl.

"You fucked my brother! That's a big deal!" Riley's legs ate up the room in long strides as he went over to the coffee table and pulled a cigarette out of a pack lying there. I hadn't seen him smoke all day, so it was a clear indicator he was stressed out. Cramming it in his mouth, he looked at me over the lighter as he flicked it on. "He's . . . touched you. That's messed up."

"So what?" I still didn't totally understand why he was so upset. "It was before I even met you."

"He's my brother!" He sucked hard on the cigarette and blew it out. "This isn't just some random guy. Every time I look at him I'm going to think about the fact that he nailed you. That he had his dick in you first."

Way to be rude about it. "Okay, I get that. But what am I supposed to do? It happened. We're adults. Rory doesn't have a problem with it and we're best friends. Tyler doesn't have a problem with being around me knowing I'm best friends with his girlfriend. None of us make it weird. Why are you making it weird? None of us walk around thinking about it."

I waved my hand in front of me to break up the cloud of smoke. "And I thought you said you wouldn't smoke in the house."

"This requires nicotine." Anger was simmering below the surface of his expression and he glared at me.

What did he have the right to be pissed about? "What do you want me to say?" I snapped. "I couldn't predict that we would wind up here. Tyler's my friend and we hooked up a few times."

"You seem to fuck an awful lot of your friends."

Oh, no, he didn't. "Excuse me?" I asked, eyes narrowing, my voice cold. He was one wrong word from finding my hand on his cheek. I'd never slapped a guy before, but this might be the perfect opportunity to go all Scarlett O'Hara on him.

"Have you fucked Nathan? I know you've fucked Bill. And my brother. What about Grant? Am I the only one you haven't had sex with? Forget about sloppy seconds, it's more like sloppy fourths."

There it went. My hand just flew up without me even thinking about it and connected with his cheek in the most satisfying slap of skin on skin. It knocked his cigarette out of his mouth and his head snapped to the side. I was shocked I actually did it, but at the same time, I was glad. Tears of anger and humiliation floated in my eyes and I blinked hard to make them disappear.

I didn't cry. I didn't. And never over a guy. Not happening.

When his head turned back, his eyes were dark and angry.

"Don't you ever refer to me as sloppy anything." I bent over and picked up the burning cigarette off the newly revealed hardwood floor and stubbed it out in the overflowing ashtray that I had been meaning to banish outside, my hand shaking from fury.

"Jessica . . ." he said, sounding contrite.

"Save it," I told him. "I'm taking my slutty ass to bed. You can go fuck yourself because I never will."

With that, I stomped down the hall. He started to follow me.

"Wait, I didn't mean that the way it sounded."

I walked faster. "You meant it exactly the way it sounded." When I sensed his arm reaching out for me, I started running. Once in Jayden and Easton's room, I slammed the door shut in Riley's face and locked it.

"I'm sorry." He tried the knob and then pounded on the door. "Let me in, Jess. I'm sorry. I don't think you're a slut."

"Yes, you do! Now go away." I wiped the tears off my cheeks with the back of my hand, my stomach tight. Asshat. He had no right to talk to me like that.

"Come on! We need to talk about this."

"Talk to someone who gives a shit." Resolutely, I put my phone in the speaker dock, blasting bouncy pop music that I knew would irritate the hell out of him.

After a minute, the knocking on the door stopped and I figured he had retreated to get away from the bubbly sultriness of Britney Spears. I could practically hear the sound of him popping open a beer, which is what I knew he would do. I had gotten to know Riley over the past week. Or so I'd thought. Okay, I could see that it might be weird to hear about me and Tyler at that particular moment, but what was he expecting? There was no purity ring on my finger, and what I did prior to him was no one's business but mine.

I could have lied about it. But I had wanted to be totally honest with him and what had that gotten me?

Sitting on Easton's bed, back against the wall, I bit my fingernail and hated on men and their goddamn double standards. When the glass of the window suddenly rose, I jumped. Riley's head appeared in the open space.

"What the hell are you doing?" I demanded, getting up to turn down the music. "Are you insane?"

He shoved the window completely up. "You wouldn't open the door," he said, like that was some kind of explanation. "We're not done with this conversation."

"Oh, I'm done." But I watched in fascination as he yanked out the screen and it disappeared behind him, and then threw his arms over the window frame and started to haul his body into the bedroom window. "What are you standing on?" That window was a good eight feet off the ground.

"The picnic table."

I refused to think this was hot. It wasn't. Or if it was, it still didn't change the fact that he was a jerk. It didn't matter that having a guy break into my bedroom to force me to talk to him was sexy, in a masculine, brutish kind of way.

He was too big for the window. He got halfway in and then he looked wedged, arms and head in, shoulders caught. There was a distinct sound of cotton tearing as his shirt caught on the aluminum frame. Served him right.

"A little help here," he said. "I'm stuck."

Help? Yeah, I could help him. So I shoved him. He barely moved, but he got my intent.

"Hey! What are you doing?"

"I'm helping you out of the window," I said, and shoved him again, harder this time, and he went backward, his shoulder finally free of the window frame. "That's what you asked for." Because it felt so good to get out my frustration, I put my hands on his shoulders and pushed a third time.

"Knock if off, Jess," he warned, as he grappled to hold on, losing his balance, his feet hitting the picnic table.

"Or what?" I pushed him yet again, high on the sensation of being in control after he'd made me feel so lousy.

His eyes narrowed, and I could hear the scraping of his boots on the house, could see the white of his knuckles as he tried to pull himself back up and not fall on his ass on the picnic table. At least his shoulders weren't stuck anymore. He should be grateful.

He didn't precisely answer the question, which was a point for him. Instead of threatening me, he simply said, "I'm not backing down until you talk to me."

"What?" I asked, cupping my hand to my ear. "I can't hear you over the flapping sound of my loose vagina."

The corner of his mouth lifted, and he almost laughed. "Is that what that noise is?" he asked. "I thought it was the air conditioner."

Ha ha. "You're a prick." I picked up a magazine, determined

to ignore him. Flipping through it, I tried to get invested in the many sexy ways Selena Gomez styled her hair, but I was too distracted by Riley dangling from the windowsill.

"I'm coming in whether you like it or not," he told me. "Now you can open your door for me or I can rip the window frame out and climb in this way. The choice is yours."

I thought about it and decided I had a perfect solution. Without a word, I got up and went over to the door to the hallway and unlocked and opened it.

"Good," he said, sounding surprised. "Great. I'll be there in a second."

Listening, I heard his boots hit the back patio, then heard him open the back door and come into the kitchen. At that point I got back up and closed my door again and relocked it.

A second later he realized I had tricked him. "Jessica! Damn it!" His fist hit the door.

I smiled. I couldn't help it. It was entertaining to get the best of him. "Yes?"

Then he did something that I wasn't prepared for. He said, "Please open the door. I really would like the chance to apologize to you face-to-face."

Crap. How could I continue being petty if he was going to be reasonable? It was a surefire way to ruin my ability to snark. With a sigh, I went to the door yet again and pulled it open. "Yes?" I asked, leaning on the door. "I'm very busy reading about sexy summer hairstyles."

He gave me a sly smile. "You have sexy summer hair." His fingers reached out and tucked my hair behind my ear.

Seducing me was not going to work. Well, it was working a little, but he still had some explaining to do. I just gave him a stony stare.

Riley dropped his hand. "I'm sorry about the comment I made. I didn't mean to suggest that you . . . well, anyway, I'm sorry. I was out of line."

"Yes, you were." Then because I didn't hold grudges, I said, "Apology accepted."

He nodded. "Thanks." Then he looked at his hand. And the floor. And behind my shoulder.

I waited, curious what brilliance was going to come out of his mouth next.

"I said that, not because I think you're a slut, but because well, I was upset that you had sex with my brother."

My eyebrows raised and I crossed my arms over my chest, the glossy fashion magazine still in my hands. "I caught on to that, yes."

"But you don't get it, do you?" he asked.

"No, not really."

"Think of it this way. What if I told you I had sex with your sister?"

"I don't have a sister."

He made a sound of impatience. "You know what I mean. Okay, say that you found out today when we were fooling around that I had sex with Kylie last year. How would you feel about that?"

A stab of jealousy pierced my chest and I asked, before I could stop myself, "Did you?"

"Ha, exactly," he said in triumph. "No, I did not have sex with Kylie, but your first reaction was one of anger. You didn't want to think that I did, because the truth is, none of us want to think that someone we care about has been naked with someone we're attracted to. Picture me with Kylie. How does it make you feel?"

I had an active imagination. Before I could put the brakes on it, an image of Riley over my roommate rose in my brain. He was enthusiastically giving her oral sex. It was a visual I could have done without. "Okay, I get it. Yes, I would be upset. Pissed."

"It just really caught me off guard," he said. "And the whole penis piercing thing . . ." He actually shuddered. "Disgusting. It's all messing with my head, making me jealous."

Begrudgingly, I loosened the death grip on my magazine. "Fine. But you took it a step too far. You didn't say the word 'slut,' but you definitely implied it loud and clear. I mean, sloppy? Ouch." I wanted him to understand where I was coming from. "I don't need to be judged, Riley. I've had my parents judging my morality my whole life and I don't have the patience for it."

"You're right, and I'm sorry. I was being an asshole. But I don't get it. Why would you and Tyler have sex? It's not like you ever had feelings for each other." Then he grimaced. "Or did you?"

"No." I shook my head. "The thing is, a lot of guys and girls are attracted to each other on some level. But that's not the same as being *attracted* to them, if you know what I mean."

"I have no idea what you mean," he said flatly.

Maybe I didn't either. I tried to explain it, frustrated by the frustration on his face. "It's not about emotional feelings. It's about physical feelings."

That I had to explain that to a guy just seemed stupid. It felt like he was purposely not understanding me. Guys were all about the booty call. But maybe what was so difficult for him to comprehend was that a girl could regard that in the same way a guy did. They were used to girls being clingers, assuming sex equaled a relationship.

"So you just get your clit licked and it's all good?" he asked dryly.

Bingo. Though I could do without the disdain on his part. I

didn't know a guy alive who didn't like to get head, given that they all asked for it and were shocked and horrified when I refused.

"Why is that so hard for you to grasp? Guys hook up with girls all the time and they don't care about them at all. Maybe, and I know it's hard to believe, but maybe sometimes girls do the same thing. Gasp. Horror. Maybe, just maybe, girls like to get off, too, for no reason other than that it feels good." I opened my magazine and started pointing to random chicks on random pages. "I bet she likes to have orgasms. I bet she does, too. And I bet this one, I bet she even masturbates." I lowered my voice. "Can you believe it?"

He made a sound of impatience and crossed his arms over his chest. "I'm not saying girls don't have sexual feelings. I'm glad they do. I appreciate enthusiasm. But I guess to me it makes sense to either be with someone you're in a relationship with or to be with a one-night stand. I don't get this crossing-the-line-with-friends thing. How do you keep it separate? It seems to me like you're just sticking your finger places it shouldn't be stuck."

I bit my lip, suddenly feeling sad. He didn't get it. And if he didn't get it, did he get me? And why did it matter that he got me? Other than that I didn't want to be put in that category of women that men didn't respect. Because I didn't deserve that. "Maybe to me it makes more sense to be physically intimate with a friend, someone who knows you and cares about you, that you trust, than to have sex with a total stranger you've met in a bar."

He nodded, but he didn't say anything, his brow furrowed.

"So what were we doing here, Riley?" I asked, the fight gone from me, a heavy sense of disappointment falling over me, a blanket of negative emotion. "It's hard to classify me as a one-night stand given that I'm living in your house."

"Oh, I don't do one-night stands," he said, and his arms dropped to his sides.

Something about the way he was looking at me . . . I felt my heart rate kick up a notch. "No?"

"No. I never have."

The magazine suddenly became a shield between us. I clutched it tighter to my chest, well aware of the goose bumps raising on my arms and the way my nipples were hard. "You've never had a one-night stand ever?" I tried to snort in derision, but it came out sounding like a shaky laugh. "Please."

"I haven't. Not my thing. I totally agree with you. I wouldn't want to have sex with someone I don't know, don't trust, don't care about."

My cheeks felt hot and I licked my lips nervously, tilting my chin up so he wouldn't see how vulnerable I suddenly felt. "So I guess you understand the friends with benefits thing better than you realized. Or maybe you would have if we hadn't been inter-rupted."

But he slowly shook his head and I shivered. "Nah. I still don't get it."

"Well, then you make no sense," I told him flatly, unnerved by the way he was looking at me. When he reached out and touched my cheek, stroking the back of his hand on my skin, I jerked away. For some reason, I wanted to believe he was making fun of me. Yet I was almost certain he wasn't. Which meant that instead of being able to retreat behind anger and indignation, I was going to have to face something that seemed scary as hell.

"I think what we can conclude here is that while I didn't say them out loud, my thoughts were running more along the relation-ship line."

"Oh," I said, though my brain had stopped functioning the minute the R word came out of his mouth.

"So what do you think? The princess and the prick . . . it could work. Or at least we could give it a shot."

My mouth filled with hot anxiety. "You want to have a relationship with me?" I asked, the very idea sending my thoughts galloping in opposite directions. On the one hand, the concept made me want to run away screaming, slamming the door shut behind me. On the other hand, there was something super hot about having Riley Mann as my boyfriend, even if that word made me want to choke on my saliva. "I thought you said you don't do relationships."

He'd said that at Nathan and Bill's, quite clearly. Maybe he had been joking. But I couldn't grasp that he would actually want to be with me, in the way you are with someone you're exclusive with. I also couldn't grasp that part of me wanted to jump straight into his arms and say yes to it. I didn't give up control like that, I didn't.

"I don't. Or I haven't in a while. Maybe we shouldn't call it a relationship then, exactly. I mean, it's only been a week we've been hanging out. Maybe it's more like dating."

The relief I felt was actually scary. It was like when you skid while driving in the snow and are sure you're going to hit the guardrail or another car and then you don't and suddenly your heart rate jacks up in relief and you gasp for air. Relationship = risk.

Yet on the heels of the relief was a profound disappointment. What the hell was wrong with me?

"What's the difference?" I asked. "Isn't dating a relationship?"

Riley shook his head. "Nah. It's totally different. Dating is what you do pre-relationship, to see if you want a relationship. You hang out, have fun together."

"Isn't that a friendship?" And were we really having this conversation?

"No." Riley leaned on the dresser and shook his head, looking totally confident in his logic. "Because when you're dating, there is an understanding you both are thinking you'd like it to be more than friendship. So even though you're not having sex, you want to and plan to."

Say what? "Wait a minute. You don't have sex when you're dating?" I wasn't sure I understood these categories. "But weren't you planning to have sex with me just now?"

He shrugged, looking a little sheepish. "I might have been jumping the gun a little. Trying to skip a step."

I rolled my eyes. "So having sex now, pre-relationship or dating, would have made us friends with benefits and we can't have that."

"No! We're not actually friends, you know. You can't be friends with someone you want to have sex with, you just can't."

"You've been saying we're friends all week! So if we're not really friends, then you want me to be a booty call, clearly." I knew he didn't, but his whole insistence that we define and label whatever the hell we were doing was completely irritating. And we weren't friends? Weren't people in relationships supposed to be friends? Or was I even more freaking clueless than I thought? And I didn't like that he had offered friendship, something I had actually really enjoyed and appreciated, and was now trying to take it away.

"No, damn it. A booty call is someone you just have sex with, nothing else. No hanging out, no conversation. You just text and make plans to hook up."

"I'm guessing you don't spend the night either."

"No, of course not." He sounded frustrated, which was exactly how I felt.

"You've given this so much thought it scares me." I tossed my magazine on the floor and myself on the bed. "You're worse than a girl and I'm done with this conversation."

I wasn't sure why I felt bad, but I did. This felt like rules, like a way for him to control me. I knew in my head he didn't mean that, he was just trying to be clear, but it just made me edgy, like I was right to stay away from relationships because I didn't know how to do this. Why did it have to be so complicated?

When he came over and tried to sit on the bed with me, I waved him away. "Just leave it for now, Riley, seriously. I'm exhausted and I can't do this."

"Can't do what?" he asked, voice exasperated. "We're discussing *us*."

"There is no *us*," I told him, feeling cranky and bitter. "You just said we're not even friends."

"You're twisting my words and you know it."

"Go. Away." I felt like I just might have a meltdown on him if he didn't leave me alone. And when I melt down, I say mean things. They just fly out of my mouth like darts, and I can't stop them. So it was better in the long run for both of us if he got the fuck out of my way.

For a heartbeat, he hesitated. Then he just nodded briefly. "Fine. Good night."

Rolling toward the wall, I closed my eyes and formed praying hands. "Night."

Yes, I was conscious that I left the "good" part out.

What can I say?

He was the one who seemed to think I was deserving of my last name.

I knew that when I was hurt, I wasn't all that nice.

And he had sliced me deep in several spots.

Which meant if he had the power to hurt me like that, I was falling hard for him, and it was better if we didn't start down a path that was going to result in me being pathetic.

It was small comfort at the moment that I was preventing myself from future weight gain due to heartbreak. Someday my ass would thank me, but now it just sucked.

# CHAPTER NINE

AFTER EIGHT HOURS OF SLEEP, I EMERGED FROM MY ROOM, hoping that Riley and I could just pretend the night before hadn't happened and go back to our easy companionship.

But he wasn't even home.

Which surprised me, because it was Sunday, and he didn't have to work. We had been planning to finish the house cleanup in anticipation of his brothers coming home on Monday. I poked around, but there was no note in the kitchen, no text on my phone from him. He just wasn't there, and empty, the house felt lonely. Which was dumb, because I'd been alone in the house before, but this was different. It felt forlorn in the aftermath of our fight, if you could call it that.

After eating a yogurt and drinking a soft drink, I showered and decided that Riley or not, I was going to finish the job I'd started. For ten minutes, I Febrezed the shit out of the couch to get the smell of smoke out of it. I dumped the ashtray in the trash bin out back and, after rinsing it with the hose, set it on the picnic table. The smoking lounge in the living room was closed as far as I was concerned.

Then I took the pictures we had printed from his phone at the drugstore as eight-by-ten-sized prints for less than twenty bucks, and the roll of bright-blue polka-dot duct tape I had bought, and started to hang them in the hallway. There was no way we could afford to buy frames for eight pictures, so I had figured the decorative duct tape would have to do. It would look like a design choice, not cheap.

It looked fantastic, I have to say, a neat row of black-and-white family shots all down the hallway, moments of joy and togetherness. I was proud of having given the Mann brothers a nicer environment to live in, to display their unique pictures on the wall, to give them a visual sense of what they already knew. But at the same time, it made me feel lonely all over again. Riley had insisted on printing our mustache shot, since he said it was my hard work that was saving his ass, and I deserved to be on the wall, but now it felt out of place. Even though I put it last, right before the door to Riley's bedroom, where the boys would never really see it, it still felt like I was intruding among the shots of Tyler and Jayden and Easton goofing off, and Riley's tattoo, cropped in tight.

Lonely doesn't sit well on me. It makes me do things I shouldn't.

Like answer Bill's random "want to hang out" text with "you should come over."

Yes, I am that stupid.

But I couldn't just wander around that house, alone, bored. There was nowhere to go. Robin was at her parents' house for church and a Sunday dinner thing. I had no car, and no desire to figure out the bus schedule to take me wherever. I had nowhere to go. Riley could be home any minute or not until tomorrow. I had no idea where he was or why he'd left without a word.

Bill was offering a distraction. I was taking it.

Not that I had any intention of messing around with him—I was mixed up about my feelings for Riley, and anyway, Bill had shut the door on that part of our relationship.

Relationship. What a loaded word. One I'd never liked, and now, after the hot mess of the night before, absolutely hated.

I figured Bill could come over, help me hang the blinds in the living room, and we could leave and go to the movies or something.

But Bill didn't know anything about hanging blinds. "What do I look like, a handyman?" he asked, dressed in plaid shorts and a polo shirt. "I'm a chemical engineering major."

"Which is why you should know how to do this," I said, shoving the instructions in his hand. "It's all math and spatial acuity."

"Forget it." He didn't even look at them. "I'm sure I could figure it out, but the answer is no." Wiping his forehead, he fanned himself. "Fuck it, it's hot in here."

"You're mean," I said. But it was a halfhearted pout. Really, why the hell would he want to hang blinds in Riley and Tyler's house? Sometimes I forgot that just because I wanted something to happen in the next five minutes, that didn't mean anyone else shared my enthusiasm or narrow focus.

I also realized that I didn't actually want Riley to come home and see Bill in the house. Regardless of how innocent it was, now that Bill was standing here, I knew it would not sit well with Riley.

Bill just laughed. "Jessica, I admit, that usually works on me, but it's too hot in here to do anything. It's like a hundred and ten degrees in this house. How are you living here without suffering heat exhaustion?"

"My room has air-conditioning. Let me go change and grab my purse and then we can leave. Come on." I indicated he should join me. I didn't want him to melt on my behalf.

"Oh my God, that's better," he said as we entered the cool sanctuary of my room. He plucked at his shirt. "It's like existing in a wet towel."

"I think I'm getting used to it." Truthfully, it didn't bother me as much as I would have expected.

"So how is it, living here with Riley?" Bill asked, sitting on my bed.

I shrugged. "It's fine." Digging through my suitcase, I found a cuter top than the shirt I had slept in. "Close your eyes," I told him.

He obeyed, but he said, "I've seen you naked."

"I know. But it's different now. We're just friends, we're not going there anymore."

"I can handle seeing you in your bra."

Why did that sound vaguely insulting? "You're the one who wanted us to be just friends. I'm trying to respect that." What the hell was with guys? No matter what I did, they wanted something different.

"But you don't have to act like I can't control myself."

Oh, for the love of God. "Fine. Open your eyes. I don't give a shit." Idiot. I pulled my knit shorts down so that I could put on denim shorts instead and rooted around in my suitcase in my bra and panties. It was like wearing a bathing suit, and he was right, he had seen me naked. I didn't feel like discussing it any further.

Why were women always being accused of being the ones who wanted to overcomplicate things? To talk them to death? Both Riley and Bill were driving me insane with their determination to define what we were doing.

And a glance over at the bed showed that Bill wasn't exactly unaffected, despite his bragging claims. He was staring at my ass.

"So why are you hanging blinds, or attempting to talk me into hanging blinds, in Riley's house?"

I shrugged. "Because he needs help cleaning up before the social worker pays a home visit." I didn't want to go too deep into the real situation. It was Riley's business, and I didn't know how much he would want known.

"How do you feel about Riley?"

I paused, my T-shirt over my head, ready to be pulled on. I eyed Bill, suddenly feeling suspicious. "What do you mean?"

Bill leaned back on his elbows on my bed, shrugging. "It just seems to me like maybe he is the kind of guy who can get you to open up a little."

"I opened up plenty for you," I told him coldly. What was he getting at? I didn't like the turn this conversation was taking.

"That's not what I mean. You never tell me anything about yourself. I don't know you at all, Jessica, not really."

"I'm not a deep, dark secret."

"Can I ask you something without you assaulting me?"

"Well, that's promising." Nerves jangling, I pulled my shirt on and down over my chest. "Sure, why not? I've been insulted on a regular basis lately, why not keep the trend going?"

"I'm serious, and this is as a friend. Why do you push guys away?"

"I don't push guys away. That's the real problem, according to some people," I said wryly.

He gave me a long look. "Okay, fine. You don't want to talk about it with me. That's cool."

"Talk about what?" I asked, totally exasperated.

"You like Riley, don't you? I've always thought you did."

That caught me off guard, and I felt my cheeks heat. "No, I haven't always liked Riley. After this week, I am more comfortable around him, but there's nothing there, trust me. He thinks I'm a slut." Just saying it out loud made me bitter all over again, and I could hear the wobble in my voice.

"Come here." Bill patted the bed next to him.

I obeyed, my shorts in my hand.

"You're not a slut," he told me as I sat down.

"I know." I leaned my head on his shoulder, wanting the comfort he was offering. "But why do I feel so bad?"

"Because having feelings for someone is a pretty miserable experience, that's why." He brought his arm around my back and hugged me to his side.

I laughed. "Apparently."

"I think a lot of guys, myself included, are more comfortable taking our clothes off with a girl than showing her how we really feel. Sex is easier than emotion."

Sex is easier than emotion. That was scary accurate.

I fumbled to drag my shorts on up over my ankles, my calves, my knees, my thighs, up, up, to cover myself. It suddenly felt wrong to be talking about this with Bill in my underwear.

Because he was right.

I could take my clothes off with any guy I was attracted to. Yet I showed no one who I really was.

How ironic that naked was more covered than conversation.

The knock on my door had me jumping. "Oh, shit," I muttered, knowing being in my room with Bill wasn't going to sit well with Riley. Fumbling to zip my shorts, my fingers trembling, I was still trying to process what Bill had said. What it meant to me.

"Jess?"

"Yeah?" I called out.

But Riley was already opening the door. "Hey, the photos look really good—"

His words cut off when he stuck his head in and assessed the situation.

My fingers were still on the snap of my shorts, having finally gotten the zipper up. I tried to tug at my shirt, like that's what I had been doing all along, but Riley wasn't buying it. He looked at Bill, the rumpled bed we were sitting on, my hand, and no doubt my guilty expression, and exploded.

*"Are you fucking kidding me?"* he yelled. "Come on! Jesus! This is how fast you move on?"

"We're going to the movies, that's all," I told him. "Calm down."

"Dude, she's telling the truth. We are just friends." Bill held his hands out in a conciliatory fashion.

Riley looked like he wanted to kick the door. In fact, his foot actually lifted, like he was contemplating it. Not wanting any more damage to the house, I jumped off the bed and rushed over to him. "Riley, stop!"

He paused and ran his fingers through his hair in clear frustration. "What the fuck is going on? For real? Last night you told me there's no you and me, but is this what you really want? Me to leave you the fuck alone so you can do whatever?"

The anger, no, the pain in his voice left me speechless.

Bill filled the awkward silence I left dangling.

"I'm just going to take off. Jess, I'll catch you later."

Normally I would have protested, said he didn't have to leave, that no one was going to chase off a friend of mine. I would have taken a stand, been defiant.

But I couldn't. Because Bill was my friend, but so was Riley.

No matter what he said about friendship being shady between guys and girls, we were friends, because that's what you called someone you cared about, right?

I cared about him.

"Thanks, Bill. Talk to you later."

Bill moved through the door. Riley didn't step out of his way, but instead glared at him. To Bill's credit, he didn't react at all, and he didn't flinch or shift out of the way. He just waved at me over his shoulder and barreled through.

"He didn't do anything wrong," I said to Riley, afraid he would take it upon himself to punch Bill at some point. "You don't have to look at him like that."

Riley just shrugged. "I can look at Nerd Boy any way I want. It's my house."

Hopefully, Bill was far enough across the living room that he didn't hear the rude slur. I wanted to tell Riley he was being a dick, but that would just take the conversation off topic. "Last night I was upset because I don't understand what it is you want from me," I told him. "First you want sex, then you want a relationship, then you say no, just dating, and no sex. I don't get it. But I like you, Riley. I really like you. So no, I don't exactly want you to leave me alone, but I can't have all these labels and expectations and rules put on whatever we're doing."

"Can you please button your shorts?" Riley refused to look at me.

That was the response I got? Anger shot through me. I shoved his chest. "You're an asshole!"

"What?" He sounded put out. "It's distracting!"

"I'm trying to share my fucking feelings, something I don't do with just anyone, you know, and you aren't even listening! You're obsessing over the fact that I might have done something with Bill despite the fact that we both said nothing happened."

He shot me a guilty look. "Well, I can't help it! The idea is killing me."

"I told you nothing happened! I just told you that I like you! Do you know how many times I've told that straight out to a guy I wasn't together with?" Furious, I held up my index finger. "Once! In my whole life! And it was to you, just now, so thanks for fucking it up."

Spinning around, I was prepared to walk away. To go where, I had no idea, but somewhere where I didn't have to look at his face, because I wanted to punch him in the jaw. Or at the very least shove him again, and I didn't want to lose control like that.

But he grabbed my arm and stopped me from retreating. "You like me?"

It was really amazing how thick-skulled guys could be. "Duh. I thought we established that last night."

"But you got mad at me."

"Because you were being confusing as hell. And I was exhausted. And then this morning you were gone and there wasn't a note or a text or anything and I had no idea where you were. I thought you were pissed at me."

"I went to work out and then to the grocery store. I got you Diet Coke and Greek yogurt. Plus a refill for the air freshener."

He had? My anger started to thaw.

"I didn't think that you would wonder where I was. I didn't think that you would, well, care."

Giving an indignant sniff, I said, "Then you're stupid."

He smiled. "Obviously. So Nerd Boy was really just here to go to the movies?"

"Yes. I was bored and lonely." So there. "I didn't want to take the bus and he has a car and offered to pick me up. That's it, though I'm not sure why you're so jealous when you're not offering me anything anyway." It wasn't pretty, but I wanted information. If I was fishing with a pole and line off a boat before, now I was wading in the river, hillbilly hand fishing. I might as well have said, "Click Like if you would date me."

Pathetic. But I needed an answer, a solid yes or no so I could move on either way. Limbo land doesn't work for me.

Riley made a sound of exasperation. "Jessica, you drive me crazy. I said I want to date you. What is so unclear about that?"

Part of me wanted to ask for clarification, but then I would be doing exactly the thing that had been making me crazy about him. So I just shrugged, pulling my arm from his touch and crossing them. "Nothing, I guess," was my stellar and petulant answer.

But I couldn't help it. Being emotionally vulnerable sucked. It was why I never did it.

Riley reached out and pried my arms off my chest.

"What are you doing?" I asked, feeling even more out of control with my chest uncovered, my arms forced down to my sides. I actually turned my head, unable to be that exposed.

But he took my hands and placed them on his waist. Then he gently tilted my head back toward him, his hand cupping my chin as I fought the urge to close my eyes.

"Hey," he murmured.

"What?" I was fighting the urge to bolt.

But then he said, "I like you, too. In fact, I like you a whole helluva lot. So let's just do this thing, see what happens. You good with that?"

There was an honest-to-God lump in my throat. It was like I'd swallowed a marshmallow. So I just nodded.

# CHAPTER TEN

RILEY GAVE ME A SOFT, GENTLE KISS THAT DISARMED ME. I didn't get kissed like that. Boyfriends kissed girlfriends that way, with a soft sense of worship. Guys tended to worship my breasts more than my mouth. I might have sighed. Or maybe I just imagined I did. I'm not sure. I just know that something shifted in me right then, something that told me what was happening between Riley and me was . . . real.

I blinked up at him, not sure what to say or do. This was all new territory for me. I hadn't had a boyfriend since my junior year in high school.

"Since you wanted to go see a movie, I can take you," he said. "We can't have you bored. You might decide to stain the picnic table or something. Which means I'll be staining the picnic table."

Air left my chest with a whoosh. He had made the moment normal again and I was damn glad. I didn't quite know how to do long minutes gazing into each other's eyes. And if he started playing with my hair like Tyler did to Rory, I was going to get twitchy. So not my style.

The movies and mildly mocking me? Yeah, that worked.

"Now that you mention it, that picnic table is shabby. Though truthfully, we should just use it to make a bonfire and have s'mores."

Riley laughed. "No."

"Just a suggestion. But yes, I would like to go to the movies. What do you want to see?"

He pulled his phone out and scrolled through the movie options. "Let me guess, you will want to see a romantic comedy."

I made a face. "Are you joking? No. Absolutely not. I find those movies embarrassingly sentimental. Kylie is the one who likes that stuff."

"Thank God. Because I was going to have to tell you no. I can't do chick flicks. What else is out?"

"Scary movies."

He looked disappointed. "Why?"

"Because they're scary," I said pointedly. "Duh."

"Come on, they're not *real*."

"How do you know?" I had been raised by a father who was absolutely certain evil and the devil existed. "If you want to watch a horror movie, you'll have to take Rory. She always watches those crime shows on TV. Every time I turn around there's a live autopsy playing on her laptop. It's brutal."

"She's pretty hard-core, isn't she?"

"Yes. Personally, I only want to see organs in living people." I cocked my head. "Wait, that doesn't sound right. Why would I be seeing organs at all?"

"My skin is an organ." His eyebrows went up and down. "As are other things."

Rolling eyes here. Though he did amuse me. I wasn't really sure why. "What else is playing?"

"Some drama about slums."

"No." My hands came out to emphasize my feelings on that one.

"Why not?"

"Because I don't want to cry." I hated crying, which is why I tried to never do it.

"So what does that leave us? Action/adventure and comedy of the Adam Sandler variety."

"I'll take action/adventure. I like to see things blow up."

"And you say Rory is brutal." But he read a movie description to me. "This starts in forty minutes, so we can make it."

"Okay, I need my purse."

Riley followed me to the doorway of my room. "So, uh, why were you buttoning your shorts up exactly?" he asked, trying to sound casual.

Really? I grabbed my hoodie and purse and shot him a look over my shoulder. This was going over what we'd already gone over, as far as I was concerned. "Because I was changing. I made him close his eyes."

He looked pained. "Damn it. I was afraid you were going to say something like that."

"Then you shouldn't ask." I crowded him in the doorway. "Because despite the fact that I'm lying to my parents about where I am, I try to be honest about my behavior."

"You know he looked. I would."

"If you're going to be jealous, we're going to have a problem. So try to keep it under control." Then because the beard scruff on his chin was so cute, I ran my fingers through it like you do with a cat behind its ears. "But I won't give you any reason to be jealous from here on out, since we're doing this thing, whatever it is, and whatever we're calling it. Cool?"

"Cool." Then he pretended to bite my finger.

I laughed.

When we went outside, I winced at the blinding sun and pulled my sunglasses out of my purse. As I was pushing them onto my face, I saw the neighbor to the left sitting on his front step, shirtless, his gray grizzled beard meeting the rounded bare belly. He eyed me boldly, then let a stream of brown tobacco juice fly from his mouth onto the hard-packed dirt and grass of his yard. He didn't acknowledge Riley and likewise.

"Good afternoon," I said, with a cheerful wave. If there was one thing I knew how to do, it was to be fake friendly with the neighbors. My mother had it down to a science.

"Christ," Riley muttered as he got in the car.

But the extra from *Duck Dynasty* actually lifted his hand and waved, calling back, "Hot as hell today, but you're a sight for sore eyes."

"Thanks. Have a great day." I climbed in the passenger seat.

"I didn't even know that guy could talk," Riley said. "In two years he's never said a word."

"A smile goes a long way."

He snorted. "Yeah, if you're a blond chick with long legs. If I smile at him we're going to end up swinging punches."

"Hm. I might need some guidance on social dynamics in your neighborhood, then. In my neighborhood, everyone kisses up to one another. It's a finely tuned ritual of hypocrisy and envy. They'll congratulate you on your son's acceptance to an Ivy League school, then trash him behind your back, mocking his looks or his intelligence, or yours. Or your new landscaping, or your vacation, or your Botox, whatever has recently been done."

"Maybe that's the difference here. No one envies anyone else, so there's no point in conversation."

That was an interesting viewpoint. I was still contemplating it when we pulled into the movie theater. There was an honesty in Riley's neighborhood. No one gave a shit about anyone else, and that was clear, whereas in my parent's neighborhood, everyone pretended to care, but they didn't really either. I wondered if there was anywhere that people did care, and looked out for one another, or if that was some small-town ideal that didn't exist. It was a depressing thought.

But then I remembered when a church member's young son had died of cancer, and the outpouring of help, both emotional and financial, for that family. There had been thousands of people at the memorial service, and that had been genuine sympathy, a real desire to ease a grief that was unimaginable. So maybe there was such a thing as community.

Maybe it was the weird, melancholy thoughts, but when Riley pressed me to see the horror movie instead of the action one, I actually agreed, for whatever reason. Maybe the scary that wasn't real could supersede the fear of the scary that was real—and what was more scary than feeling that everything is one big cynical joke?

Riley pulled out his wallet to pay for the tickets and I scrambled to get out my debit card. "Don't pay for me."

"I got it," he told me. "You don't even want to see this movie, the least I can do is pay for it."

"But . . ." I wanted to say I knew he didn't have a lot of money, but that would sound so patronizing and elitist, no matter what my intention was, that I cut myself off.

"But nothing." He handed the girl behind the counter a twenty and got his change and our tickets. "You just spent a ton of money making my house less of a shithole. I can take you to the movies."

"That was different. I only spent eighty bucks. That's like rent for the week I've been staying with you."

"Rent?" Riley shot me an amused look as we moved into the lobby area. "That's hilarious."

I started toward the ticket attendant to enter, but he said, "Hold up. I need popcorn."

He bought a tub of popcorn that was basically the size of a beer keg. And a soft drink equally as insane. "Want a drink?" he asked as he encouraged the employee to pump more oil or fake butter or whatever that was on his popcorn.

"I'll just share yours. It looks like you'll have plenty." Especially considering his snacks cost as much as the tickets themselves.

Riley had to sit in the middle, both at the theater and in the aisle, so we climbed over a couple in their fifties. We settled in, and he slumped down, his legs wide, turning off his phone and then proceeding to throw giant handfuls of popcorn into his mouth.

My own mouth watered. I hadn't eaten lunch and that looked good. It smelled good.

"Aren't you going to have any?" he asked.

I took one piece and put it in my mouth. Damn. That was some buttery goodness. Fake butter or not, it tasted like victory in my mouth. Like triumph and glory and the finish line. I chewed slowly, afraid I was going to reach out and just bury my face in the tub.

After an excruciating minute, I let myself take another piece. Riley didn't say anything, which I appreciated. I was struggling, and I didn't want to hear the typical male attitude, which was "dieting is stupid," yet they could not deny that they wanted women to look a certain way.

All these various thoughts I was having were all just a little too heady for a Sunday afternoon.

Fortunately, Riley pulled my hand into his, which sufficiently distracted me. He also gave me a buttery and salty kiss that had me leaning extra close to him, tucking my feet under my legs.

"Mm," he said. Then he popped a piece of popcorn into my mouth and I didn't even count the calories.

I just giggled as the opening credits started.

Twenty minutes later there was no giggling going on. The movie was creepy. Like hide-my-eyes, suck-my-soul-out-of-my-chest, whimper-in-the-dark scary as fucking hell. I was practically sitting in Riley's lap. He had put his arm around me and tucked me into his chest and armpit, but it wasn't enough to combat the freaked-out factor as the girl in the movie screamed the eeriest scream in the history of screams. A demon was possessing her, and in the most horrific of ironies, her name was Jessica.

"Really?" I had asked Riley when we had first learned her name. He had just laughed. "It's a common name."

While I had never seen *The Exorcist*, this seemed to me like that movie, but with modern special effects and camera angles. I wasn't entirely sure I believed in demon possession, but I couldn't say with any certainty that it *didn't* exist, and if it did, I imagined it would look exactly like this. Snot and sweat and weird limb angles.

Something shot across the room in the film, and I jumped. I may have whimpered, because Riley moved his popcorn to the opposite side so that he could pull me closer. "You okay?" he whispered.

"I don't think so," I whispered back. "I think I'm going to run out of the theater screaming."

"Just remember it's not real. It's just a story."

Someone in the theater shushed us. I was tempted to throw popcorn at them. I was having a crisis here, a little sympathy, please. Besides, what did you need to hear in a horror movie? The dialogue all focused on the normal people being disbelieving, e.g., "Just go back to bed, Becky. It's the wind." And then the evil creature/character whispering ominously, "Murder, murder, murder." Or whatever the case was.

In this movie it was things like, "I've been watching you, Jessica" and "We're in this together, Jessica, in your body and your soul." What, like I needed *that*?

By the three-quarter point, I had my head buried in Riley's shoulder and I was clutching his shirt with both hands.

It wasn't pretty.

But neither was Satan.

By the time the lights came on in the theater, I was sweating and breathing hard, my hands clammy. When I released Riley's shirt, there were wet spots from my anxious fists palming him.

"Maybe this wasn't the best choice," he conceded, rubbing my arms. "I stand corrected."

"You think?" I said, actually shivering from fear.

"You really are afraid. I thought you were exaggerating."

"I don't exaggerate," I said with great dignity.

He snorted. "It's the sledding all over again. I didn't know you were really such a chickenshit. I thought you were making it up."

Oh, yes, the sledding. I didn't think it was that weird to be twenty years old and afraid of flying down a hill on a piece of cracked plastic, but he had seemed to think I was just stalling to be annoying. So Riley had pushed me, and I had almost fainted from lack of oxygen, a scream frozen in my lungs. "Well, from now on, you should believe me."

As we stood up and left the theater, I added, "And I'm not a chickenshit. There are just certain things I'm afraid of, high speeds and demonic possession being two of them. You have to be afraid of something, too, everyone is."

"Nope."

"Whatever." I rolled my eyes for emphasis. "You're not afraid of heights or small spaces or spiders?"

"No."

"Flying?"

"I've never been on a plane, so I'm not one hundred percent sure, but most likely no."

"Death?"

"Not particularly. I'm too busy trying to live."

"You're unnatural," I declared. "Everyone is afraid of something."

Riley held the door open for me as we stepped out into the heat and sunshine. "You know the one thing I'm afraid of."

I glanced back at him, and I knew what it was—losing Easton. "That's not going to happen," I told him firmly. "The house looks great and Easton is happy. He feels safe with you, and he'll tell the social worker that."

Riley nodded. "And demons aren't going to possess you, Jess. I don't believe in guarantees, but in this case I'm willing to guarantee it."

"I'm willing to guarantee that you're going to hang those blinds when we get back to the house."

He made a face. "What are you majoring in? Management?

Because you're really good at telling me what to do, while you watch me and point."

"Ha ha." I hesitated to tell him my major, because it sounded so stupid to me. Like a waste of a giant pile of money. For more than a year, I hadn't even told Kylie and Rory that I was doubling with religious studies. They had just thought I was a design student until Rory started to get suspicious as to why I was taking so many theology classes and I had confessed the truth.

I wasn't even sure what I wanted to do post-college exactly, and that felt like such a failure. It made me feel guilty, too, that other people didn't have the luxury of going through the motions of a degree. They had to pay bills and survive and here I was, getting a degree to placate Daddy.

The freedom I was working so hard to ensure wasn't really all that freeing if I was going through the motions with my classes, and aimless otherwise. I was halfway done with college and knew less about my future than I had when I'd graduated high school. Scary shit.

Fortunately, Riley was not the kind of guy who wanted me to cough up all my personal details or my feelings. Probably because he didn't want to do that in return.

There was a safety in spending time with him, laughing and eye-rolling and teasing, with occasional moments of serious conversation. There was no prying, no judgment.

He hung the blind. Maybe because he knew that it would look a lot better than the sheet that was currently tacked to the wall. Or maybe he just wanted to get me to shut up. Either way, in ten minutes, he had the brackets mounted to the wall and the blind clicked into place.

I clapped. "It looks awesome in here." I had thrown away the pillows on the couch when he wasn't looking and had replaced them with two red pillows we had scored at the dollar store for five bucks a piece. Mostly my goal there was again to cut down on the lingering smoke smell.

"I have to admit, it does look a lot better. You are a genius, my friend." But he swatted my hand when I tried to open the window. "Down, girl."

"Argh! Your logic makes no sense! It's boiling in here!"

"You're cute when you're annoyed," he told me, and kissed the tip of my nose.

Damn him. I forgot about the window. "Kiss me," I ordered.

"There we go with the bossy thing again." But he obeyed, taking me into his arms and kissing me thoroughly.

Everything inside me melted, and I rubbed my breasts against his chest as his breathing grew slower, louder, our mouths colliding with a hot intensity, his fingers gripping my hair on the back of my head. I went for his zipper.

Riley stopped me. "Uh-uh. We're just kissing. No skipping steps."

What steps was I missing? Kissing led to naked, which led to sex. I wasn't sure what else there was supposed to be, but I didn't want to get into a breakdown of sexual dynamics and dating again. Those conversations were boring and annoying. So I just moved my hands to the small of his back and bit his bottom lip to show him what I thought of that.

"Ow."

"Be quiet," I said in response to his clearly fake complaining. "It wasn't that hard."

"You know, there is something else I'm afraid of," he said, his brown eyes crinkling in amusement.

"What?"

"You."

That earned him a smack on his chest.

He laughed, and that was the end of our romantic kiss. He pulled away and dug his phone out of his pocket. "I'm starving. I'm going to order Chinese food. What do you want?"

A magic pill that would allow me to eat as much food as he did. Jesus. "Steamed vegetables."

"Gross."

"Like your face."

He laughed. "Touché, pussycat."

Hell, if this was dating, I could do this, no problem. It wasn't that much different than how we had been two days ago. I felt a little more relaxed about the weightiness of the word "relationship." Obviously it meant different things depending on the people involved, and Riley and I were not moony-eyed, let's-carve-each-other's-names-with-knives-on-our-forearms kind of people. Nor did we need to be constantly petting and grooming each other like Tyler and Rory, or using smoochie-woochie, fakie-wakie words like Kylie and Nathan.

We were awesome, as Riley had stated, and we ate Chinese food (well, he ate Chinese food, and I nibbled on broccoli) and played video games and made out, his Szechuan breath killing my desire to stick both my hands in the food containers and shovel scoops into my mouth.

Riley kissed me old school, his hands staying outside of clothes, on my waist. I have to admit, it was making me crazy, but in a good way. He was stirring my arousal, making it simmer low, and I knew if he kept this up, I would be boiling. I tried to arch my breasts as an enticement but he ignored me.

Then he smiled at me. "I need to go to bed. I have to get up at six tomorrow to be on site by seven."

I blinked. "Are you serious? It's only ten." I knew that because I had been clock watching earlier for our war of the windows. I had just opened the living room one a half hour before.

"I know. But I want to get home early tomorrow and do something with the boys when they get back. Jayden loves the zoo, and I hate the zoo, so I need a good night's sleep to have the patience for that. All that walking and animal shit and Jayden pointing out their balls in a voice that is way too loud for public."

Nice. "That sounds fun. Sort of. I can't say I'm that interested in giraffe testicles myself." I realized I didn't know what my role in any of this was. "I should probably pack up my stuff tonight. I'll see if Robin can drive me to the apartment I'm subletting." I was supposed to move out the next day, when the boys came home. That's what we had agreed on. But now that seemed like a whole lot of no fun. I didn't want to be in an apartment by myself with a strange roommate. I wanted to be here.

"Want to go to the zoo with us?"

"I have to work."

"Bummer."

It was a bummer. All of it. I didn't expect him to offer for me to stay. Where would I? The only room I could stay in would be in Riley's with him and that was like basically living together. Real living together. That was skipping steps, and maybe not appropriate for Easton's impressionable mind. Of course, Rory stayed there all the time, so what the hell was I worried about? That wasn't really the point. The point was you don't move in for reals with someone you started dating five minutes earlier. Plus Riley knew I'd rented this apartment already. It would seem weird if he suggested I stay.

So why did I want him to suggest I stay?

He was turning me into a neurotic freak. Maybe it was better I was moving out.

"When will I see you again?" he asked.

"Wednesday is my first day off." Hm. That was a long time to not see each other. In a week I'd gotten used to him being around, and I felt a pout coming on.

"Text me your new address and I'll pick you up after work, and we can do something. That cool?"

"Yep." Sort of. I guess it would have to be.

"Good night." He kissed my forehead. "Talk to you tomorrow."

So apparently I was supposed to sleep in my room. I wasn't sure how I felt about that. Actually, yes, I was. I thought it sucked.

I really hated it when he closed the door to his room and I realized how dark and quiet the house was. I got up and checked the front and back doors. The front had been locked already but the kitchen wasn't, and I did a quick search of the closets and the pantry to make sure no one was lurking there, having snuck in while the door was unlocked all afternoon. Then I closed the living room window because really, anyone could just pop the screen out and climb in. It was huge, unlike the bedroom windows.

Trying to watch TV, I bit my fingernails and told myself there was no such thing as demons and that the weird scratching sound was the cat who came and went at random through the pet door. He must be back in the house, wandering around. My feet were on the coffee table and I was hot now that I'd closed the window, yet I shivered like something had touched the back of my neck. Spinning around, I expected to see the cat on the back of the couch, but nothing was there.

Suddenly the room had shadows everywhere, and the kitchen

looked like a big yawning black hole, the back door glass giving off a weird reflective shimmer.

The scratching got louder, and I went from slightly unnerved to scared on a level of pure panic.

When the scratch was followed by what I swear was a sinister whisper, I shut off the TV, jumped off the couch, and went down the hall, my back sliding against the wall so nothing could attack me from behind. Reaching Riley's room, my heart racing, I whispered, "Riley?"

He didn't answer.

I lightly knocked. "Riley?" I had to keep it down. I didn't want the demon to know where I was precisely. Or the serial killer. Whichever it was.

When he still didn't answer, I turned the knob and slowly pushed the door open. "Riley?"

"Yeah?"

Thank God. He wasn't dead in his bed.

"I heard a noise. In the living room. Like a disembodied voice whispering." I didn't wait for his response. I was already moving into his room, closing the door behind me and locking it. "I think someone is in the house."

He sighed. "No one is in the house."

"How do you know?" I tripped over something in the dark and stumbled into the bed. "Fuck." I crawled up onto it, accidentally putting my knee down on Riley's shin.

"Ow, Jesus, what are you doing?"

"I'm scared." I started climbing Riley, trying to get over him to the free side of the bed. We were a tangle of limbs, my balance off as we rocked slightly. "Why are we moving? OMG, is this a water bed? Who the hell has water beds?"

"People whose mothers were fourteen in the eighties and in love with hair bands." The light from his phone suddenly glowed in the dark. I could see his squinting eyes looking less than pleased.

My elbow went into his gut and he made an *oomph* sound as the air left his lungs. "Sorry. But there's someone in the house."

Riley helped me off of him, tucking me along his side. "There is no one in the house."

"You keep saying that but you have no way of knowing if that's true or not. I heard scratching."

"That's the cat."

Pulling the sheet over me, I threw my leg over his, wanting the reassurance of his masculine body. He could probably beat the crap out of a serial killer. Or at least stall him so we could escape. A demon I wasn't sure about, but I still felt a lot better being next to him. "Cats don't whisper."

Riley sighed. His phone went dark, and I could hear him set it down on the nightstand before sitting up. "I'm never taking you to see a horror movie ever again."

Thank God. I grabbed his arm. "What are you doing?" I knew I was being insane, but I couldn't help it. I was scared and I didn't want him to be killed. Nor did I want to be left alone.

"I'm going to check the house to give you peace of mind and to give me sleep."

I started to get up, too, but he added, "Just stay here."

"That's what they always tell the female protagonist to do in movies and that's when she gets killed."

"You're not coming with me. Just lay down and I'll be back in two minutes."

I didn't lay down, but I did obey him, despite my desperate urge to jump on his back like a baby monkey. That would hinder him from fighting off a killer, though, so I cursed my stupidity for leaving my phone in the living room and rested on my knees, peering through the open doorway, trying to see and hear what was happening. I was wobbling from the water bed, but Riley flicked the lights on as he went, which helped my state of mind.

In a minute, he was back, filling the door frame with his near-naked sexiness before he flicked off the hall light. "There is nothing and no one in the house. The cat isn't even here."

"Oh. Are you sure?"

"I've never been more positive of anything in my life." Riley got into bed, further rocking me.

I held on to the headboard for balance. "Well, that's good."

"Come here, princess." In the dark, his arms reached out for me.

Grateful, I tumbled back onto the bed with him, letting him pull me against him in a spooning position. His arm was heavy and comforting tucked under my breasts, his legs warm, the cotton of his boxer briefs soft against my thighs.

"You okay?" he asked, his breath a hot whisper above my ear. He sounded sleepy.

"Yes. Thanks." I hadn't been planning to go to bed this early, but I was reluctant to go back out there by myself. I knew if I heard another random noise, I'd flip out again.

Besides, it was nice being with him like this. The rhythm of the bed was soothing. I wished I could take my bra off but I didn't want to disturb him, any more than I already had, that is. Feeling a little sheepish, but mostly relieved, I wrapped my arm around his and snuggled my ass into his crotch. It wasn't meant to be a come-on and he didn't respond in any way, his breathing light on the back of my neck. It was more that I wanted to be close to him.

"Night, Pita," he murmured.

"Pita? How am I like a Middle Eastern flatbread?" Was that better than princess? I wasn't sure.

"It stands for pain in the ass."

"Oh." I wasn't even particularly insulted. I was a pain in the ass. I didn't mean to be.

He kissed my bare shoulder.

And it felt more intimate than oral sex.

I shivered in the dark.

# CHAPTER ELEVEN

WHEN RILEY CLIMBED OUT OF BED AT SOME UNGODLY HOUR, his alarm having gone off with a vicious squawk, I vaguely responded with an "Mm," when he said good-bye. Then I promptly fell back asleep and didn't wake up until I heard shouting and door slamming and altogether too much freaking noise for anything earlier than noon.

It sounded like the boys were back from their jaunt in the suburbs.

I pried my eyes open and wished coffee would miraculously appear in my right hand. I'm not so much a morning person, but with caffeine, all things are possible. Yawning, I started when I realized there was a pair of eyes staring at me from the doorway.

Easton. The kid moved like smoke. It was freaky.

"Where's Riley?" he asked, looking at me like I had swallowed his brother whole.

"He's at work. How was Rory's house?"

"Fine. Who are you?"

Yeah, I needed coffee. I sat up. "I'm Jessica, Rory's roommate. We've met a couple of times."

"Hm." He sounded like he thought I was lying. About all of it. His brown eyes stared at me, unblinking.

I stared back, not sure what to say. I didn't have Rory's way with kids. It didn't come naturally to me.

After a second, he turned on his heel and left. He must have narced on me, because Tyler appeared. "Hey."

"Hey. How was the fresh air?"

"Chilly with the disapproval of Rory's father. But I have to give the guy credit, he's trying to ignore the fact that his daughter is dating a convicted felon."

"Well, you are innocent." I yawned and stretched my arms.

"I'm not sure how much that matters. So what the hell happened to the house? It looks almost nice."

Jayden's head popped up behind Tyler, his mouth split into a grin. "It's fucking awesome!"

I laughed. "I'm glad you like it."

Jayden disappeared again, probably back to the kitchen.

"You did this, obviously," Tyler said. "Riley would never hang the word YUM anywhere except maybe off his dick."

Rolling my eyes, I climbed out of bed. "Yes, the ideas were mine. Riley was the labor."

Tyler coughed and lowered his voice. "So, uh, why are you sleeping in here? Your stuff is in the other room. Did you and Riley . . ." He made a gesture that was supposed to indicate sex, obviously, but it looked more like he was changing a tire.

"No. We didn't." I mimicked the gesture so he'd see how stupid it looked. "But we're doing something. Just not that. Yet. And FYI,

I had to tell him that *we* have, and he was none too happy about it. He didn't know and I wasn't going to hide it from him."

Tyler winced. "Awkward."

"Big time," I agreed.

"So, you like him or whatever?" he asked, clearly curious. "He likes you?"

"I guess. You'd have to ask him. But yes, I do." I felt more than a little defensive. "Is that okay?"

He shrugged. "Yeah, sure. Whatever makes you both happy. I just didn't think that you two were going in that direction."

"Me either," I answered truthfully.

"Don't break his heart, Jessica, that's all I'm asking."

I glared at him. "Shouldn't you be worried about my heart being broken? I'm the girl here."

"Yeah, but you're not exactly sensitive. Riley doesn't really get out much, you know. He's not one to get involved with someone lightly." Tyler scratched his tattoo, the one that read TRUE FAMILY, just like Riley's. I wondered if he even realized he was doing it, a subconscious gesture as he worried that I might gut his brother emotionally.

"I think you're giving me more power than I have." Truly. "And why does everyone think I'm so hard-core? I have feelings, too." I did. Buried deep down underneath a layer of self-tanner.

"You can handle yourself."

"Thanks." Not. "Now are you going to move out of the way, or am I trapped in here all day?"

"See? You're not afraid to say what you think."

I was so not flattered. "I'm not afraid to punch either."

Tyler put his hands up in front of his face, boxer style, and bounced on his feet, grinning. "Give me what you got, Jess."

"Weirdo. Now I need coffee before I kill someone."

Jayden and Easton were in the kitchen, Jayden's hand in the cookie jar. "Did you see this, Jessica?" he asked me. "Cookies!"

At least he remembered me. His amazement made me smile. "I know, cool, huh? I told Riley that when it's empty, you should very nicely ask Rory to make some more."

"Except Rory won't be back until next month and there is no way these will last that long," Jayden said earnestly.

Tyler laughed. "Those won't last until tomorrow. Slow down, U."

I still didn't understand why sometimes Riley and Tyler called Jayden "U," but I had given up trying to figure it out. "So you guys like the house? I'm glad. And I told Riley no smoking in the house anymore." I directed this at Tyler. "The ashtrays are out on the picnic table."

"What, you paint the kitchen and suddenly you're the boss?" he asked.

"The social worker is coming tomorrow," I told him, trying to sound casual. "Probably a good time to start keeping the second-hand smoke outside."

He made a face. "Shit. Okay. You're right. It seemed pointless to smoke outside before because my mom always smoked in the house. It just became a habit."

"Well, with the carpet gone, the smell is almost gone, too, so this is a fresh start, as cliché as that is."

"How come Riley didn't tell me?" Tyler asked in a low voice, coming up close to me to ask as I pulled out a coffee filter.

We were both very much aware of Easton fingering the candy wrappers on the YUM art just a few feet away.

"I don't know. He probably didn't want to ruin your vacay."

"Yeah, but I need to make it look like I don't live here. You know, again, the whole convicted felon thing." Tyler leaned on the fridge, his arms crossed, looking worried.

I hadn't even thought of that. "Okay. We'll just move all your clothes and stuff to Riley's room and they'll assume it's his. We'll make your room look empty. But don't you have to give an address for your parole officer and stuff like that?" Though truthfully, I had no clue what I was talking about. That was just an assumption I was making based off TV.

"I gave them Nathan's address. If they show up there, Nathan just says I'm at work and then texts me, though it's only happened once."

"That sounds illegal."

"I'd rather violate my parole than have them deny custody to Riley." He nodded his head in Easton's direction. "He won't do well in foster care."

No, I didn't imagine he would. I didn't imagine any kid would, but Easton was quiet, thin. He would be an easy target without his brothers there to protect him. "All right, let me drink this coffee and then I'll help you move your stuff." I dumped grounds in without measuring them in any way.

"Really?" Tyler sounded surprised.

"Sure. Rory is stuck out at her dad's working her summer job, and I'm here. I can help."

He was looking at me like I'd just parted the Nile.

"What?" I growled.

"Nothing." He shook his head. "Nada."

"Then stop looking at me like that." I poured some water haphazardly into the coffeemaker. Truthfully, I had been surprised the Manns had a coffeemaker. But apparently it had been handy for hiding drugs, so their mother had bought it at a garage sale, according to Riley. I hoped there weren't any lingering drug bits in there, though I was too naive to really know what she had been hiding and/or doing. Sure, I'd popped a Vicodin here and there and had smoked a blunt or two, but it wasn't like I really had any clue about having a real drug habit other than what I had seen on intervention shows.

Ever since the funeral, though, I had decided that getting an occasional itchy high from a pill or two wasn't worth the risk of addiction. Who was to say when it might go too far, and I didn't want to do that to myself or to my family. So not worth it.

"By the way, the pictures in the hall?" Tyler smiled at me. "Nice touch, Jess. It means a lot."

"You're welcome," I said, feeling uncomfortable with his praise. I was used to compliments on my appearance, not on my actions.

He studied me as I reached for a mug, looking like he wanted to say more.

"Yes?" I snapped.

Tyler laughed. "God, you're as big of an asshole as Riley."

Now that I was more comfortable with. "Watch what you say or I'll freeze your underwear when we're cleaning out your room. One of the many skills I learned at Bible camp."

"How do you freeze underwear?" Jayden wanted to know.

Tyler rolled his eyes. "Oh, great, Jess, thanks, way to give him an idea."

I grinned. "You dunk them in water and put them in the freezer, Jayden."

Jayden cackled at the thought. "Watch out, Tyler, or I'll freeze your underwear, too."

"If anyone freezes my underwear I'll beat the shit out of you." Though Tyler looked more amused than pissed.

Jayden's response was to flip his brother off. I figured that was as good of a comeback as any, so I followed suit. Jayden and I met eyes and laughed.

"I like you," he told me, expression honest and guileless.

I can't even begin to say how much that wiggled inside my heart and pleased me. I'd never thought of myself as particularly senti-mental, but Jayden's open approval made me feel awesome. Nor-mally I avoided hugs and casual contact at all costs, but I found myself reaching out and actually initiating a hug with Jayden, pull-ing him close. "I like you, too."

It was a toss-up who was the most surprised—me, Jayden, or Tyler.

Easton wasn't paying attention. He was resting his head on the table and tracing his finger over the cookie jar, speaking quietly to the Mystery Machine.

And maybe for the first time in my whole life I felt protective.

So I turned and poured myself a huge mug of coffee.

THAT NIGHT I SAT IN MY SUBLET APARTMENT AND TRIED TO concentrate on the TV. When I had seen the apartment, I had liked that two girls lived there and were clean, their furniture pretty and shabby chic, the dishes in the kitchen matching. But now with my suitcases tucked away in the one free bedroom, it felt frilly and too perfect, and empty.

Lonely.

The girl, Maggie, who lived in the other bedroom, was already in bed. It was midnight, and I was still keyed up from work, and worried about the social worker's visit the next day. But I knew I couldn't text Riley because he would be asleep. So I had nothing to do but sit there wide awake and stress out.

My phone buzzed with a text message. Riley.

U awake?

Yes. U ok?

No. Can't sleep.

It's going to b ok, promise.

Wish u were here Pita.

That made me inhale sharply, a giddy thrill. It was a new feeling. Usually if a guy said that, I laughed or rolled my eyes, knowing he was just talking about sex.

But this had nothing to do with sex.

Me too.

Then I shocked myself by adding, Pick me up?

Just three little words that hung out there, making me feel as stripped down and vulnerable as I ever had. How selfish and stupid and pathetic was that request?

He had a social worker coming the next day. He didn't need to be dealing with me. And why would he want to get out of bed, drive over to my place, and bring me back just to lay in bed together? I knew he wouldn't want to have sex. It so wasn't the right time for that, especially for our first time together.

Panicked, I was going to add a "haha" to make it seem like I was joking. But he responded before I could.

Be there in ten.

Huh.

K.

So I stuffed a change of clothes in my purse, along with my toothpaste and deodorant, and went downstairs to the lobby to wait for him. He was actually there in nine minutes and I pushed open the door to the building and climbed in. "Hey," I said, a little breathless from running down the stairs and from nerves.

"Hey." He leaned over and slid his hand to the back of my head before kissing me. "Thanks." Resting his forehead on mine, he sighed.

"For what?"

"Coming back."

I liked the sound of that, like my leaving had been a big deal. "You might change your mind when you see me in the morning without makeup."

He gave a soft laugh and pulled away, putting the car in drive. "I doubt that. You're beautiful, and I'm going to keep telling you that until you believe me."

"Okay," I agreed. I was down with that. "Twice on Sundays would be great."

"Brat."

For some weird reason, I reached out and rested my hand on the back of his neck, stroking up into his hair. I had no idea why I was having such a touchy-feely day, but he seemed to like it. "What time is the social worker coming?"

"Ten. I think I scared Easton. I was trying to prepare him, coach him, you know? I was giving him examples of questions she might ask him and how he should answer and he started crying. Then he denied it and locked himself in his room."

"Well, you had to tell him what was going on. And of course he's scared. You're all scared. But he'll tell the truth and it will be fine." I massaged his neck, feeling the tension in his muscles. "I mean, it's sad to say, but since your mom passed, there hasn't been any drama in the house. What could he say that would damage your case?"

"I don't know. What if he drops an F bomb or something?"

"I doubt that will be the first time a social worker hears a kid swearing."

He sighed. "I guess I can speculate all fucking night. Nothing can be done about it. This paper pusher has me by the balls. I don't want to talk about it anymore." Riley reached for a cigarette from the half-empty pack by the gearshift.

I didn't even consider complaining about the smoke. Let him have that. It was better than the whiskey escape of the other night.

"What do you want to talk about then? I can recite a poem for you if you'd like."

"You do not know any poems by heart."

He had a point. "You're right. I don't. But I do know Bible verses."

"Oh, God."

"Exactly."

Riley laughed. "I guess that makes you a good preacher's daughter."

"Good is a loose, all-encompassing term."

"Do you believe in God?" he asked, sounding genuinely curious, taking a drag on his just lit cigarette.

"Yes. I just don't believe in using religion as an excuse to hate or exclude others, or as a self-righteous shield." I had thought a lot about the hypocrisy of religions, or rather of the people who professed to practice it. It didn't sit well with me that you could claim yourself a devout Christian, then plot revenge on your neighbor for his dog destroying your flower garden. And that was on the small end of the scale.

"I don't know what I believe." The smoke rose in front of his features, his eyes troubled, jaw set.

"You believe in your brothers."

"Yeah. I do." Riley pulled into his driveway and turned off the car. He looked at me. "I know that my life as it is right now is how it will always be. I'm cool with that. But I want better for them."

I nodded. "I know." I did. I could see his sincerity. Knew that he lived his life to take care of everyone else but himself. Until Tyler had gotten arrested, most of Riley's income had gone to pay Tyler's tuition. It had been their plan to secure Tyler a decent paying job. But then their mother had dicked them over by planting her drugs on Tyler to avoid her own arrest.

It was clear Riley wasn't really sure how to adjust to the new reality, how to create a new plan. I didn't know what my plan was either. We totally had that in common, though his stakes were way higher. Mine were just my own future, not the responsibility of other human beings.

"Sometimes I picture the future my parents want for me, and I feel like I'm drowning," I told him. "But I guess I deal with it by telling myself to just live now."

"What future do your parents want for you?"

"Arm candy for a junior minister. Social coordinator for the church. Donation solicitor."

His eyebrows shot up. "For real?"

I nodded. "I'm double majoring in religious studies and interior design. Their call, not mine. I get to choose my husband, but only from a church member."

"Holy shit." He looked astonished. "Then what are you doing here with me?"

"Living in the now." I wanted him to understand, to hear what no one had ever heard. "I won't be able to do it, you know. I'll fail. At some point, I will be kicked out by my family. It's just a matter of when, of when they figure out that I can never be good enough. Pure enough."

"They'll really cut you off?"

"Without a doubt." It was something I had never said out loud before, but it was the truth, I knew it.

His hand stroked my knee. "I guess we're both fucked, huh?"

"Looks that way."

"Then I guess it's a damn good thing we found each other."

It was.

# CHAPTER TWELVE

BY THE TIME RILEY FINALLY CALLED ME AT ELEVEN THIRTY the next day, I was clammy from anxiety. My temporary roommate, Maggie, had been trying to chat with me after Tyler had dropped me off that morning, but I had been so lame and boring, she'd given up.

"Hello?" I said, already pacing back and forth in the small kitchen.

"It went good. The social worker said everything looks fine. That it was a clean and 'pleasant environment' for four guys our age."

"Yes!" I gave a fist pump, letting out a sigh of relief.

He laughed. "She had Easton go through the pictures in the hallway and tell her about them. When he got to the one of you and me, he said, 'That's Jessica. She says no one is allowed to smoke in the house.' The social worker said that was a good rule."

"My work is done here," I told Riley, highly satisfied. "Though I didn't even realize Easton heard me." Or remembered my name.

"He hears everything. It's his superpower."

"What's your superpower?"

"You haven't seen it yet."

Oh, my. The night before we had just spooned again. No making out, no nothing. It was like Riley had been too worried to be turned on. I had tried not to find it weird, but the truth was, I found it weird. Most guys I knew used sex as an excuse to avoid anything and everything. Or it was the one thing that could distract them from something they didn't want to deal with. Riley was different.

"Oh, yeah? That sounds ominous."

"Nah. Superpowers are always a positive thing." There was a pause where I could tell he was lighting a cigarette because there was a muffled rustling as his shoulder connected with the phone.

I wondered when his birthday was, because I wanted to buy him a nicotine patch.

"The cookie jar was a nice touch, by the way. Jayden reached in and got one out and he actually remembered to offer one to her. I don't know how he pulled manners out of his ass at the right second, but it was golden."

"That's awesome. I'm really happy it went so well." Happy and relieved.

"Thanks, babe. I owe you one."

Hopefully it would be in the form of a giant orgasm. "What are you doing now?" Maybe we could celebrate.

"I'm heading to work. I'll at least get a half day's pay."

Ick. So much for thoughts of celebration. "Hey, I forgot to ask, how was the zoo yesterday? Did you actually make it?"

"Yes. And it was ninety degrees there. It was like doing laps in ball soup. We saw a gorilla eat his own shit and two lemurs fucking."

"Hm. Sounds delightful."

"But for whatever reason Jayden and Easton loved it. They must be seeing something I'm not."

"I never liked the zoo either. It's a lot of walking to look at dirty and bored animals."

"See? That's exactly what I'm talking about. How come you and I are the only ones who get it?"

"We're an island unto ourselves." I paced again, suddenly overcome by the urge to call off work and be at the house when Riley got home.

The thought was alien. I had wanted to ditch work plenty of times, but not for the simple reason that I wanted to see a guy. It was scary. I was sharing my feelings with him and wanting to be with him all the time.

I was pretty sure this meant that I was emotionally invested, aka emotionally screwed.

He laughed and it ended in a cough, a real hacking sound that was not normal for a twenty-five-year-old. "Sorry," he said when it petered out. "The tuberculosis is kicking up."

"Ha ha. Maybe you should try quitting smoking."

"Maybe you should try quitting nagging."

I was nagging. I sounded like a bitchy wife. "Doesn't mean I'm not right." Let him argue with that logic.

"I'll quit someday. Just not today. Besides, I can just about guarantee I'm in better shape than you. I haul roofing materials all day and I go to the gym."

"You also eat fried foods. And I'm reasonably athletic," I protested. "I was on the volleyball team in high school."

"I'm doing a Warrior Dash on Saturday. Want to do it with me?"

"What's that?" I asked, suspicious. I was fairly certain I was being tricked into something heinous.

"It's an obstacle course, where you scale a wall and stuff like that. Once you finish, they give you beer. People of all ages and levels of endurance do it, and there are no high speeds or demons."

He was just a regular Jimmy Fallon. "I could probably do that." Though I didn't exactly sound enthusiastic. "I like beer."

"You don't have to," he said. "It requires determination and a willingness to get dirty. But maybe you can come and just cheer me on."

Hello. Just because I was blond didn't mean I was going to be relegated to the role of cheerleader in a tight T-shirt. "I can get dirty. I'm determined. Screw you, Mann. Tell me when and where."

I could practically hear him grinning. "You are so easy to manipulate."

How amusing. Not. "Dick." Though I had walked right into that one.

"What?"

"You know. But fine, I'll still do it. Now I have a point to prove and maybe you'll stop calling me princess."

"I already have. Pita."

"How about no nicknames unless they start with Sexy?"

"No. That shows no imagination."

Winning. "I'm okay with cliché as long as it references my beauty."

"We can talk about your beauty later. Right now I have to go to work."

"Work sucks."

"Tell me about it. I'll call you later." He made exaggerated and obnoxious kissing sounds into the phone.

I laughed. "Oh, God, never make that sound again."

WEDNESDAY NIGHT AFTER HE PICKED ME UP, WE WENT BACK to his house and played video games in the hot living room. "So who do you normally hang out with?" I asked, thumbs moving fast on my controller.

"I don't know. I'm either at work or the gym or with my brothers. Sometimes I grab a beer with the guys I work with."

"Maybe we should invite some people over sometime."

"You mean, like a party?" he asked, glancing over at me.

"No. I guess we really can't do that. Not with the boys and social workers and all that. I meant more just like, maybe you could introduce me to your friends." The minute it was out of my mouth, I wanted to retract the statement. It was so "girlfriend." So needy.

"I don't have any friends. I have coworkers I grab a beer with. I have Tyler and Nathan and that's about it. You're dating a loser. There is still time for you to bail if you want."

"Don't be self-deprecating. It's not a good look on you." I dodged a missile on the screen. "I don't have a lot of true friends either. Just Rory and Kylie and Robin." The rest were fringe.

"Robin's the hot one, right?" he asked, voice teasing.

"I will cut you if you say that again."

"And you were worried about my jealousy? Damn."

"Maybe we could have a cookout or something for your friends and my friends." Why was I still pushing this? I wasn't even sure what I was pushing.

"Why do we have to be with other people? Can't I just be with you?" He paused the game and tossed his controller on the coffee table. "Come here, weirdo."

He pulled me into his arms and I settled with my back against his chest. "What are you really asking for, Jess?"

"I don't know," I told him honestly. "I don't really have any idea how to date someone. I haven't had a boyfriend since my junior year in high school."

"Well, I've never had a boyfriend so you're one step ahead of me."

Oh, God. I rolled my eyes even though he couldn't see them. "Cute."

Tyler came into the living room from the kitchen. He saw us sitting together and made a face.

"What?" I asked.

"I miss Rory."

"It's been two days," Riley protested. "How much can you miss her?"

"Easy for you to say when you have Jessica's ass resting on your junk."

Suddenly Riley stiffened. "Hey, look, man, I know I'm supposed to be all cool with whatever you and Jess did before, but the truth is, I'm not. I'm trying but it's hard, so just leave my girlfriend's ass out of our conversations, okay?"

My cheeks started to burn. I wanted to protest that Tyler hadn't said anything suggestive at all, that he was talking about missing Rory, but my gut said that would make it worse. Instead, I just linked my hand through Riley's, trying to convey that I was with him and he needed to chill.

"Girlfriend, huh?" was what Tyler said. "I never saw that one coming, but I have to say, the two of you make sense together."

Now I was really embarrassed. I turned to Riley. "Yeah, girlfriend?"

He shrugged. "You got a problem with that?"

It was so utterly unromantic that I grinned, feeling much better about the whole thing. He was just as awkward as I was, and it was a huge relief. I didn't feel so insane for suggesting he introduce me to his friends.

"Dude, you have no game," Tyler told him.

"Fuck you," Riley responded. "She never wanted to date you, did she? Yet she's dating *me*."

Fortunately, Tyler just laughed, throwing his hands up. "True. See, it all worked out the way it was supposed to. Now can you just accept that Jess and I are friends, always have been, and stop making her feel uncomfortable?"

"Can you just go away?"

Easton came streaking out of the kitchen in nothing but a pair of basketball shorts, running out of the front door. "Where the hell are you going?" Riley roared after him.

"He has a bug up his ass about catching fireflies since Rory's dad showed him how to catch them and release them before they croak."

For some reason, Riley sighed. "You know the next time the social worker shows up, it will be an unannounced visit."

"So?" Tyler shrugged. "It's all going to be fine. Easton has gained ten pounds since Mom died and he's grown like half an inch. He even talks more. His teachers at the end of the year said he was doing better. Don't borrow trouble, man."

I found it interesting that the dynamic in the house had changed since the boys were back. Riley was less relaxed. While he had been worried about Easton and the impending social worker visit, he hadn't been on edge like this. That Tyler was always so calm seemed to make Riley wind tighter. I sensed a wall kicking in the near future.

That tension was why he wasn't interested in having sex with me. That's what I told myself when Riley drove me back to my apartment an hour later and just idled the car, his good-night kiss distracted.

"Wear clothes that can get dirty for the Warrior Dash," he said. "I'll pick you up at eight Saturday morning."

Gross. I wished I'd had that information before I'd said yes. I also wished that he would show the slightest bit of interest in seeing me between now and then. It was only Wednesday. And if we had to get up at the crack of dawn on Saturday, wouldn't it make sense for me to stay over with him Friday night?

And have sex?

I wasn't sure how to approach the subject, though, without looking needy. "What are you doing Friday?"

"Working. Sleeping."

Not the answer I was looking for. Apparently I needed *some* romance. Not a lot. But an ounce.

But I was not about to beg for it. I climbed out of the car. "Talk to you later."

"Bye."

That was it?

I slammed the door shut behind me, climbing the stairs to my apartment with angry stomps of my sandals.

My new roommate was in her room and clearly not alone. The

sound of desperate moans of pleasure, interspersed with male grunts, filled the air.

Fabulous. Everyone was getting some but me.

"I GUESS I WASN'T CLEAR ON THE DRESS CODE," RILEY SAID, eyeing my hot-pink sports bra and black volleyball shorts as I climbed into his car Saturday morning.

"What? You said it's an obstacle course. This is my workout outfit."

"I also said it should be something you don't mind getting dirty. This looks like you're going to film an erotic workout video."

"What the hell is an erotic workout video?" I lifted his coffee mug out of the holder and sniffed. "Is this from today or is it old?"

"It's from today."

I took a sip.

"Yes, you can have a sip."

That would be my tongue sticking out at him.

"I'm serious. You should go change."

"Is this some jealousy thing again?"

He ran his fingers through his hair and rubbed his temples like I gave him a headache. "Just get a T-shirt. Please."

"Can't I just wear yours? I don't feel like climbing all those stairs again."

Riley gave me a long look. "You don't want to take the stairs. But you're about to enter a Warrior Dash."

"I'm saving my energy. We can T-shirt share. Like a time-share, only less expensive."

"You make me want to drink and it's only 8 a.m."

"Then my work is done here." I stared him down.

Finally, he sighed and put the car into reverse. Ha. I won.

Except it was an empty victory when I saw what the obstacle course actually looked like. "Riley! You did not tell me I would be crawling through mud!"

"I said wear clothes to get dirty."

"Dirty and covered in mud from head to toe are two different things." I was watching in horror as person after person dragged themselves on their bellies through a sloppy pit to touch dangling flags. Then there was the wall scaling. And the jumping over a line of fire. What the hell?

"What about this is supposed to be fun?"

"It's sweaty, messy fun."

"That's sex." Of which we were having none.

He frowned at me. "You don't have to do it."

"Well, of course I'm going to do it. I'm just a little surprised. Besides, I like to complain."

"Really? I never noticed." He laced his fingers through mine. "I bet you make this obstacle course your bitch."

Holding hands in public was a new thing for me, and I had a weird appreciation for why people did it. It made me feel . . . wanted. Taken care of. I can't say I'd felt that way in a long time. On the other hand, it felt a little like gloating—like look at me with my hot boyfriend. But I was okay with that.

Riley had taken off his shirt and yanked it on over my head. I don't think it was a total coincidence that he did it after a guy in his thirties was checking me out. With my free hand, I traced the tattoo on his chest, trying to make sense of the dark figure and all the shading. "What is this, anyway?"

"I'm not telling you."

"Excuse me? Why not?" I leaned forward to study his chest a little closer. "Wait a minute. Is that a demon? With wings?"

"It may or may not be a demon or it may or may not be the devil."

"Holy crap!" Horror rushed over me. I had been okay with thinking it was a weird werewolf or a monster from a video game or a comic. But the devil? The Big S? The ultimate demon of all demons? "How am I supposed to cuddle on your chest knowing my head is resting on Lucifer?"

"It wasn't something I particularly planned out," he admitted. "But if it's any consolation it's meant to symbolize conquering your demons."

Now that I knew what it was, there was no denying it. It was hard to see why I hadn't been able to pick that evil face out of the black swirls before. I stared at it so long, the lines started to blur. The devil had particularly menacing teeth. "I'm speechless."

"Now I know my secret weapon to get you to shut up."

I twisted his nipple.

"Ow, Jess." He rubbed his chest. "You fight dirty."

"Remember that." I looked back at the course. "Okay, so how does this work?"

"You're in the eighteen-to-twenty-four age bracket. They run heats of competitors in each bracket so everyone isn't out there at once."

"I'd rather go up against the sixty-year-olds. But okay, fine."

He explained the course, and in another five minutes, they were calling us for line up. I had been hoping I would get to see Riley do it first, but no such luck.

"You got this," he told me, sounding way more confident than I felt.

But I was nothing if not stubborn. I figured I could power my

way through the course. Which is what I did. Leaping over the fire
was no big deal. The wall wasn't that tough either, and I gained
ground on some of the other competitors by showing no hesitation
in just dropping the five feet from the top down the other side,
landing with an *oomph* on the soft ground. Only one other girl
just free-fell like I did. The others eased themselves down, and I
felt a certain triumph. What I had loved about volleyball was the
jump, the hit, the power. The pure adrenaline that came from
rushing the net and stuffing an opponent.

The control.

I pushed it hard, the buzzing in my ears, the crowd yelling, and
the rush of my burning lungs. Okay, I'm not going to lie. When I
dropped in the mud pit, the first slap of hot sludge sliding over me
made me want to gag, and an army crawl through slop is harder
than it looks. But using my elbows and my thighs, I hauled myself
through and scrambled to my feet, my hair falling out of my pony-
tail and slapping me in the cheek with a wet layer of mud. For a
second I couldn't see, but as I ran in the general direction of the
finish line, I swiped at my eyes with the one spot on my forearm
that was clean. I saw that Riley was at the finish line yelling for
me, a grin splitting his face.

In my wave of competitors, I finished second, behind the girl
who had jumped with me. Stumbling to a stop, I sucked in a few
deep breaths and slapped Riley's hands, which he had raised for a
double high five. A high ten.

"Babe, that was awesome!" he said. "You killed it!"

"Told you," I wheezed. Then I leaned forward and wiped my
muddy hands on his chest.

Instead of being pissed, he laughed. He grabbed both my dirty
cheeks and gave me a kiss.

"When is your turn?" I asked, still breathing hard. "I'm dying of thirst and I want to steal your beer."

"I think I have a few minutes."

"Okay." I peeled off his T-shirt and slapped the muddy mess against his chest. "Here's your shirt back."

He cocked his head. "Oh, you are just asking for it."

"Yes, I am." I grinned before throwing my arms around his neck, rubbing my body against his, the shirt wedged between us. "Kiss me."

Riley laughed and ran his hands all over my muddy ass before letting them rest on my back. "Too bad there are a hundred people around us."

That was what I had been waiting to hear—that there was some hint he wanted me the way I wanted him.

But his kiss was sweet, not intense.

Damn the crowd.

When Riley's heat went, I was stunned watching him. His focus and intensity were unreal. He didn't look at any of the other guys, and his trajectory was completely straight, his feet eating up the course at top speed. He was up the wall in two leaps, and down the other side. I wondered if he had played sports in high school because he moved like an athlete, his arms tucked in close to his abs. Unlike me, he didn't flop into the mud like a tripped hippo, but he crouched low and covered half the pit with one leap forward.

Sexy. I was warm from more than the hot sun beating down on me.

Shielding my eyes so I could see, I slipped in between two women in their forties to watch him overtake the guy in front.

"Yummy," the one said to the other. "I love me some tattooed boys."

Normally, I would have just listened in silent amusement. But I felt a wave of territorialism and the need to claim and brag. It was a foreign feeling, and before I knew it I was blurting out, "That's my boyfriend."

They glanced over at me, smiling. "He's very pretty," the one said. "And with such a hard body. What a perfect combo. Enjoy him."

She was right, but wow, that was pure objectification of another human being. I knew my friends and I did that, too, but hearing it said about Riley made me realize girls were no better than guys when it came to checking out the opposite sex.

So I said, "Thanks. He's very sweet." Which just made them laugh.

But then I had no time for them because Riley finished the race in first place, looking barely winded.

"See?" he said when I made my way over to him. "Smoking doesn't even affect me."

I snorted. "That is the worst justification I've ever heard." But I reached for his hand. "But that was an awesome job. You were like a mud ninja out there."

"Thanks. We need a picture of us. Where's your phone?"

"In my fanny pack," I deadpanned. "In the car, where do you think?"

"God, you're such a brat. Go get it while I get my beer. Of which you can have none because you're underage."

Like he wouldn't cave if I asked him for a sip. Feeling happy, sticky, and proud of myself, I took his keys and went to the car to get my phone. When I came back he was holding a giant beer stein and wearing a Viking hat.

"Wow, you've never been hotter." And I kind of meant it.

"You came in tenth out of forty-five in your age bracket," he said. "Good job."

"Thanks. That's not bad considering I didn't know what I was doing. How did you finish overall in your bracket?"

"Second."

"Woot." I gave him another high five. "You are awesome."

"Thanks." He kissed me, and I tasted the beer on his breath.

"So. Thirsty. Dying."

He grinned. "Take a sip, but if you get caught, I'm not bailing you out of jail."

"Yeah, right." I took a quick sip, shielding myself from view by leaning over and letting my hair fall in front of me. The cup was down by his waist.

"This looks really inappropriate," he said. "I'm getting a boner because of it."

About time. "Then let's go home." I stood up and eyed him. "I'm feeling dirty," I said in a flirty voice.

Riley put his arm around me as we headed toward the car. "We can fix that."

He better mean fix it in the way I wanted to fix it. "How about a hot, wet shower?"

I wasn't exactly being subtle, but he didn't respond in the way I wanted him to. He just said, "I need food first, I'm starving."

"Of course you are." Not exactly what I wanted to hear.

I was consoled by the fact that when we got in the car, Riley showed no concern for his upholstery and pushed me backward, kissing me with a ferocity he hadn't shown since our first real make out session, his hand brushing over my breast.

Yes. That's what I wanted. That hot, deep slide into oblivion, that tingling over my skin, wet tongues and tight nipples.

But he pulled back just as I was getting into it. As he put the key in the ignition, I was sideways, knee up, on my elbows, breathless and unsatisfied.

WTF.

# CHAPTER THIRTEEN

"THAT'S A GOOD LOOK ON YOU," TYLER SAID WHEN I WALKED
in the front door. He was reclining on the couch, his phone up to his
ear, a burger bag on the coffee table. "By the way, Rory wants to
know why you're not answering her texts and if you're avoiding her
for some unknown weird girl reason. Those are my words, not hers."

I kicked off my shoes by the front door. "I'm not avoiding her."
Not much anyway. Just slightly, because I didn't want to talk about
Riley with her. I didn't know what to say. We like each other? That
felt so lame. Nor was I going to share my fear that Riley didn't
want to have sex with me. Rory would say he was respecting me
or some such crap like that, but I knew that even guys who respect
you want to bang you.

Besides, I wasn't comfortable sharing my emotions. What I was
feeling was new and different and I wanted to keep it in a private
little box labeled Mine, Mine, Mine. If I tried to talk about Riley,
I wouldn't be able to express myself, because I didn't even understand completely what I felt.

But I didn't want my friend thinking I was mad at her. "Give me the phone." I held out my hand.

"No. You're covered in mud. Besides, I'm talking to her. You can call her later."

"Rory, your boyfriend is a controlling dick," I said loudly so she would hear me. "He's keeping us apart for no reason."

Tyler laughed and threw a balled-up fast food napkin at me. I caught it. Riley put his own fast food bag down next to Tyler's and was about to sit on the easy chair when I said, "Halt! Change your shorts first."

"I'm dry," he protested.

"No. You'll crumble and flake off all over the furniture." I wasn't budging on that. I couldn't regulate his appalling diet, but I could force him to keep the house clean.

"Who is the controlling dick in this room?" Riley asked, but he just stood over the coffee table and started eating his burger hovering there.

"Can I borrow some clean clothes?"

"Yep. Everything is going to be too big on you though." Riley took another huge bite of his burger.

"Whatever. I'm taking a shower." I paused, pointedly.

"Okay."

That was it. Riley was still focused on his beef. Tyler, who had gotten off the phone, seemed to get that I was extending an invitation. He raised his eyebrows and looked at his brother like he was an idiot. It was a small consolation.

"You can come with me," I said, going for flat-out obvious.

"I'm eating." A fry went into his mouth.

And that would be the cold slap of rejection. Defeated, I turned on my heel and headed to the bathroom. "Fine."

"Dude, what the fuck is wrong with you?" Tyler asked him.

I paused down the hallway, eavesdropping, wanting to hear Riley's response.

"What do you mean?"

"You're turning down a shower with your brand-new girlfriend? And don't tell me it's because of U and Easton, because they're throwing a tennis ball they found at the garage door."

"Mind your own business."

"I've known Jess longer than you."

Riley snorted. "No shit."

Ugh. I was never going to be forgiven for not having the psychic abilities that would have allowed me to avoid sex with Tyler before I met Riley.

"Fine. I was just trying to help."

"I didn't ask for help."

That seemed to be the end of the conversation, so I went into Riley's room and rooted through his drawers for a shirt and basketball shorts. I chose a shirt that said "Bacon is the question and the answer" with two strips of bacon on it. Somehow I didn't think he would miss that one if I didn't get it back to him right away. I may have slammed the drawer harder than was necessary. My visions of a porn star shower for two were not going to happen, so I went into the bathroom and washed the mud off my body with aggressive scrubbing and efficiency.

When I came out, thankfully swimming in Riley's clothes, because no girl wants to discover her boyfriend's clothes are tight on her, Riley was done with his binge eating. "Can you drive me home?" I asked, finger combing my wet hair before twisting it up into a bun to let it dry off my head.

He looked puzzled. "You have plans or something? I thought we were hanging out."

"I already had plans with Robin to go to a party tonight. You and Tyler can meet us there if you want."

"Where's it at?" Tyler asked.

"Shit Shack."

"Okay, cool."

But Riley frowned. "I don't want to go to a college party at some place called the Shit Shack."

"I went to the Warrior Dash," I pointed out. I could hear the mean creeping into my voice, and I wanted to go home before it got worse. My wounded feelings were notorious for driving me into bitchy mode, and I didn't want Riley to be on the receiving end of that mood.

"True. Okay. What time?"

"Ten at the earliest."

Riley stood up. "Can I shower before we go?"

"Sure." Even though I really just wanted to crawl into bed at my apartment and feel bitter.

When he passed me he reached out and squeezed both of my breasts. "Mm. Bacon."

Yeah, that didn't improve my mood.

I turned and Tyler was watching me, and he gave a short laugh. "Don't look at me, seriously. I don't think I'm allowed to talk to you about, you know." He jerked his thumb in the direction of the bathroom Riley had retreated into.

Glaring at him, I said, "You're supposed to be my friend."

"Okay, all I'm going to say is this—now you know what it's like to date you."

"What the hell is that supposed to mean?"

"Just think about it." Tyler got up and grabbed his pack of cigarettes. "I'm going outside to smoke, and frankly, I don't want to be alone with you. I don't think Riley and I bloodying each other is going to look good in our custody case."

I followed him, because I didn't want to sit in the hot house by myself. As Tyler blackened his lungs, and Easton and Jayden played some undetermined game involving a tennis ball and a sad piñata that looked like they had found it in the trash, I sat at the picnic table and reflected on Tyler's words.

Apparently he thought Riley and I were similar personalities.

I could see that. Snarky. Emotionally closed off.

But it didn't explain why Riley was giving me the brush-off. He hadn't even tried to touch anything on me that was within twelve inches of the erogenous zone. Well, unless you count smacking my ass in triumph or tweaking my bacon boobs. Funny how the one thing I'd always been confident about with other guys was the thing I had no handle on with Riley.

The tennis ball bounced off the garage and nailed me on the side of the head.

Fuck me, that hurt. My eyes teared up.

Easton looked horrified and like I might beat him. "Sorry, sorry, sorry!"

"It's okay. Shit happens." Which probably wasn't appropriate to say to an eleven-year-old. I turned to Tyler. "Got any beer? I think I need one."


CRACKING OPEN A BEER AT FOUR WAS HOW I ENDED UP DRUNK by the time I arrived at the Shit Shack, tottering in my heels. Holding on to Robin for support, already regretting my shoes, I shoved open the screen door and scanned the crowd, alcohol buzz ringing in my ears.

After Riley had dropped me off, Robin had come over with a bottle of vodka and cranberry juice, and it seemed the beer had broken the seal and it was a fabulous idea to start drinking. We had killed half the bottle while getting ready and eating a twelve-pack of Reese's Cups. Considering I hadn't really eaten all day, it was a miracle I didn't blind myself with my mascara or electrocute myself with the hair dryer, because I was drunkity-drunk.

Alcohol—worst coping mechanism ever.

But at least I looked good. Or I thought I looked good puckering up in front of my mirror, fluffing my hair and adjusting the cleavage on my strapless red jersey shirt. I had on tiny denim shorts and sky-high wedge sandals in a red and hot-pink stripe. For some reason I felt compelled to put on seventy-two bracelets and carelessly discarded my cross necklace on the dresser. I wasn't in the mood for Jesus.

I was in the mood for dancing. For laughing. For flirting.

Maybe Riley didn't think that I was hot, but other guys did. It wasn't going to hurt to look good and have a little appreciation tossed my way.

"OMG, it's crowded here," Robin said, her huge earrings shaking as she scanned the room for the action.

"Good." It had taken twenty minutes to walk from my apartment to the house, since Robin was in no shape to be driving. You would have thought my buzz would have slowed since I hadn't been able to drink since we'd left, but if anything I felt more drunk than I had when we started walking.

"Jessica!" A big, brawny guy called out, holding up his arms. "Give me some love."

Aaron was a guy from my Dead Sea Scrolls class last semester.

Like me, he was also getting a secondary degree in religious studies. Like me, he was also drunk.

"What's up?" I asked, giving him the hug he was requesting.

"Want a drink?" He gestured to the toilet in the corner that
had a pony keg resting on it.

The Shit Shack had gotten its name from the many toilets and
plumbing fixtures left over from its former life as a shop. Now it
was a dumpy college rental where a revolving door of frat guys
lived, and it was notorious for killer parties.

"Sure," I said, because my mouth was hot and dry. "This is my
friend Robin."

"Stellar." Aaron held up his hand to Robin for a high five. She
giggled and gave him one, her tiny palm swallowed by his massive
one. He gave her a look of pure sexual interest and entwined his
fingers around hers so they were holding hands.

She let him.

Fabulous. I was not jealous of my friend, but what was with the
Robin Effect lately?

Ten minutes later, I actually was jealous. Robin and Aaron were
making out and I was trying to shove myself down the narrow
hallway to the back door, wanting some fresh air. My beer sloshed
over the rim of my cup as someone jostled me. "Hey!"

"Sorry." Though the guy didn't even look remotely sorry.

I clung to the wall and checked my phone, almost dropping it.
No text from Riley. That just further spurred my desire to have a
good time. Fuck him. These were my classmates, and we were
having fun. When a guy I vaguely knew from previous parties
pulled me out into the yard where everyone was dancing, I let him.
He tried to bootygrind and I laughed, pushing him away, keeping
an arm's length between us.

So he changed tactics, doing some kind of swing dancing thing, flinging me around and around in circles so that I was breathless and laughing hard.

"Dancing with the Sig Eps!" he yelled in a frat battle cry, lifting me up at the waist and spinning me around.

"Shit!" I cried out when he lost his balance and we started to slice through the crowd, beers sloshing and bodies scattering. He ended up on his ass, and I landed with a knee in his gut.

But it didn't really hurt because I was trashed. Even seeing the other knee that had hit the hard-packed dirt now covered in blood and grass clippings, I didn't really feel any pain. I just laughed and offered my hand to help him up off the ground. But when he stood, his own laughter died out and he shifted in front of me in a protective gesture. I glanced around his body to see why his tone had changed and I realized that in the middle of a crowd of colorful tops on the girls and polo shirts and cargo shorts on the guys, Riley and Tyler were standing there in black T-shirts and jeans. They looked like a metal band that had been dropped onto a college campus for a free concert. Riley's shirt featured Ozzy Osbourne in his infamous bat-biting shot, and Tyler had a lock on a chain around his neck above his Metallica shirt. Neither looked like they belonged. Neither looked happy.

"Can I help you?" Frat Boy asked.

"Yes, you can," Riley said. "You can move out of my way so I can say hello to my girlfriend." He sounded deceptively calm. But I could see the tension in his jaw.

But I was too drunk to sense the danger. I was just stupidly, ridiculously happy to see him. I shoved around the guy and said, "Hi, honey," and threw my arms around him, wanting a kiss.

He did kiss me, but he pulled back and met my eyes. "You're drunk."

"Duh." I laughed.

"So why were you on the ground with that guy?"

"We fell dancing." I eyed my knee with a squint. "I think I'm bleeding."

"Yes, you are." He took my hand firmly and turned to his brother. "Do you see anyone you know?"

"Nathan's over there. And Bill."

"Really?" I said, excited. "I didn't know they were here. I should say hi!" It didn't seem to occur to me that if Riley didn't look at all pleased, then he probably wasn't pleased.

I did catch on when he frowned though. "What's the matter?" I asked, scratching his cheeks and chin, liking the feel of his beard stubble.

He sighed. "This isn't really my scene."

"Do you have a scene?" I asked sincerely. In my drunken state, I was just remembering him saying he didn't really have any friends, and I felt sad about that.

The corner of his mouth lifted. "No. How much did you drink?"

"A lot of vodka cranberries. But it's okay because I ate six peanut butter cups."

"Oh, yeah, that will totally prevent you from getting trashed." Riley shook his head. "Come on, let's find Nathan. Hell, I'll even be glad to see Nerd Boy in this crowd. I feel like I fell into a prep school. I've never seen so much pink cotton in my life. And I'm about to choke on the smell of wasted money."

"There's drunk money here?" I asked. It made sense to me.

But Riley gave a snort of laughter. "Shh, Pita, don't talk."

I stuck my tongue out at the back of his head as he pulled me along through the crowd. I was aware of the other partygoers blatantly staring at us, though they parted rapidly, like they didn't want to come into contact with Riley.

*My boyfriend*, I mouthed to a group of girls who were looking scandalized. Then I winked.

Robin had come outside with Aaron, who didn't seem to fear Riley. He called out to me, "Shalom, Jessica."

"Right back at ya," I told him with a point of my finger. Only in turning to talk to them, I didn't notice Riley stopping. I ran into his back and bit my tongue. "Shit."

Riley glanced back at me. "What the hell are you doing?"

"I'm walking."

"When did you get so tall?" he asked me.

I lifted my foot to show him my high-heel wedges, only I lost my balance. I would have gone down if he hadn't grabbed me and held me upright. "Oops."

But in the movement, I had accidentally kicked a guy standing by the garbage can filled with barf booze, the miscellaneous alcohol punch that anyone could pour into, and only the brave and stupid would drink out of. Before I could apologize, he shot me an angry look and said, "Watch it, you drunk cunt."

"Ah!" I was stunned at his venomous dig. Normally I would have a quick comeback, but I was too drunk to be quick-witted.

But before I could do anything, Riley had dropped my hand and stepped in front of me. "Excuse me?" he asked the guy.

"You heard me," Douche Bag said, his hair flopping in his eyes, lip in a sneer as he eyed me. "She's a cunt."

Then Douche Bag's face was in the barf booze and it was Riley's hand and arm shoving it there.

Robin screamed, and Aaron dragged me backward out of the

way as there was gurgling and splashing and scuffling. Tyler was wedging himself between Riley and the guy, and he was saying urgently, "Come on, man, bad idea."

Riley pulled the guy's head back up and yanked him by the hair hard, tossing him to the side. Douche stumbled and sat down on the ground, swearing. "Asshole!"

"You don't call my girlfriend a cunt," Riley said. "You're lucky I didn't knock your fucking teeth out."

"Trailer trash. She's just slumming for a thrill, you know."

For a second, I thought Riley was going to kick the guy in the chin with his boot, but he took a few deep breaths and clenched and unclenched his fists.

More sober, I realized that a fight was the last thing Riley needed right now. I reached out and touched him. "Hey, let's go, sweetie. This asshole isn't worth it." I inserted myself between them and urged Riley backward.

I'm not sure I would have turned my back to the guy on the ground if I hadn't been making friends with vodka all night, but fortunately, he didn't do anything in retaliation. There was some grumbling and exclamations, but for the most part, everyone else seemed to want to stay out of it, so we cut across the yard. I snagged Robin by the arm on our way by and she resisted, tugging herself out of my reach.

"I'm staying. I'll get a ride with Nathan."

"Okay. Text me when you're home safe."

"K." She blew me a kiss.

I had to walk fast to catch up to Riley, who was eating up the sidewalk with long strides. "Hey." I tried to take his hand but he shook me off.

Tyler just shook his head at me, indicating I should leave Riley alone. My ankle turned in my dumbass shoes, and it was Tyler who grabbed me this time, not Riley.

Since I wasn't exactly sober, and I definitely didn't appreciate the silent treatment, I stopped walking. "I'm going back to the party."

Riley came to a dead stop. He turned and glared at me. "Are you fucking kidding me?"

"Well, you're ignoring me."

"I'm pissed off! I'm trying to calm down so I don't go and beat that guy's face in."

"I didn't mean to kick him," I said. It just seemed like the right thing to say.

Riley's frown softened. "I know. Which is why he was so far out of line."

Tyler pulled out a cigarette and lit it. "I think Riley is a little old for the Shit Shack, Jess. He doesn't have the patience for drunk idiots."

"Like me?"

Finally the tension in Riley's shoulders eased up. "No. You're the only drunk idiot I *can* tolerate. Everyone else there can go to hell."

"I'm sorry." I felt sad, and I wasn't really sure why.

He sighed. "Do you really want to go back? Were you having fun?"

Was I? Not particularly. I just had a good buzz and didn't want to waste it. But I'd rather be with Riley. I shook my head. "No."

"If you don't want to go home yet I'll take you to the townie bar and we can play the jukebox."

I wasn't sure if that sounded fun or not. I wasn't sure I even knew what a townie bar was. Standing there, not even moving, both ankles gave out from my drunken wobbling, and I fell off my shoes.

Riley laughed. "All right, come here. Hold my shoulders." He squatted down and grabbed my ankle.

"What are you doing?"

"I'm taking these stupid shoes off your feet before you break your ankle."

I held on to his shoulders, digging my fingers into the fabric of his shirt to stabilize myself as he undid the straps on my shoes. "I'm fine." On the spectrum of fine I was probably right in the middle, and that was good enough for me. "The ground is icky. I don't want to be barefoot."

"Tough."

Then my shoes were in his hand and I was on stable ground. Or as stable as the ground is when you've basically had a vodka IV in all day.

"Where is your phone?" Riley asked me. "Did you bring a purse?"

"Oh, poop!" I felt my pockets and my boobs. "I had a wristlet. I think I set it on a toilet."

"Do you remember which toilet? There were about twenty laying around that yard."

I burped and tried to pretend I didn't. "The pink one."

"All right, come on." Shoes in one hand, Riley used the other to pull me back toward the yard.

Tyler followed a step behind and I turned and made a goofy face at him for no apparent reason. He laughed and shook his head.

As we moved through the crowd I noticed a girl from my design class was letting a guy do a shot from between her breasts. "Hooter tooter!" his friends were chanting.

She was giggling and bending over as his head tipped back so that tequila and her tits fell into his face. So maybe I could see why this wasn't Riley's kind of party.

Riley didn't say anything, though. He just wove us through the crowd from toilet to toilet. I wanted to offer advice on where the toilet had been, but I couldn't quite remember. I was actually doubting that I had even left my purse on a toilet. I might have set it down when I had refilled my drink. Or when I had been dancing. But after a few minutes Riley pointed. "Is that it?"

My little red bag was on a pink toilet lid. Yay, me. "Yes!"

He leaned over and snagged it from between two girls. The one glared at him, but he ignored her. I held my hand out to take the purse but he just kept it tucked in his palm along with my shoes dangling from his fingers. I was starting to think he didn't trust me to have my shit together tonight.

I was starting to think he might be right.

Because I actually walked into a neighborhood bar with Riley barefoot with no concern whatsoever to what might be sticking to the bottoms of my feet.

# CHAPTER FOURTEEN

"HEY, WHAT'S UP?" THE BARTENDER SAID TO RILEY WHEN WE walked in.

Riley waved and pulled out a stool for me. I eyed the bartender, expecting him to card me, but he looked more interested in checking his phone than preventing underage drinking.

So this was a townie bar. It was dark, with a full display of liquor bottles behind the bar, the chairs cracked vinyl. It was nothing like the dance clubs we always went to, but more like what you see in movies, where hairy loggers are grabbing a beer before the zombie apocalypse.

Spinning on my barstool to get a view of the room, I lost my balance and almost wiped out. I wasn't sure why I was having so much trouble staying upright.

Riley laughed. "Settle down over there. I'm going to get a beer. I hesitate to ask this, but do you want something?"

"Let's do a shot," was my brilliant answer. It seemed to sound like a fabulous idea. We had dropped Tyler back off at the house, and I was thinking that tonight Riley and I could finally have sex. I was thinking a shot might increase the probability.

"Only if I can do it off your tits," he said, with a look that said he clearly thought that was about as cheap and ridiculous as you could get. He gave a mock fist pump. "Hooter tooter. Dickwads."

"Ha ha."

"So who's your friend here, Mann?" the bartender asked Riley, eyeing me with blatant curiosity.

"Maybe you should sit down," Riley told him. "Because this is Jessica, my girlfriend."

The guy laughed, stroking his long beard. He was bald and heavily tattooed. "No shit?" He held his hand out to me. "Well, it's nice to meet you, Jessica. I'm Zeke."

I shook his hand and gave him what I assumed was a charming smile. "Nice to meet you, too." Then I nudged Riley. "Why is it so hard to believe I'm your girlfriend?"

"I don't bring girls to bars."

"So how did you two meet?" Zeke asked. "At the mall?"

Was I being insulted?

Riley just laughed. "Screw you. No, Jess is Tyler's girlfriend's roommate. We've known each other for about a year I guess."

"Six months," I corrected.

He shrugged. "Six months."

"Nice. Make Tyler do all the hard work of scoring a girl, then you just shop from her friends. I admire that."

What, was I a pair of jeans? But I had to assume Zeke was joking.

"Yeah, well, I'm working with a handicap here." He gestured

to his face, then eyed me. "Okay, how about one shot of vodka, since that's what you've been drinking all night? Zeke, you going to do one with us?"

"Why the hell not?" was his opinion as he reached back for a bottle. Shot glasses appeared from under the counter.

"Now if you're going to do a shot," Riley instructed me, "you have to do it right. None of this sipping on it crap."

"I know how to do a shot." I gave him a dirty smile. "Open my throat."

His eyebrows went up. "You good at that?" His knee nudged mine.

"Oh, yeah." Yes, I was flirting. Yes, I was lying. I could do a shot no problem, but I never gave blow jobs. Ever. So the implication was false, but I figured he wouldn't care once we were naked and I was offering other alternatives.

Our three glasses filled, Zeke handed one to me. Riley took his and we lifted them. "Cheers!" I said.

Zeke just nodded and raised his glass to his lips.

I knocked my glass into Riley's. It was meant to make a sweet little *chink* sound. Instead, I overestimated my strength and half of his shot sloshed over the glass onto his hand. "Oops. Sorry." I leaned over and licked his hand. "Trade me." I switched our shots and then drank the halfsie one down.

He drank his in one tilt, wrinkling his nose. "You want something on the jukebox?"

"Well, yes, I do." The vodka was warming me down into my inner thighs and I wanted to dance with him. After I got a little closer. I leaned over to his stool, hands on the countertop, feet on the footrest bar, and kissed him.

He kissed me back, hand firm on the small of my back, gradually shifting down onto my ass. He broke away. "Every woman in here hates you right now."

"Why? Because I'm kissing you?" That was a little arrogant on his part. Not that it was untrue but yeesh. I glanced around and saw that of the ten people in the bar, nine were watching us. The men were all in their fifties except for one and they were all gawking openly. The women were of the big-hair-blinged-butt-jeans variety and they were shooting me glares. What did I do, besides have a hot boyfriend?

Riley patted my butt. "No. Because you have legs that are a mile long and the shortest pair of denim shorts in the history of the world on and you look smoking hot."

"Oh." Well, that was okay then. As long as he thought I looked hot. I licked my lips. "Thanks."

"You're killing me." He stood up. "Come on, let's play pool."

We did. Or rather, he did, and I tried, but all I succeeded in doing was almost taking my own eye out. But it had the added benefit of forcing him to lean over me and help me with my strokes. No one in the bar bothered us, and I decided I liked it there, in the dark, smoky quiet. Everyone was disregarding the no-smoking law and just puffing away, and while I didn't love the smell, I liked the haze.

Dark and seductive, that's what it was.

The jukebox took negotiation. "No way in hell," Riley said to a pop song.

I flipped and pointed.

"Lame. No. Over my dead body."

"You pick one then," I told him, pinching his arm.

"Hey. You can't just pinch me."

"Yes, I can." I did it again.

He laced his fingers through mine so I couldn't touch him any-more and grinned. "You are asking for it."

"You say that all the time," I murmured, "and nothing ever happens."

"You say that like you want something to happen," he said, eliminating all the space between us.

My lips parted.

He bent, his expression intense. When he kissed me, he nipped at my bottom lip and I closed my eyes. I wanted him so much, the alcohol making my body feel liquid and hot, and I shifted so that his thigh was between my legs, my hips bumping against him.

His eyes darkened, the corner of his mouth tilting up. "I'm picking the song."

He did and it was something I'd never heard of. It sounded like it was a fuck-me song masquerading as a love ballad from the seventies. Or rather a love ballad from the seventies masquerading as a fuck-me song. Something like that.

Riley pulled my arms up to rest around his neck, and right there, in the skeezy bar, with Zeke and bullet-bra-wearing women watch-ing, he slow danced with me. He actually had good rhythm.

I sighed. "This is better than prom." My date had been Tweeter Brinkley and he was nice enough, though with a serious sweating problem. But he had been in love with Chelsea Zane and had spent the whole night following her around while I had gotten drunk in the restroom with Kylie. At one point, I pulled out my hair exten-sions and wrote on my arms with a Sharpie, brilliant things like *Seniors! Prom Blows!* And *Troy Trojans . . . because she rode the wrong horse*. My parents were not amused the next day, even though I insisted I had been held down forcibly against my will.

"I didn't go to prom," Riley said.

"You didn't miss a damn thing."

"What I was missing was you," he said.

My breath caught. Everything inside me melted. I had never felt more female in my entire life than I did right then and I felt softer, languid.

Like I was falling in love.

"Let's go home," he said as we swayed to the song that was now my favorite song ever, because it had created this moment.

"You always have the best ideas."

Riley pulled me toward the bar. "What do I owe you?" he asked Zeke.

"It's on me," the bartender said, drying a glass in his hand. "Thanks for the entertainment."

They fist-bumped.

"Got everything?" Riley asked.

"I left everything in the car."

His hand rubbed my knee during the three-minute drive home, and I wouldn't have thought such a simple thing could be so erotic, yet it was. It just went in slow circles over my bare skin and it felt as sexy as that slow dance.

As we went down the hallway to his bedroom, Riley paused once to kiss me, cupping my cheeks with his hands. "God, you're so beautiful."

Not only did I feel beautiful with Riley, I felt like a nicer, better person, softer, like melted butter. Maybe it was the vodka, maybe it was dark hallway or our whispered voices, the boys all asleep, but I felt like I was going to crawl out of my skin if I didn't get to have sex with Riley in the next five seconds. When he stripped off his shirt, after carefully closing his door and locking it, I yanked off my shirt and tossed it on the floor. I took my bra off, too.

He turned to me and actually jumped a little. "Holy shit, Jess." His voice was strained.

"What?" I undid the snap on my shorts and started to take the zipper down.

"Slow down."

"No." I wanted to feel his skin on mine.

But Riley pulled me down onto the bed with him before I could finish taking off my shorts and he kissed me deeply, with tongue, so that I groaned, hips arching to meet his erection.

"Not tonight, honey," he told me, breathing hard, his eyes agonized.

I froze in the act of humping his crotch, astride his body, my breasts scraping along his chest. "What do you mean?"

"I mean we're not having sex tonight. I don't want our first time together to be when you're shitfaced."

It was like a slap. Hot humiliation rushed into my mouth, a thick bile, and I sucked in a few deep breaths, suddenly feeling like I was going to be sick. "I'm not shitfaced," I protested. "I know exactly what I'm doing."

But he still shook his head. "I don't want it like this."

He didn't want *me*. That's what I heard. I rolled off of him and curled up against the edge of the bed, feeling as rejected as I had when I had been cut from the cheerleading squad in seventh grade for fucking up a back handspring.

"I want you to remember it," he said.

"What I'm going to remember is that you're a prick," I said venomously.

"Don't be irrational." He touched my back and I swatted at him.

"Don't touch me."

"Fine."

"Whatever." I closed my eyes, willing myself not to cry. No tears. Jessica Sweet didn't cry. It was the golden rule.

My body was aching with the need for an orgasm and my stomach was roiling from the alcohol. I tried to breathe quickly in and out of my nose, nausea climbing. The damn water bed was moving, further contributing to the bed spins from all the booze. It was like being on the deck of a ship. For a second I thought I was going to be okay, but then Riley rolled over and the whole bed undulated. I grabbed the lip of the frame and felt my stomach heave in protest.

Game over. I sat up and fumbled my way out of bed and along the wall.

"Where are you going?"

I didn't bother to say anything, just clawed at the door until I yanked it open and dashed into the bathroom, topless, my shorts unzipped. I flicked on the light, blinding myself, and barely had time to flip up the lid on the toilet before I threw up, the stench of peanut butter and chocolate making me cough and choke as vodka and Reese's and bile expelled from my stomach.

Riley appeared behind me and I waved him off, not wanting him to see me like this. After the heaving stopped, I still clung to the toilet, on my knees, drool dangling from my mouth.

He lifted my heavy hair off my face and smoothed it over my back. "You okay?"

I nodded. As good as anyone can be, horking topless in front of her boyfriend who won't have sex with her. Sinking backward, I shifted my legs and sat on my ass, leaning against the wall, wiping my mouth with my arm. My eyes were watering, and I noticed how badly torn up my knee actually was from falling. There was dried blood dripping down my leg.

The faucet turned on and suddenly Riley's hand was in my face, and he was gently wiping my mouth, eyes, cheeks with a towel. Then he dried me off and shifted to my knee, dabbing at the dirt and blood. When he put a T-shirt over my head and dressed me like a doll, carefully pushing my arms through the holes, I wasn't any help to him, but I didn't resist either.

I waited for the recriminations, the judgment over taking that last shot.

But he didn't tell me I was stupid.

That was the voice in my own head, not his.

"Are you going to throw up again?" he asked, squatting in front of me, knuckles gently drifting down my cheek.

"I don't think so."

"Let me help you back to bed then."

"I can't sleep on that water bed. It's moving." Just the memory of it made me gag a little.

"Okay, you can sleep on the couch. Come on." He lifted me under my armpits and dragged me to my feet.

With his help I stumbled to the couch and collapsed, pulling one of the new pillows under my head and sighing. I closed my eyes, but that made the spinning start again, so I kept them resolutely open as Riley draped a blanket over me. It was too hot for the blanket, but I left it, appreciating his care.

"I'm sorry," I said.

In the dark room, he leaned over and gave me a half smile. "Vodka happens. No big deal."

That wasn't what I meant. I was trying to tell him that I was sorry for being me. I shook my head. "No. For everything." For not being good enough for him, because I knew that I wasn't. I was a liar and afraid to stand up to my parents, passive in my life, and far too willing to put out instead of make emotional connections with people.

My last name shouldn't be Sweet, it should be Sour. Jessica Sour. That was me.

A big tart, mouth-puckering, acidic mess.

That was my last drunken thought before I drifted off to sleep, Riley still petting my hair.

I WOKE UP OUT OF A RESTLESS SLEEP BURNING HOT, MOUTH dry. I jerked when I realized that Easton was sitting on the coffee table watching me. "Hey," I mumbled, my throat sore. I checked under the blanket to make sure I was wearing clothes, because I had a memory of being topless while puking.

But I was wearing a soft T-shirt, so I kicked the blanket off with my feet, boiling hot, hair damp with sweat.

"Hey," he said. "If you give me ten bucks, I'll go to the store and get you Red Bull. That's the best thing for a hangover, my mom always said that."

Wonderful. I was sending him back into memories of his hard-partying mother. "That's nice of you, but I'm okay." I also thought Red Bull was probably a poor choice for dehydration, but what did I know? There hadn't been a lot of nights where I had hit it like I had the night before.

His leg bounced. "Are you sure?"

Suddenly suspicious, I swallowed hard and studied him, picking at my left eye, which seemed gummed shut with mascara. "Do you want to go to the store?" I asked carefully.

He shrugged. "I don't mind."

"Are you conning Jessica?" Riley said, coming into the room in basketball shorts, no shirt. "Beat it, punk."

Easton sent me one last meaningful look that I didn't understand and ran past his brother, darting out of the way as Riley tried to rub the top of his head.

"Why does he want to go to the store?" I asked, trying to pull myself to a sitting position with a sigh.

"He takes a cut of the money and buys himself candy. Plus I think the dude at the 7-Eleven lets him look at the latest issue of *Playboy*."

"Oh. At least he's enterprising."

Riley laughed. "I guess you could call it that. How are you feeling?"

"Like shit."

Jayden came into the room. "Oh my God!" he exclaimed when he saw me. "What happened to you? You look like butthole!"

Perfect. Even Jayden recognized a hot mess when he saw one.

"U!" Riley frowned at him. "That's a pretty goddamn rude thing to say to a chick."

"Oh. Sorry." Jayden looked at me, his apology looking and sounding sincere. But then he added equally truthfully, "But you do look terrible."

I couldn't help it. I had to laugh. "I'm sure I do. This is why vodka has a warning label."

Jayden either didn't get it or didn't care. He lost interest in me and turned to Riley. "It's hot as balls today. Can we go swimming?"

Riley looked like he would rather have his nails torn out, but he nodded. "Give me at least an hour, though. And no harassing me about it in the meantime. You drive me crazy when you follow me around sighing."

"Okay!" Jayden moved off down the hall singing a Lady Gaga song at the top of his lungs.

Riley shook his head. "God, what song is that? It's a good thing I love them. Because otherwise I might drive them out into the country and leave them in a cornfield."

"You would not." My head was throbbing, but I knew he was full of shit. He would do anything for them. He already had.

"Nah. I wouldn't." Riley moved into the kitchen. "I have coffee for you," he called out as he disappeared from view. "I iced it."

When he brought me a cup of chilled coffee and a yogurt I made a face. "Drink it. Eat it. You'll feel better, trust me."

I took a tentative sip. It was cold and wet and all that was wonderful. "Thanks. Where's my purse? I want to see if Robin got home okay." I should have texted her from the townie bar and made sure she had a ride. But I was too fucked-up to think about it.

"You threw this on the floor when we got back." Riley bent over by the front door and handed my wristlet to me.

Unzipping it, I took another coffee sip and checked my phone. No relevant texts. I tapped out a message to Robin and closed my eyes again briefly. "I'm sorry about last night."

"What was that all about?" he asked, sitting on the coffee table where Easton had been earlier, resting his elbows on his legs.

"I got drunk."

"No, I mean, what was that all about, later? Were you really upset with me for wanting to wait?"

I wanted to lie and shrug it off. But it did bother me. A lot. "I felt—no, I *feel*—rejected."

"Why would that make you feel rejected?" He looked genuinely confused.

"Because you don't want me." If I hadn't been feeling like ass, and obviously, according to Jayden, looking like it, too, I never would have said it. But I was pretty much so low I was crawling on the dirty ground of the townie bar, so what difference did it make? It wasn't like I had an ounce of dignity left.

His jaw dropped. "Are you joking? Of course I want you! I want you so fucking bad it hurts. But you were loaded last night. You weren't going to wake up today and think that was an awesome sexual experience."

"It's not just about last night. You don't ever try to . . . you know." I was having a hard time extracting words from my sluggish brain.

"What? Stick it in you after zero effort on my part? Bend you over the couch after five minutes of dating? No. I don't try to do that. Because I care about you. I want to take some time and get to know each other and each other's bodies, together." He shifted closer to me, his brown eyes earnest. "I want to explore you and your body, not use it."

"Oh." I wasn't sure what to say to that, it was so totally foreign to me. "But I want to have sex with you. Don't make me feel bad for that."

"I'm not trying to. I think it's awesome that you want to get naked with me." He raised his eyebrows up and down. "Trust me, I'm looking forward to it. But it's like cramming a whole ice-cream cone in my mouth and swallowing it whole. What good is that? It's over and done in a second. I want to really taste it, to lick it slowly. I want to savor the ice cream, you know what I'm saying?"

Holy crap, it was hot in the living room. "So this isn't about you punishing me for sleeping with other guys before I met you?" Because that was my ultimate fear.

Riley took my hand and put his palm so that it faced out and he laced his fingers through mine. "No. Absolutely not. But I have to admit that I do want to be important. Not just another guy, but *the* guy. More important than my brother, than Bill, than whoever else." He kissed my knuckles. "I want to be the man you love."

The thing was, I thought maybe he already was. Who else could make me feel like this? So special, so beautiful, so cherished, when I was laying in my sweat, vomit still in my hair, breath smelling like the bottom of a trash can. I nodded enthusiastically, because I didn't trust myself to speak without crying. There was a tightness in my chest, my throat, and I squeezed his fingers tightly.

I thought and discarded a few different things to say as wrong or over the top and settled on, "You are more important than any of them. Ever."

For the first time ever, I caught a glimpse of vulnerability in Riley. He looked like he couldn't speak now, and he gave a short nod, his jaw working. Then he said, "Good. Okay. So we're on the same page now?"

I nodded. "Though I still want to have sex."

He laughed. "Me, too. But it's been two years, I figure I can last a few more weeks."

Weeks? God save the queen, was he for real? And wait a minute. He hadn't had sex in two years? That made my self-control seem virtually nonexistent. I had to step it up. "Oh me, too, of course. I was just testing you."

"Jessica, you are amazing." He leaned forward and kissed me. "Now eat your yogurt so we can go to the pool later. You're coming with us, right?"

"Wouldn't miss it." I swung my legs around and forced myself to stand. "Though I don't have a bathing suit with me."

"We can stop at your apartment." Riley gave me a look. "And

maybe you should just pack a whole suitcase. It's a little inconvenient to have your stuff there when you're always going to be here."

Hello. He was suggesting I stay with him. Not quite living with him, but there would be extended periods of time where I didn't go back to my apartment. That might seem fast, except for the fact that we had started out living together. It didn't seem weird to me, it just seemed awesome. "Good point," I told him, just as casual as he was. "Now I have to go pee."

"After all that booze I'm surprised you didn't wet your pants last night. I have to hand it to you, you can hold your liquor."

"I puked in your bathroom. How is that holding my liquor?"

"But you did it with such style. Topless. That's classic."

I could only imagine. "Before the whole throwing-up thing, I had a great time with you. Well, after you shoved that guy's face into a garbage can of booze. Everything in between was a lot of fun."

"Actually, I had fun at the bar with you, too. Next time let's skip the frat party and go straight there."

"Deal." Relieved that not only had I not ruined our relationship, we seemed to have taken it to the next level, even without sex, I went into the bathroom and checked out the horror reflecting back at me in the mirror. Yep. Train wreck. My face was swollen and dry, mascara streaking down both cheeks. My hair was stringy and sticking up in the back. Chapped lips. Filthy, dirty feet and a scraped-up knee. Yep. Adorbs. That was me.

I didn't even bother to brush my hair or wash my face. I figured everyone had already seen me looking like ass. I used the toilet and padded back out to the living room, grabbing the yogurt and coffee. I could hear the guys all out on the back patio and I wanted to sit with them. The sun might feel good. Wincing when I opened the door and the sun hit me in the eyes, I shuffled over to the table and plopped down next to Riley.

Tyler was on the other side and he took one look at me and said, "Wow. Good morning, pretty girl."

"I hate you," I said.

He laughed. But he did call out to his brother, "Hey, Easton, go grab your sunglasses for Jess. She needs them."

Easton went streaking by.

"That kid never walks, does he?" I said, scooping up some of the yogurt and forcing it into my mouth, even when I thought I might gag.

"Nope."

Riley was straddling the bench sideways, and he reached out and started rubbing my shoulders, easing the drunken knots out of them.

"Oh my God, that feels so good."

Easton came back and flung a pair of plastic sunglasses on the table before going back into the yard shirtless to poke at something in the corner with a stick. "Thank you," I called after him.

Then I opened them and realized they were twin dollar signs. Nice. I put them on my face and Tyler and Riley both started laughing.

"Wow, big pimpin', Jess." Riley took a sip from my coffee.

"It does help with the glare," I said. "I can't really look any worse, so what's the difference?"

"I think you look cute," Riley said, reaching out and brushing his fingers over my lip.

Oh, my. Heart. Melt.

"Suck-up." Tyler coughed into his hand.

I looked at Tyler, thinking about how happy he was with Rory, thinking about how I really liked him as a friend, but now, next to Riley, he was like, well, a brother to me. It was almost impossible to remember what it felt like to see and feel him naked, his body inside of me, and instead of shoving that away, ignoring it, I wanted to examine those feelings and memories. I wanted to be honest with myself.

It was a weird phrase, "inside of me," when you thought about it, as if sex were an invasion. An alien moving in your body. It didn't factor in the emotional side of sex at all.

Because I knew in that capacity, no one had ever actually been inside me.

So if I knew then what I knew now, would I still have sex with Tyler? It was hard to remember the exact circumstances that had even led to it to the first time. So it was hard to say. Probably no. But I wasn't exactly sure.

All I knew was certain was that like fabric fades in the sun, so had the physical part of my relationship with Tyler, and neither of us would ever miss it. In some ways, it was already like it had never happened.

Which gave me my answer. Because if you could look back on sex with someone and say it was like it had never happened, then it never should have in the first place.

It should matter.

So while it wasn't regret I felt as the sun beat down on me on the patio and Tyler smoked me out with his ever-present cigarette, I knew that I was looking forward to me and Riley.

To a relationship that mattered.

# CHAPTER FIFTEEN

"DON'T SPOIL THEM," RILEY TOLD ME AS I LET JAYDEN AND Easton fill my convenience store basket with a variety of candy and soft drinks. Easton seemed to have a thing for grape soda, and how could I argue with that? He was a guy after my own heart.

"It's not spoiling them to let them get something to take to the pool. I'm not going to just buy stuff for me and then eat and drink in front of them. That's so rude."

Riley eyed my basket. "Hangover food?"

"Yep." There was chips, chips, and more chips in there. Plus Twizzlers and orange juice and grape soda for me in addition to Easton's. Jayden had picked bottled iced tea, which struck me as seriously gross. You could see things floating in there.

I had showered at Riley's house, then we had swung by my apartment and packed one of my two suitcases. It wasn't awesome that I was paying rent on a place I was almost never going to be in, but whatever. The high cost of a relationship. But now I was in my yellow bikini, hoodie and shorts on over it, fortunately wearing

my own sunglasses, making our pit stop before the pool. I tossed
two trashy magazines and a fashion one in the basket.

"Are you done?" Riley asked me, eyebrows raised.

"Can I get gum?" Jayden asked.

"No," Riley told him. "You already have a drink and chips.
Money doesn't grow on trees, U."

"It should," was Jayden's opinion on that.

I laughed. "Totally."

When we got to the pool, I blinked. "Holy crap, there's a ton
of people here."

Okay, I can admit that I had never been to a public pool before.
Why would I? My parents had a pool and so did the country club
my dad golfed at. But this was more seminaked bodies together in
one place than at the last night we'd gone clubbing.

"It is Memorial Day weekend," Riley said. "I'm not surprised
it's crowded."

"Chair." Tyler pointed to a free chaise and Easton darted off
to claim it, his scrawny limbs allowing him to dodge and weave
around other people. He dove onto it with a move worthy of pro-
fessional wrestling.

"Impressive," I said.

What was even more impressive was that all four of the Mann
brothers agreed I should have the chair. I was touched to the bottom
of my cynical heart. "Really?"

"Sleep off that hangover," Tyler told me.

"Thanks, guys." I spread out my towel and sat down, then set
down the plastic bag with our haul. "Who wants their stuff?"

"I'm going in first," Riley said. "I'm boiling." He peeled off his
shirt and I eyeballed those muscles and his tattoos.

Yummy. Biting a Twizzler, I said, "Put on sunscreen."

"Jessica, I am on the roof of a house every day without a shirt on." He flipped his waistband down to show me the difference in his skin tone. Yep, he was whiter down there. "I don't think sunscreen is going to matter at this point."

"It's never too late to prevent skin cancer."

"Put it on Jayden instead. He's practically transparent."

He was. His skin tone was at least two shades lighter than Tyler's and Riley's. "Sit down here, Jayden, and I'll put it on your shoulders."

He squawked in protest when I sprayed him. "It's cold!"

"Wimp," Tyler said.

"Shut up."

I rubbed it into his skin and Jayden made sounds of enjoyment.

Riley grinned. "You should see his face right now, Jess. I think he's working up a chub."

"Don't be disgusting," I told him primly. "You're going to embarrass Jayden."

"No, it's actually true," Jayden said, glancing at me over his shoulder.

His brothers almost died laughing.

Nice.

I wiped my hands on my towel. Easton was digging through the bag and I saw he was eyeing my fashion magazine, which had a topless model on the cover, artfully covering her breasts. I remembered what Riley had said about *Playboy* and I decided I needed to intervene.

"Find your stuff?" I asked him, peeling off my hoodie so I could spray sunscreen on my chest and arms.

He just nodded without looking at me and dropped the bag.

"Ready?" Riley asked him, rubbing the top of his head so that Easton rocked back and forth.

He nodded again.

I sprayed the tops of my breasts and started rubbing them. Riley made a sound in the back of his throat. "Need any help?"

"No, thank you." I wasn't going to subject myself to that kind of contact in public. I was so hot for him I'd probably be foaming at the mouth by the time he was done. "Easton's waiting."

Tyler was kicking his shoes off and I asked him, "Hey, have you heard from Robin at all? I'm getting worried. She never answered my text."

He paused pulling his shirt off. "Robin's fine. I saw her leave with Nathan."

There was an odd look on his face. "What?"

His expression was guarded. "Nothing. What, what?"

"I don't know. You look weird."

"Nope." He dropped his shirt and headed straight to the water. Huh. That was not normal.

"Put my wallet behind your ass," Riley said.

"What?" I said, distracted from Tyler's weirdness by my boyfriend's weirdness. "Did you just tell me to stick your wallet behind my ass?"

"Yes. So no one steals it. My phone, too."

Suddenly I had Riley's cell phone crammed behind my butt. Followed by his leather wallet. Yeah, this was comfortable.

But I figured he would know the risks involved with leaving valuables around at the pool more than me, so I tucked my own phone in my bikini top. Not comfortable either. But the sun was warm and as I lay back I dozed in and out of sleep, the alcohol effect still lingering.

Until ice-cold water droplets fell on my bare stomach. I jumped, my eyes flying open. All four Mann boys were standing around me, dripping wet.

"Does anyone notice they're dripping on me?" I asked.

Apparently the answer was no, and they didn't care, because no one said anything.

Riley ran his hand through his hair and nudged me with his knee. "Scoot over."

"Scoot over to where? The ground? This is a chair for one."

"You can lean against me."

"Can I at least spring your wallet from my butt then?"

"Yeah, put it under the chair." Riley put his leg behind me to straddle the chair as I leaned forward. He sat down.

Water dripped down my back. And I swear his junk smacked me in the back of the head. When I leaned back onto his chest, his arms coming around me, cold and wet, I winced as goose bumps rose on my body, but I didn't really mind. It felt fantastic to be this comfortable with him, to have a place to spend a Sunday.

"Ah, this is a perfect day," he said, echoing my thoughts, kissing the back of my head. "Now if only a burger would appear in my hand."

"All we have are chips." I leaned to the left and snagged a bag. Yanking it open, I held a chip up over my shoulder. Riley pulled it into his mouth hands free, his tongue flicking over my fingers. A shiver went through me that had nothing to do with pool water.

I popped a chip in my own mouth. His hands were resting on my hips. Easton had perched himself on the bottom of the chair and he was inspecting a scab on his knee. Tyler and Jayden were laying on a couple of towels on the ground next to us, Tyler with a shirt over his face.

"So Jessica Sour, huh?" Riley asked, his voice amused by my ear.

Oh, shit. I had actually said that out loud? "What are you talking about?" I went for innocence.

"You don't remember calling yourself that?"

"Nope."

"Bullshit." His arms were locked together under my breasts and he squeezed me. "I don't think you give yourself enough credit. I believe we have our names for a reason. I mean, think about it . . . Riley *Mann*. I've certainly earned that title."

I snorted. "And you're modest about it, too."

"The truth is the truth," he teased. "And Jessica Sweet. It's perfect for you."

"If you say so."

"I know so."

"Even though I'm lying to my parents?"

I could feel his shrug. "You have your reasons."

I snuggled against him. "If you could do anything in the world, say, if you didn't have to be in construction and could go to college or whatever, what would you do?"

"I have no idea. None whatsoever. How about you? What if you could pick your own major in college, what would it be?"

Glancing back at him, I grinned. "I have no idea either. So it seems pointless to take a stand on it if I don't have an alternative in mind." I had thought a lot about it and what interested me and I hadn't really come to any conclusions. It made me feel lazy and indecisive.

But today I didn't care about being lazy. Riley seemed to like me exactly the way I was.

"I figured why think about it when it can never happen? Waste of wanting, for me. It is what it is."

"Does that bother you?"

"Nah, not usually. Everyone has a part to play and this is mine. It's what you make of it. Sometimes I let my temper get the best of me and I struggle with that, but I can't complain. Not with your ass rubbing against me right now."

"Pure poetry," I told him.

"If you want poetry go read Shakespeare."

"I'd rather stick my finger down my throat than read Shakespeare. I think we're good." I never understood poetry, truthfully. It was like a trick, every word meaning something other than what it was originally intended. A mind fuck, that was poetry. Who needs that?

"Hey, if you married me your name would be Jessica Sweet Mann. That's literally the best name I've ever heard."

Or the worst. OMG. It was awful. Yet the fact that he said the word "married" in a sentence referring to me and him made me breathless. He didn't mean that, obviously. I mean, ludicrous. But why would his mind even go there? It had to be a point-A-to-point-B-to-point-C kind of thing, but if he could even mentally cross that bridge, even to tease me, well, that made me shift even closer to him, a girly glow settling over me.

"That name is balls."

He laughed. "I think it rocks."

My phone vibrated against my boob. I pulled it out. Robin had finally answered. Im fine. Hungover.

Did you hook up with Aaron?

No.

Want to meet us at the pool?

No.

K. ttyl

She didn't answer that.

Looking up, I realized that Easton was throwing Cheetos at a woman's very large backside.

"Hey, stop wasting those," Riley told him. "They're expensive."

"That's your teachable moment parenting response?" I asked him, amazed. "Nothing about not throwing snack foods at women's butts?"

"Yeah. That, too." Riley shrugged. "I told you I'm not that good at this parenting thing. I keep him alive, don't I? The finer points sometimes elude me. Besides, I would have done the same damn thing when I was eleven. It's a pretty substantial ass and she's wearing hot pink."

I had no problem picturing him as an eleven-year-old, with a smart mouth and a lust for freedom. He had probably been trying to sneak off to try to get tattooed. "You do deserve credit for keeping him alive. But maybe you should all try to remember that he isn't in his twenties."

"I know that. He'd have a job if he was. And he'd be taller."

Eye rolling. That's all that demanded. "Easton, why are you throwing Cheetos at her?" I asked, curious to figure out what was going on in Easton's head.

But he just shrugged. "Because it's big and right in front of me. I wanted to see if they'll bounce."

That's what I got for asking. The truth, which wasn't that pretty. "But if she realizes what you're doing, you're going to hurt her feelings. No one likes to be made fun of, and you're basically making fun of her."

Easton didn't answer me. He just threw the Cheetos back in the plastic store bag and went back to the pool, jumping in cannonball style.

"Well, that went well." I felt bad. "I guess I shouldn't have said anything. It's none of my business." Who did I think I was, telling Riley how to handle Easton? Telling Easton how to behave? It wasn't like I was some model daughter. Clearly. Just ask my parents.

"Don't sweat it."

"I don't want him to hate me." He was an odd little kid, but I was getting fond of him, and I wanted him to like me.

"He doesn't hate you. And you're right, he probably does need better manners, but I've been more focused on keeping him. I hate to say it, but it's better for him since Mom died. Less swearing, less drama, no drugs, no violence. I figure the other stuff will catch up later."

"I'm sorry. I'm a horrible, pretentious, elitist bitch. Thinking I can come in and clean your house and help you with Easton." My chest felt tight. "Next time just tell me to shut up."

"Jess, stop being so goddamn sensitive. I know you're only trying to help. I appreciate that. And I don't find you elitist. Maybe a little inexperienced when it comes to the, you know, real world, but if you were elitist, you wouldn't be with me, and you wouldn't be living in my house, or be seen riding around in my piece-of-shit Impala. Or at the public pool."

Maybe he was right. Just because I had grown up in a bubble didn't make me pretentious. Just inexperienced. It was my mother who liked designer labels, not me. That had never been a priority to me. "I don't mean to be sensitive. I've never thought of myself that way."

"Well, no one wakes up and says 'I'm going to be sensitive today.' It's probably because you're tired. I always get pissed off when I'm hungover. Every little thing irritates me."

"I don't remember you acting that way at all. You pulled up carpeting hungover and never complained."

"Okay, you're right. I am awesome."

I laughed. He always managed to make me feel better.

He tipped my head backward and I almost went cross-eyed looking up at his super cute face. "You're more awesome-er," he said.

While I didn't believe it, I believed that he believed it.

And that was good enough for me.

When he kissed me, I realized that falling in love with Riley was just like having my head tilted backward—blood rushing, dizzy, hot and desperate, the world spinning.

IN BED THAT NIGHT, OUR BODIES CLOSE AND WARM, RILEY'S hand firmly on my hip, pulling me tighter into him, I tried to re-member his analogy. Food. This was like food. Like me eating a slice of loaded pizza—pick one piece off at a time and savor it, let all the flavors work their way around my mouth. It wasn't about efficiency or eating to be finished.

So wearing sleep shorts and a cami but no bra, Riley shirtless in his boxer briefs, I tried to appreciate the now and not the later. We weren't going to have sex, not yet, not tonight. That was un-derstood between both of us. So I relaxed, letting the tension I usually felt as I raced toward penetration fade away.

"I love your mouth," he murmured. "Your lips are perfect." His hand was on my chin and we were lying sideways, looking into each other's eyes.

The water bed had the smallest of a rock to it, allowing us to move together, his fingers drawing my leg over his hip. It was still creepy to me that we slept on a giant fluid-filled sac, but in moments like this, I could appreciate the motion of the ocean. I sighed, enjoying the ease with which we fit together, lips teasing and melding, my fingers splaying over his hard chest.

"I love your body," I told him sincerely. "You're so nice and hard everywhere." I brushed over his nipple and enjoyed the sharp intake of breath he gave. Ah, the power. "I just wish I wasn't groping Satan right now."

"Think of it more like there's a little devil inside all of us."

"I wish there was a little devil inside of me," I told him, teasing my fingertips lower to the waistband of his boxers.

He gave a soft laugh, nuzzling into my neck. "That wouldn't be little then."

"Of course not." But truthfully, I didn't actually mind that we weren't going there. This was intimate, close, allowing us the time to tease and talk, and I was learning that I could be more aware of my body and my arousal than I had ever realized.

As Riley kissed me and rocked me onto him, I gave soft moans and realized that I trusted him. That's what was different. I trusted his words, his feelings, his touch. That was actually a bigger turn-on than any porn star move guys had pulled with me. It wasn't kinky, bold, or worthy of a scandalous bucket list, but it was more real than anything else I'd ever experienced.

And an hour later I discovered that I could come to orgasm just from kissing, clothes on, with nothing but whispered words of encouragement and a complete understanding of every inch of my body.

"Oh, God," I breathed into his mouth, blinking in shock and wonder. "Riley . . ."

"Mm," was his response. His tongue slid across my bottom lip as we cuddled. "Night, Pita."

He sent me to sleep like that every night, though each time our fingers moved further into new territories, brushing over every inch we could with clothes still intact, and his lips started to stray down my shirt. By night four I was rocking onto him in nothing but my panties, my breasts pressing into his chest, my body alive and zinging, my heart full of a feeling I had never experienced before.

The first time his tongue touched my nipple, the first slide of a finger down into my panties, I felt like I had discovered something entirely new, that the simplest of touches could be the most electric, the most satisfying, when desire was so heightened.

I stroked him with fingers that trembled from my own hot need, goose bumps on my skin in the darkness of the narrow room, wanting to give him in return what he was giving to me. When I started to peel down his boxers, he didn't object. It was the first time I'd seen him bare to me, his erection thick and throbbing beneath my touch. It was too dark to really see what he looked like, but I was learning his body by exploring every line, every muscle, every hair, and I did the same now, taking my time, from top to bottom, feeling, stroking, learning.

"Does it get your stamp of approval?" he asked.

Even though he said it in a teasing voice, I knew that it was an important question. Guys compared. They needed to know that they measured up, literally and figuratively.

"It's perfect," I told him honestly. I kissed the tip of his penis and then retreated, having learned how to do that from him. "You're perfect." I covered his mouth with my own and tried to show him with my lips how amazing I thought he was and how I had never been happier in my entire life than I was with him.

He groaned, gripping my hips hard, bringing my body into grinding contact with his dick. "Jess?"

"Yeah?"

"Would you be okay with it if I fell in love with you?"

My heart squeezed and I paused, my mouth a hairbreadth from his, as I took in his words, as if I could breathe them into my mouth, my heart, my soul.

"Yeah," I whispered. "I'd be very okay with it."

It must have been the right answer, because without warning he flipped me onto my back and kissed down the front of me until suddenly he was kissing between my thighs and I was burying my head into the pillow as I cried out.

I wasn't even naked, his mouth working me through cotton, yet I was more open to him than to any other guy I'd been with.

And I knew without any doubt that he was *the* guy.

# CHAPTER SIXTEEN

FRIDAY WAS MY DAY OFF AND I WAS HAVING DINNER ON RILEY'S lap. We were in the kitchen sharing a grilled cheese sandwich I had made, along with a pickle that I couldn't resist doing suggestive things to.

"Seriously?" Tyler asked, eating a bowl of cereal. "You guys are making me throw me up in my mouth."

"It's paybacks, asshole," Riley told him, shifting me on his legs so he could see his brother. "For a year I've been forced to watch you and Rory hang all over each other."

"Six months," I corrected him, kissing his temple. He was adorable when he was wrong. He was adorable when he was right. And I was as bad as every girl who'd come before me and fallen head over ass in love.

"Six months," he repeated. "Either way, Tyler can suck it up."

Tyler couldn't really argue with that. But he did roll his eyes and say, "I'll give you five bucks, Jess, if you sit in your own chair."

Hell, yeah. "Deal." I jumped off Riley's lap and held my hand out.

"Fuck." Tyler grumbled, but pulled out his wallet and gave me a five.

Riley laughed. "Dude, you should know better. This is *my* girl-friend, not yours. Rory isn't about the angle, but Jess should count cards in Vegas. She's a *play-uh*."

"Thanks, baby," I said, because he made it sound like a compliment. I dropped down into my own chair and tore off a piece of the sandwich and popped it in my mouth. "So what do you want to do tonight?"

"Movies?"

"Nothing scary."

"Uh, hell, no, nothing scary. I won't make that mistake twice. Having you crawl up my asshole has never been a particular fantasy of mine."

"I wasn't that bad."

"You ran into my room crying because you thought there was a demon in the house."

"You're exaggerating!" I said, laughing. "But only a little." My phone lit up and the ringtone was "Gangnam Style."

"Oh my God, whose ringtone is that?" Riley asked.

"It's my brother's. Because this song is almost as annoying as he is."

"Are you going to answer it?"

"No." I hit Ignore. Why was my brother calling me? He never did. He knew I was supposed to be in West Virginia and out of cell range. I started to worry that maybe something had happened to my parents. That's the only reason I could think of for him to call. "Maybe I should have answered," I said, frowning.

"Did he leave a voice mail?"

"No." Did anyone leave voice mails? But then my phone buzzed for a text. I opened it and my heart sank when I saw the picture he'd attached. "Shit." I didn't even have to read what he'd written to know it would be a threat, but I did anyway.

WV huh? Location says Cinci and your face says wasted. How much $ to keep quiet?

Yep. That was a threat. Technically blackmail. I stared at the picture that he had clearly lifted off of my Facebook page. Someone had posted it and I hadn't been on my page in days so I hadn't noticed. It was me dancing with the guy at the party at the Shit Shack. I had a beer in my hand and a goofy, drunk expression on my face. My cleavage was exploding, and his hand was lower on my hip than I remembered it being.

I was so busted.

"What's the matter?"

"My brother has a picture of me at the party last weekend. He says he'll tell my parents if I don't pay him off."

Riley's jaw dropped. "Your *brother* is trying to extort money from you?"

"I told you, he hates me for no apparent reason."

"How bad is the picture?" Tyler asked. "I mean, your parents have to know you party a bit at school, right?"

"No. They do not." I pushed my phone over to him so he could see it. "They also think I'm in West Virginia building houses for the poor with a church mission group."

Tyler choked on his cereal. "Are you shitting me?"

"No, I am not." I felt sick. Like throw-up sick.

Riley squeezed my knee. "Hey, it's okay. What does your brother want, like fifty bucks? Just pay the little prick. Or let me talk to him." There was a gleam in his eye that suggested he wanted to do more than talk.

"You think I should pay him?"

"Well, if you want him to keep quiet, it's your best option. Though I would personally prefer to beat the piss out of him. What kind of a shit thing is that to do to your own sister?"

How much? I typed to Paxton.

Two grand.

I laughed in disbelief. "He wants two thousand dollars!"

"What? Fuck him." Riley waved his hand. "Tell him to suck my dick."

You're insane. I don't have 2k.

You have thirty minutes. You can transfer the $ to my acct or I'm going to mom.

That he said Mom instead of Dad was a good indication he was serious. Dad would be profoundly disappointed, but Mom would be pissed.

Why do you care what I do?

Though I already knew it was pointless to try to talk him out of it. Paxton had been looking for the big score, the way to topple me, for years, and he had found it. I had basically handed it to him via vodka cranberries.

Because you're a bitch.

Well, there you go. My brother thought I was a bitch so he was going to ruin my life. "This is bad. This is so bad. My parents are going to freak." The grilled cheese sat like a lump in my gut and my mind raced, trying to anticipate the fallout.

"Obviously they're going to be pissed you lied, but they can't really punish you. I mean, you're twenty years old."

I shook my head. "Oh, they can punish me. They'll cut me off."

"Rory's dad threatened to stop paying her tuition and he didn't," Tyler said. "He knew in the end hurting Rory's future wasn't worth it."

But Rory's father was different from mine and I knew that. Rory had stood up to her dad, and I had admired it when she'd done it. It couldn't have been easy to tell him she was going to intentionally disobey him. But Rory also knew that at the end of the day, her dad had her back. It was just the two of them, and he loved her.

My father loved me. Sure. And he was a good man in so many ways, a good leader, with deep moral convictions. But those convictions would prevent him from indulging what he would consider the path of my moral destruction. My mother was just like Paxton—she was spiteful. Once she was angry, it took a lot to earn back her affection.

The combination of both of them upset with me was going to result in an order to come home or be cut off. I knew it.

Both of which made me feel like I couldn't breathe.

"Rory's dad compromised because he didn't want to lose her. Mine won't. I know it." I tried to give a shrug. "I guess it was going to be impossible not to get busted at some point. I can't keep pretending to be the perfect daughter. Frankly, I'm surprised they haven't figured that out already."

"Maybe they have," Riley said, reaching over and pulling my hand into his. "They might know more than you realize."

My phone rang again. This time it was "Material Girl" by Madonna. My mom's ringtone, and my sense of irony on display. "Wow. Paxton moves faster than I thought. He must have been planning to tell the whole time."

Resigned, heart thumping, hand shaking, I picked up the phone, wondering if I genuinely felt guilty that I lied, or if I was just sorry I'd been caught. "Hello?"

"If you're going to mastermind that you're off doing mission work, then you should have the good sense not to post pictures of you partying like a trashy whore on the Internet."

How was that for a greeting? "Mom, I'm sorry, I didn't mean for you to find out like that."

"You didn't mean for me to find out at all. But I'm not discussing this with you on the phone." Her voice was cold, her anger barely contained. She wasn't yelling, but she wanted to be. It sounded like she was trying to not completely lose her shit on me.

I just waited, because there was going to be more. "I'm sorry," I repeated.

She took a breath and continued. "I don't want to hear your insincere apologies. Tomorrow night is the fund-raiser. You will be there, and you will do your part to help this family. Then we will discuss your behavior."

"Mom, I have to work tomorrow," I protested. I didn't want to go home. They might not let me leave again. I supposed my parents couldn't lock me in the house, but they could use emotional manipulation.

"And I don't give a damn," she said. "Be at the house by five at the latest and I want zero arguments from you."

Then she hung up on me. Probably to go throw something to let out all that simmering rage.

"That was fast," Riley said.

"She said I have to come home tomorrow and go to a fundraiser. Then we'll discuss my behavior."

"Are you going to?" he asked.

"I don't have a ride."

"I can take you if you want to go. Though maybe showing up with me isn't going to help the situation. I don't imagine I'm your dad's idea of the right guy for his daughter."

No, he wouldn't be. But he was the only person who could give me a ride, and if the truth had to come out, then maybe I needed to be a little braver like Rory had been and own up to everything. I wasn't ashamed of Riley. He was a good guy. I was completely happy with him, and I didn't want to keep our relationship a secret.

The real question was, did I want to go? I definitely didn't want to, but I knew I had to. I couldn't hide from my parents or from my lie. I had to face them and be totally honest. Mature and responsible for my own actions.

"Unless my dad handpicked you, he won't think any guy is right for me. But it would be awesome if you could take me. I could use the support."

"If she wants you to go to a fund-raiser, maybe she's not that pissed," Tyler said, obviously trying to cheer me up.

But she was pissed, there was no doubt about it.

This was not going to be a fun weekend.

WHEN I CAME OUT OF THE BATHROOM ON SATURDAY DRESSED to go home, Riley blinked at me. "I'm sorry, I thought my girlfriend was in the bathroom. Who exactly are you?"

"Ha ha." I was wearing a long floral maxi dress with a sweater over it, buttoned at the top so it pulled over my chest to cover the bare skin there. The only jewelry I had on was my cross necklace. My flats were yellow, like the flowers in the dress, and I had tied my hair up in a simple bun. No makeup. "I'm trying not to piss them off the second I walk in the door."

"You look . . . pale." Riley came over and kissed me on the forehead. "Like a watered-down version of you. I don't like it."

"Me either." But I was trying to be respectful. Either that, or I was still being a wimp. "You ready to go?"

"Yep. Let's do this. It's going to be fine." He stroked my cheek and smiled. "Who can resist forgiving a face like this?"

Even Riley's optimism started to crack when we pulled up to my parents' house, though. "Holy shit," he said. "This is where you grew up?"

"Yes." It was a big redbrick monstrosity, with white pillars and a fountain out front. I had never actually thought it was pretty, though as a kid I'd loved the fountain. But by the time I was in middle school, I found it pretentious and embarrassing. Even more so now, seeing it through Riley's eyes.

"Apparently the God gig is a good one," Riley said, parking the car. "I admit, I'm feeling a little intimidated."

"Don't. It's just a house that the church paid for. I've always thought it was on the verge of tacky." I took a deep breath and stared at its stillness. "But I know I was really lucky to have material things as a kid. I always got what I wanted, within reason." Which was probably part of the reason I was so aimless. I'd never really had to work all that hard at anything to have a comfortable life.

Just smile, and say your prayers in public. That's all that had been expected of me.

"Now I'm really amazed that you agreed to stay at my place. Damn." Riley shook his head.

"You have a better sense of family in that house than there is in this one," I told him sincerely. "I like being there, with you and the boys." Even though I didn't belong, not really, I felt like I did.

"You ready to do this?" he asked me, taking the key out of the ignition.

"I guess I have to be." What I really wanted to do was run away and never face the disappointment that was going to be on my parents' faces.

Riley walked behind me, his boots creating a steady rhythm that soothed me. I was actually really relieved he was with me. I didn't think that I would have the courage to go inside if he hadn't held my hand, squeezing it in reassurance. The house was hushed and quiet and I figured my dad was in the library, reading before the social night ahead. The main hallway was two stories high and had more columns, with a winding staircase. I led Riley past the stairs to the wooden double doors to the library. They were open, and my dad was exactly where I had expected, on the sofa already wearing a suit, book in hand.

He looked up and saw me and his rigid expression showed his displeasure. But then astonishment replaced that as he took in Riley's hand in mine. I knew the picture Riley made to a man like my father. Riley was wearing a Doors T-shirt, the leather straps of his bracelets wrapping around below his tattoos. The fact that he was twenty-five years old was evident in his jaw, the sun crinkles around his eyes, and a glance showed that he looked tense, edgy. His adorable dimples were nowhere in sight.

"Jessica. Come in. Introduce me to your friend."

Dad sounded polite, in control. I wasn't sure if that was better or worse. He sounded . . . remote. We went into the room and sat down on the opposite sofa from my father.

"Hi, Dad. This is Riley Mann." I paused a heartbeat, then went for it. "My boyfriend."

The manners evaporated. "Is this why you lied to us? Is this why you wanted to stay in Cincinnati for the summer, to be around some guy?"

Of course he would conclude that. I realized I was going to have a hard time convincing him otherwise. "No. Absolutely not. We weren't even together yet."

It was like I didn't even speak. My father set his iced tea down carefully on the end table and eyed Riley. I didn't like the way his eyes narrowed. He was a tall man, broad in the shoulders, graying at the temples. He was intimidating. I had always been a little afraid of him. Not because he'd ever hurt me in any way, but because he was imposing. As a little girl, he would always say he had God's ear, that he was a shepherd leading God's flock of sheep. Somehow I had decided that God's ear was actually in my dad's pocket, next to his wallet and the change that jangled when he put his hand in there and moved it around subconsciously. I had always been afraid it would fall out and I would see it, a torn-off celestial ear piece listening to all my words and thoughts like a big tattletaling megaphone to God.

"Are you having sexual intercourse with my daughter?" Dad asked Riley, bluntly and out of nowhere.

I uncrossed my leg and sat up straight. "Dad! You can't ask him that." I turned to Riley. "Don't answer that!"

But Riley ignored me just like my father did. He met my dad's hard stare with one of his own. "No, sir, I am not."

I wasn't sure how entirely accurate that was, considering we did dry hump on a regular basis, but I was just so appalled by the question that I wasn't even sure what to say.

"But you want to." It wasn't a question, but a statement.

Riley nodded. "Of course. Jessica is a beautiful woman and I care a great deal about her."

Heat rushed to my cheeks. Did anyone notice that I was still in the room while they sat there and discussed me?

"Dad, my sex life is none of your business," I told him firmly.

It was at that point that my mother walked into the room. "What on earth?" she asked, coming to a complete stop in the doorway, her hand going to her throat. "Jessica, what sex life? What the hell is going on here? Have you lost your goddamn mind?"

Mom was swearing. And saying the word "sex" out loud. Now I really knew I was in trouble.

"No sex life," I said firmly. "We are not having this conversation."

"Who is this?" My mother eyed Riley like he was mold growing in the shower grout.

"This is her boyfriend, she says. This is why she lied to us, she clearly wanted to spend the summer with him."

"That is not true," I insisted, feeling this spiral out of control even more. I was trying to be honest for the first time in, oh, ever, and no one would listen to me. The irony was frustrating. "I lied to you because I didn't want to come home for the summer and deal with having to do what you want me to do."

My mother said, "What, like helping with Sunday school? You'd rather be getting drunk and dancing suggestively with random boys?"

Well, when she put it that way it didn't sound very good. "No. I just want to be able to make my own choices. I'm not interested in the legacy of the church. I'm sorry, I know that hurts you, but I'm not going to marry one of your staff, Daddy. I can't. I would be horrible as a preacher's wife and the thought makes me want to scream at the top of my lungs."

I hadn't meant to get so specific. I had intended to just explain why I hadn't come home, but I guess the truth was it was all interconnected. I couldn't explain without being completely honest. "I don't want to study theology and I don't want to pretend to be someone I'm not when I'm with you."

My mother made a sound of annoyance.

My father studied me. "Are you saying you've lost your faith entirely?"

"No." I fingered my cross necklace. "I believe in God and I believe in Christian kindness. But I don't believe in judging other people and I don't believe that I'm a bad person because I do things you may not like." I wasn't a bad person. I really wasn't, and I realized that maybe with the freedom to be myself, I would become an even better person. That I would discover my purpose, my passion.

"So basically you'd like a personalized Jessica Plan, with the rules changing with your mood? Whatever you like is okay morally?" Dad said. "Moral ambiguity is a slippery slope to Hell."

Uh. No. I had firm beliefs and that sentence sounded super snarky. This conversation was not going to go in my favor. Though why I had thought it would was beyond me.

"I don't understand why you couldn't just come to us and say you didn't want to come home," my mother said, her bobbed hair not moving an inch even though she was shaking her head rapidly.

"Come on, if I had done that, you wouldn't have let me stay in Cincinnati."

Neither disputed that.

"Where are you staying?"

"I subletted an apartment."

"So you're not living with him?" my father asked, gesturing to Riley.

"His name is Riley," I said pointedly, because I was super embarrassed by my dad's pretentious treatment of him. "And no, technically I don't live with him, but I spend a lot of time there. And yes, sometimes I spend the night."

"Are you still pure?" was the awesome follow-up question.

The implication that if I wasn't a virgin I was impure—dirty—made me flinch. But I held up my head and said clearly, "No." Let them vilify me.

Riley made a sound in the back of his throat.

My mother made a sound of horror and she looked at me with such disgust that I dug my nails into my legs, a sense of shame that I didn't want to own rushing over me.

"Him?" Mom asked, gesturing to Riley. "This is who you gave your virginity to?"

"This doesn't have anything to do with Riley." It could be amusing to think that we hadn't even had sex yet, but I was too upset to appreciate the irony. "This is about me trying to explain to you that I can't be who you want me to be."

"What, modest? How many boys have you slept with?" Mom asked. "Please tell me it was just the one."

"I'm not discussing this with you." And I would keep saying it until someone heard me. "What I'm trying to get you to understand is that I get it that you think of women as fitting into two categories—whores and the Madonna. But I'm neither. I'm just Jessica, somewhere in between, and I love you and I want you to accept me." Tears formed in my eyes and I could hear the pleading in my voice and it horrified me. Being vulnerable wasn't easy, especially with Riley sitting next to me seeing my humiliation.

"So in other words, it was more than one." My mother's mouth pressed into a thin line, her red lipstick disappearing into her frown.

My heart sank. So that was that. That was her response and it wasn't even close to what I wanted, no, needed, to hear.

My father cleared his throat. "You have two choices, Jessica. You can stay here for the rest of the summer under our roof with our rules and go back to school for the coursework we agreed on together, you and I"—he pointed back and forth between us—"or you can stay in Cincinnati now and lose our financial support. I cannot condone your lifestyle choices with my wallet."

My mother was crying now, silent, pretty tears that wouldn't wreck her makeup.

"I understand," I said, feeling very calm all of a sudden. Hadn't I been expecting this for years? I couldn't pretend forever that I was going to walk the path they had chosen for me and in a sense it was a relief to know I wouldn't have to anymore. "I don't want to waste your money so I think it's best if I withdraw from school for a while. Can I get my stuff from my room?"

"So you're leaving?" my father asked.

I nodded.

"If you leave this house I don't want to speak to you ever again," Mom said.

That almost got me. My fingers jerked, and I took a second to make sure my voice was controlled. "I hope that isn't really true, Mom. I love you and I still want to be a part of this family."

"Don't overreact, Donna," Dad said.

It was too late for that. My mother wiped her tears and told me in a shaky voice, "I want you to know that you've broken my heart."

Way to drive the knife just a little deeper, Mom. I didn't say anything, because what could I say? Nothing was going to matter or make her feel any better.

But Riley's hand gripped me more firmly and his body shifted closer to me like he could protect me from those words.

She got up and left the room when I didn't burst into tears and declare myself a born-again virgin.

Dad wasn't smiling, but he didn't look like he hated me either. "Your mother is just disappointed," he said. "Give her time. And yes, you can get your stuff. You can always come home—I want you to know that. In the meantime, just remember that if you stumble the Lord will always pick you up. But you have to allow Him near you to do that."

I nodded, throat tight. Without meaning to, my fingers went to my cross, and I fingered it, seeking comfort. My father noticed and it seemed to give him reassurance.

"I'll be praying for you, Jessica." He stood up and held his arms open for me.

I sank into his hug, the crispness of his suit jacket sliding over my skin as I buried my face in his shoulder. He smelled like Dad, like cologne and whiskey. He had spiked his iced tea. I wondered if my mom knew how often he did that. "Thanks, Daddy."

Then he stepped back, and he actually held his hand out to Riley to shake it. Riley did, giving my father a nod of acknowledgment. I had to admit, my father was impressing me with his calm control. I guess that was part of what made him such an amazing minister.

"Take care of her," Dad said. "It takes a man to sit here and answer my questions with honesty and respect, and I appreciate that. I also appreciate you not interfering. I don't approve of what Jessica is doing, but I won't hold that against you. Maybe you can be a positive influence on her."

Seriously? How effing misogynistic was that? All the positive feelings toward my dad that I had been having evaporated. How nice that Riley wasn't tainted by association with me.

I didn't trust myself to speak. Turning on my heel, I started toward the door, reaching up to yank my hair down out of the constricting bun.

Riley scrambled to follow me. "Jessica, wait."

"I'm done with this conversation," I told him, ripping my sweater off and letting it fall to the floor in the hallway. What was the point of dressing the part to please? "Did you hear him? I can't do anything to make them happy."

"I'm sorry, babe."

Running up the stairs, I stomped down the hall, trying not to scream, or throw something, or in any way show my parents that I was the out-of-control loser they thought I was. Paxton was coming out of his room and he stopped short, giving me a sneer.

"Fuck you," I told him.

Shoving the door open to my room, I eyed it with displeasure. It was a princess palace and it didn't reflect me at all. It was expensive furniture and mirrored surfaces, in pinks and ivories. Whatever clutter I had left behind over Christmas break had been removed. It was like a perfect guest room for a perfect person who didn't exist.

My boxes from school were neatly stacked in the corner and I went over and tried to lift two at once, pure adrenaline fueling me.

"Are we taking all of these?" Riley asked. His voice was carefully neutral.

"Yes. These six plus the vacuum."

It took two trips, but we got everything shoved into the back of the car. On the second trip, Riley bent down to pick up my sweater.

"Just leave it," I told him brusquely. "I don't want it."

He looked like he going to say something, then thought better of it. He carefully set the sweater down on the console table my mother used to sort mail and display fresh flowers.

Then I walked out the front door with no idea if and when I would be there again. Eighteen years of my life lived there, and all it took was an hour and six boxes to walk away from it.

No one came to stop me. No one came to say good-bye.

I turned to look back, to take in the foundation of my childhood, and I felt sadness, regret, longing.

But I also felt hope. That in leaving, I could find my place.

# CHAPTER SEVENTEEN

"DO YOU WANT TO TALK ABOUT IT?" RILEY ASKED AFTER twenty minutes of silence.

I was stewing, staring out the window as we drove down the highway. "Not really."

"Okay." He was quiet for a minute, then he said, "I don't want you to worry about money or anything. We'll be fine. I don't need to sell a kidney yet."

I hadn't even thought far enough ahead to realize that without my parent's financial support, I was going to have to live off my waitress tips. Yikes. I thought I would be okay, but what did I really know? I'd always had a backup bank in my father. "I'm not your problem, Riley. I'll just pick up more hours at work to help pay for stuff."

"You're not my problem, you're my girlfriend. We're in it together, Jess."

I nodded, throat tight.

"I have to tell you, I'm not even sure I totally get what it is you did to deserve being kicked out. It's not like you filmed a porno."

Now there was an image. "There's still time," I said, because I was exhausted. I just wanted to snuggle on the couch with Riley and watch stupid YouTube videos, and I didn't really want to talk about it anymore.

He got the hint. "I do have porn star gonads, I must say."

I laughed. "Gross. I don't even want to know what constitutes porn star, you know." The word gonads made me squeamish.

"I don't either, to tell you the truth," he admitted. "But let me assure you, my nuts are class A."

"I'm reassured, thanks. Of course, I do find it ironic that my father is worried about my salvation but he thinks you're just awesome." I didn't blame Riley for that, but I did find it frustrating as hell.

"He didn't say that. And he's never heard me swear or seen me kick a wall. I'm sure if he knew the full story he'd be praying for me, too."

I sighed. "It doesn't matter."

"Well, I think it does matter. Plus I owe you an apology. I thought you were exaggerating about your parents, but you weren't."

"Thanks." There was more I wanted to say, but I wasn't sure how to articulate my feelings. "They're not bad parents," I said, because they weren't. They wanted what was best for me, I knew that. They just thought their way was what was best for me.

"No, of course not," he agreed. "Everyone makes mistakes and none of us know what the fuck we're doing. We just take it one day at a time. Hopefully Easton will remember that when he's thirty and in therapy."

SWEET                    237

"Easton is probably going to grow up to be the most normal of all of us."

Riley laughed. "We can only hope."

When we got back and went into the house, Tyler was playing video games with Easton. "How did it go? I didn't think you'd be back so soon."

Riley just shook his head, carrying one of my boxes. He started back toward the bedroom.

"I'm your new permanent roomie," I told Tyler. "I'll try not to hog the bathroom."

"Shit, it didn't go so good, huh?"

"Nope."

"You're moving in?" Easton asked, glancing up from his controller.

"Yes."

He made a face of disgust.

Fabulous.

"I wish it was Rory instead," he said.

Now that hurt. I blinked hard, feeling tears fill my eyes. So I didn't really belong or fit in here either. Rory was the preferred girlfriend.

"Hey! That was really rude," Tyler told him, shoving Easton's knee. "Say you're sorry."

He shrugged like he didn't know why it mattered. "Sorry."

Yeah, that was believable. I set my box down and fast-walked out the front door to the car for another box. Riley came into the living room as I was leaving.

"What did you guys say to her?" he asked them in an accusing tone.

I didn't wait for the answer. I just strode down the driveway, just in time to see a guy stealing my vacuum out of Riley's open car.

"Hey! Drop the fucking vacuum or I will hurt you," I screamed. It was a bit melodramatic for a twenty-dollar Dirt Devil, but I was not in the mood. Besides, I was broke now.

Apparently I looked scary enough that he eyed me and ditched it in the grass. He was about sixteen and skinny, dark circles under his eyes. I took a step toward him and he ran. I chased him, screaming at the top of my lungs the whole time.

Riley and Tyler came tearing out of the house. "What the fuck?" Riley shouted. "Jessica, stop chasing him!"

Considering we were actually just running in circles around the car, it did seem pointless. I came to a stop, breathing hard. "He tried to steal my vacuum."

I saw Riley and Tyler exchange a look, both clearly trying not to laugh.

"David, go home before I beat your ass," Tyler told the guy.

"He lives next door," Riley explained.

"Your bitch is crazy," David said, shaking his head.

"That's right," I told him. "Batshit crazy. So stay out of our yard."

Feeling like I might cry, and not wanting to lose it in front of an audience, I leaned in the car and grabbed another box, ignoring everyone as I carried it into the house with as much dignity as I could manage on a day like I was having.

"That was cool," Jayden told me when I shifted past him in the doorway. "You're a baller."

Awesome. "Thanks."

"I guess I'm not the only one with a temper," I heard Riley say. "The only thing that would have been better is if she had tackled him. I would have paid money to see that."

"You don't have any money!" I yelled over my shoulder.

Riley laughed.

I STAYED UP LATER THAN I SHOULD HAVE, BUT I WAS EDGY, anxious. Riley was already asleep when I came to bed, climbing up the water bed from the bottom so I wouldn't disturb him. I had been staring at the TV for the last two hours and texting with Rory, though I didn't tell her about my parents. I didn't want to talk about it. I'd never been one who dealt with stuff by discussing it endlessly.

Riley stirred. "You okay?" he murmured.

"Yeah." I was pretty sure I was okay, even though I felt agitated. That was normal, I would guess, when your whole world has changed. I had thought about not going to school, about seeing all my friends studying and going to class with their backpacks and me not being a part of that. About working at the restaurant an extra two or three shifts to pay the bills. About the fact that I didn't even know what constituted "the bills."

But mostly I had thought about me, my choices, and what I would do differently. Not from a place of regret or guilt, but an analytical viewpoint. But it was like a squirrel with a nut—I kept turning it all around and around and I couldn't figure out how to crack the code on how to please everyone. If I made myself over to please my parents, I was miserable. If I apologized for being sexually active, then I insulted the choice of women to be in control of their bodies and I insulted myself. Maybe my dad was right—maybe I was trying to be a Christian on my own terms, but wasn't that what being twenty years old was about? Figuring out what I believed, what my opinions were?

I couldn't please everyone, there was no way to do that. But I could please myself.

That was my conclusion, and I knew what pleased me. Having the freedom to make my own mistakes, to learn, to grow, to become a better person. Being here, in this house, with this guy, pleased me. My friendships pleased me. My hoodie made me happy. It was all the simplest of things that mattered, and the future didn't have to be decided tonight.

"Go back to sleep," I said, slipping under the sheet and peeling off my T-shirt.

He rolled over and kissed my bare shoulder. "Mm. Sorry today was so rough."

"Thanks. Thanks for being there."

The air-conditioning unit hummed and I kept one leg outside of the sheet.

"So what *is* your number?" he murmured.

"What?" I frowned in the dark, not sure what he was talking about.

"You know, partners. What is your number?"

I went completely still for a split second. Then I exploded. "Are you freaking kidding me? How can you ask me that?"

I couldn't see his face clearly in the dark room so I sat up and leaned over to the dresser and turned on the lamp.

"Ow, fuck," he said, covering his eyes.

"Get over it. Answer the question—how could you ask me that, after what I went through today?"

"I'm just curious. You can ask me."

I shook my head in disbelief. "I don't want to ask you. I don't give a shit. It has nothing to do with me. Whatever you did before me is your business, not mine."

Going up on his elbow, he said, "Come on. You're not even like a little bit curious?"

"Of course I'm curious. But again, it's none of my business." Why was that so hard to grasp? I didn't want to know. It would be like a slippery slope into comparisons and jealousies. I had no desire to do that to myself. I put my back against the wall, wanting to be sitting up. The anxiety crawled up my neck like a spider.

"I don't mind telling you my number."

"Well, great, but I don't want to hear it! And I'm not telling you regardless. The truth is, you know it's more than one. You know it's more than two. And anything more than that for a girl is getting into questionable territory according to the world we live in. What if it was ten? Twenty? Forty? What would you say?"

"Forty is a lot of guys to be fucking, that's what I would say." He looked appalled.

"See, that's my point. Everyone has this number that they decide is too much, and what if I say a number and it's past your magical line in the sand? Then what? I have to watch the respect drain away from your face?"

"It's not forty, is it?" He looked like he actually might be sick. His face was white and he was swallowing hard.

"No. It's not." Truthfully, I wasn't sure what it was. I didn't stop and finger count. Each one had been taken for what they were and who they were, not a sum total of sexual parts. If I had to quick guess, I would say six or seven. "But it's not two. I can't re-virginize myself, Riley. I don't even want to."

"Is it less than ten?" he asked.

That was it. I got out of bed and pulled my T-shirt back on.

"Where are you going?"

"I'm leaving." I was already tapping a text to Robin asking her to pick me up.

"You can't leave. Where the hell are you going to go?" He jumped out of bed and tried to head me off.

I darted around him and grabbed my purse off the dresser. When he touched my elbow, I shook him off, his hot grip feeling violating. "Leave me alone."

"Jess. Come on. Stay. Please."

In the living room, I whirled around to face him. "You aren't any better than my parents! You are judging me the same way they are, and that really freaking hurts!"

"I just get jealous, I'm sorry, I can't help it." He put his hands onto the top of his head, staring at a spot on the wall behind me.

I wasn't going to be swayed by how amazing he looked in his boxer briefs, that damn demon tattoo moving as he moved his arms, the skull screaming down his side.

Anger and hurt coursed through me and I was breathing hard, my chest heaving. So I did the one thing I knew would hurt him as much as he had just hurt me. I held out my thumb and said, "Bill." Then the index finger. "Tyler." Another. "Adam." I flipped backward through my college years and held up another finger. "Carter." My pinky went out. "Dude whose name I don't remember because I got super drunk at my first party at college." Second hand thumb. "John." Last one. "Matthew. He was my first at church camp. Yes, church camp. We were counselors. There, feel better now?"

"Not really," he said, his jaw working and his nostrils flaring.

"I didn't think so." I was so angry I was fuming. "But now you know."

He clearly felt the same way because without warning he picked up the lamp and threw it across the room. It hit the wall and shattered in an explosion of ceramic and glass.

I shrieked. "Riley!"

Tyler came rushing out of his bedroom. "What the fuck is going on?"

"Ask your brother," I snapped.

"Dude, what the hell?" Tyler asked him, then looked at me. Pulling me back from the broken glass, Tyler asked, "You okay?"

I nodded.

"Get your goddamn hands off her," Riley said, taking a step toward Tyler, hands clenching into fists.

"Whoa." Tyler looked at his brother in shock. "Take it down a notch, Riley."

"I'm going outside," I said, striding through the kitchen and shoving the back door open and plunking myself on the top of the picnic table, my feet on the bench. I checked my phone. Robin had answered.

For real? I can be there in 10.

Thanks.

There was a pack of cigarettes lying on the table and I picked it up and took one out. Cramming it in my mouth, I grabbed the lighter and flicked it on. I sucked hard, and immediately I got a bit lightheaded. Blowing it out, I took a shuddering breath and tried to calm down, the blood vessels in my head feeling like they were constricting in response to tension and nicotine.

The back door opened and Tyler came out. He looked at the cigarette and shook his head. "What are you doing?"

"Nothing." I took another drag. It tasted like total ass, and the cloud rising in front of my face was hazy and stung my eyes, but I was feeling defiant. "What is he doing in there? He didn't wake the boys up, did he?"

"Of course they woke up. Riley said he tripped on the lamp cord and they went back to bed. Now he's cleaning up the mess and swearing up a blue streak. Then if I had to take a guess, he'll go in the basement and lift weights for an hour, then he'll start drinking." Tyler sat down next to me. "What the hell happened?"

"Doesn't matter," I said, staring at the burning end of the cigarette. Amazing how quickly the paper could burn, without me even doing anything to it. "I called Robin to pick me up. She'll be here any second."

I half expected Tyler to try to talk me out of it, to suggest that I go into the house and work things out with Riley, but he didn't.

"That's probably the best thing for tonight. When Riley's temper explodes, it's better to give him space. He is like our father in that way."

"I don't think Riley wants to be compared to your father."

"No, I'm sure he doesn't. Doesn't make it any less true. But the difference is, Riley doesn't mean to hurt anyone. He just says things, and he doesn't always think through how it will be taken, you know what I'm saying?"

So this was Tyler trying to tell me to go easy on his brother. "Just because he doesn't mean to doesn't make it hurt any less," I said, handing Tyler the cigarette. I didn't want it.

He took it from me and put it to his mouth. "True. But I have to tell you, Jess, Riley doesn't let girls get close to him. He's put himself out there for you."

I looked at my feet, still bare from getting into bed with Riley. I needed to redo my pedicure. The paint was chipped. "I know. I've put myself out there, too. And Riley used that against me."

The back door flew open, and Riley stood there, looking enraged. "We need to talk."

"I have nothing to say to you."

"Get in the goddamn house," he said.

Like that was going to make me comply? I bristled. "Screw you."

"Not tonight."

That was so out of line, I grabbed the pack of cigarettes and threw it at him.

He caught it in his left hand.

I should have whipped the glass ashtray at his head instead. It would have been a lot more satisfying to knock him unconscious.

Headlights flooded the driveway and I hopped off the table, grabbing my purse. "I'll talk to you later, Tyler."

Tyler didn't say anything.

I gave Riley a glare. "You, I don't want to talk to at all."

"Don't walk away, Jessica, I'm not kidding."

He started toward me and I ran.

ROBIN AND I CURLED UP ON HER SOFA UNDER A SQUISHY COM-forter and drank chocolate milk, watching *The Notebook*. She was crying. I felt numb.

She was already living in the house that we had rented for the following school year with Kylie and Rory. The previous tenants, graduating seniors, were still living there, but Robin had the one empty bedroom that had belonged to an overachiever who already had secured a job in finance and moved into a trendy apartment.

My parents were supposed to pay for my portion of the rent once the fall semester started, but I had no idea if I was going to be able to manage that on my own now. I had figured I would let

my friends rent my spot to someone else and I would stay with
Riley, but how could I do that now?

I wanted to cry, but it was like the tears were trapped inside me,
along with a scream of frustration. It was like my heart had actually been removed from my body and left back at Riley's, beating
on the kitchen table. I was feeling weird and morbid and not like
me at all. Like I was so angry that it was smothering all my other
emotions.

Robin hooked her arm through mine and leaned on my shoulder. "Do you ever wonder if you have any idea what you're doing?"
she asked, her voice melancholy.

"Um, yes, daily." That was the problem. I was sure I had convictions, but I couldn't figure out who I was supposed to be. Who
I wanted to be. Who I could be.

Riley was blowing up my phone with "I'm sorry" and asking
to see me. I wasn't answering. I didn't know what to say. I didn't
know how to explain that what he had done had seemed like a
huge betrayal. That I had spent my life seeking approval, and never
getting it, and I needed it without question from him. I needed to
trust that he not only loved me and was attracted to me, he *liked* me.

"I did something awful," Robin said in a small voice, her eyes
red and weepy, hair falling out of her sloppy bun.

Looking at her curiously, I said, "What?"

She shook her head. "It doesn't matter. But I'm wondering if I
even know myself at all."

"You do," I reassured her. "But we all fuck up sometimes. It's
okay. You just have to forgive yourself."

"We need to forgive other people, too," she said, giving me a
long look. "Stop being so angry all the time."

That was a direct hit at me. I knew there was truth to it.

Anger was an easy emotion to control. It was a powerful one. It didn't allow you to be passive or dominated or hurt. You couldn't be vulnerable if you were lashing out at someone.

Yet it also kept me from ever reaching that place of trust I was looking for, the place I was demanding Riley arrive at, without me.

But if I opened up that box I tightly kept my emotions in, who knew what might come spewing out?

# CHAPTER EIGHTEEN

IN THE MIDDLE OF MY SUNDAY NIGHT SHIFT AT WORK, MY HAIR slipping from its bun, I rushed to the table that had just been seated. "Hi, my name is Jess—"

I cut off when I saw that it was Riley sitting at the table by himself, giving me a sheepish smile.

"Hey," he said.

"What are you doing here?" I asked uneasily, glancing around the restaurant. No one was looking at us.

"Eating?" He shrugged. "You won't answer my texts or my calls. I needed to talk to you."

I should have known that he wouldn't accept my silence. Truthfully, I knew I couldn't keep ignoring him, but I needed more than a few hours to get my head on straight. The plan had been to talk to him on Monday, after he got off work. "This isn't the place."

"What was I supposed to do? Look, I'm really, really sorry about last night. I talk before I think and shit comes out that shouldn't. I was half asleep, it just slipped out."

He wasn't getting it. That wasn't really the problem. "Except that you obviously were really bothered by the idea of how many guys I've been with, so I needed to hear that, to know that. You obviously don't respect me."

"No, it's not that." His hand came out, like he was going to take mine, but he stopped himself. "It's pure jealousy, which is totally different from judgment. I know being jealous is wrong, I know that, and I want to get ahold of it, but the thing is, Jess, I've never felt the way about a girl the way I feel about you. I love you."

Oh, God. I took a deep breath, my heart squeezing. It was so hard to think when he was looking at me like that, his brown eyes so big and sincere and pleading.

"I want to be *important* to you. Special." He shook his head and gave a soft laugh. "Do you know how stupid I feel saying that? I think my balls just dropped to the floor."

My fingertips were shaking, and I wanted desperately to kiss him, to lean forward and feel his mouth on mine. He loved me, and I believed him. "It takes a real man to be honest. And you are important to me. The most special guy I've ever met. *The* guy. But last night I needed you to be there for me, and you put that jealousy on me."

"I know, and I'm so sorry. Please come home tonight. Please. I'll pick you up after work."

"It's not my home," I said, though I wasn't even sure why I said that. It wasn't the time or the place to get into it.

"Yes, it is. And I owe you a true apology in it."

"Jessica!" One of the other servers went rushing past me, giving me an exasperated look, her tray filled with drinks. "Table thirty-seven."

Shit. "Give me five." I rushed off to the bar to put in orders from the table I had greeted before Riley came in, and I ordered a beer for him.

"Who is the hottie you were talking to?" Mandy the bartender asked, with a speculative look over at Riley.

"That's my boyfriend," I told her, because I already knew I was going to go home with Riley and I was going to listen to what he had to say. I was going to give him the ear that I never got with my family, the right to explain himself without having already made my decision.

"Oh, wow, lucky you."

She had a point, because how many other guys did I know who would have come to a restaurant by himself to beg me for forgiveness? None. Tyler was right—Riley had put himself out there for me.

So I walked carefully in the shoes I had borrowed from Robin, which were a half size too small, since I'd run out without clothes, and went back to Riley's table. "Okay, you can pick me up tonight. I'll come home with you."

"Really?" He looked so ridiculously pleased that my heart swelled. "Cool. Awesome." He picked up the bottle of beer a server over twenty-one had brought him. "Thanks for the beer, by the way."

"Well, I had to order you something or people were going to think it was really weird that you were sitting here by yourself not eating or drinking anything."

"Yeah, but you knew the right brand. That was sweet."

Or observant. But I smiled, because he was just so gorgeous, and he understood me. He saw in me something more than anyone else did and that was an amazing feeling. "Sweet, that's me. Jessica Sweet. Now you have to order some food or I'm going to get fired."

He grinned. "Can I have some hot wings? And mozzarella sticks? And maybe some potato skins. Suddenly I'm hungry."

"Oh my God. I hate you," I told him with an exasperated laugh. "Fine. But when you die of a heart attack, I'm going to say I told you so."

"As long as you do a shot of whiskey over my casket, it's all good."

"Don't die," I said, suddenly serious. "Don't leave me."

His expression changed, too, and he shook his head solemnly. "I won't leave you. Trust me, that is the last thing in the world I want."

AFTER GETTING YELLED AT BY MY BOSS AT THE END OF MY shift, I had to promise that my boyfriend would never show up at the restaurant again. Then I went into the parking lot, Riley's car idling as he waited for me.

"I got bitched out," I told him as a greeting. "Apparently other customers don't think they should have to wait for their dinner while you and I work out our personal shit."

"Selfish bastards," he said, before leaning over and giving me a soft kiss. "Sorry. I really am. For everything."

"I know." I did.

"I want to show you something before we go home," he said. "Do you mind?"

Suspicious, I eyed him. "Is it perverted?"

"No. It's fucking romantic, that's what it is."

I pressed my lips together, wanting to laugh. "Well, in that case, absolutely."

He pulled out and started to drive out of Hyde Park, a neighborhood of families where the chain restaurant was, and up the winding streets of Mt. Adams, an artsy area of young professionals. My friends and I never went there because it was for the martini-and-Ann-Taylor crowd, tapas bars and top-shelf liquor. I started to worry that Riley was trying to impress me with a nice dinner out or something, though I couldn't imagine where we could eat at eleven at night. I was in no way dressed for public. I wasn't even dressed to clean the house. I had on skinny jeans, a white T-shirt with a marinara stain on it, and the Converse that were pinching my feet.

"Where are we going?"

"Don't sound so scared." Riley glanced over at me. "We're going somewhere private. I never told you about my grandmother, did I?" he asked, in a total change of subject.

"No."

"My grandmother was this tiny Irish woman who was the toughest woman I ever met. She worked two jobs and she buried two alcoholic husbands." He shot me a rueful glance. "I guess addiction runs in the family. But she was fair and loving and even though she died when I was seven, I think she taught me more about being a decent person in that short time than my mom did in my whole life."

"That's awesome. It's good you had her in your life."

"She was Catholic, even though I didn't know what that meant exactly when I was a kid. I just thought it meant you had to wave your hand around your face when something bad happened. It also meant you got to drink wine at church. But anyway, she lived in the neighborhood we live in now, but before every Easter, on Good Friday, she would take me to the church here, in Mt. Adams, for what they call Praying the Steps. People climb the ninety-some steps to the church starting at midnight, praying the rosary or the stations of the cross. I didn't know what any of that meant, and frankly, I still don't." Riley pulled the car over and pointed. "Those are the stairs. See how steep they are? Picture being five years old and seeing thousands of people winding up those steps, murmuring. It was how I first understood what it means to believe in something. Because that was faith."

I nodded, my throat tight. "I know exactly what you mean. It must have been beautiful."

"It was." He turned off the car and studied me, his hand brushing my cheek. "I want you to know that what I believe in is us. You and me. Will you walk up the stairs with me? The view up there is amazing. The whole city."

"Yes," I said, understanding that he was asking more of me than that. He was asking if I was in, with him. "I would love to." My throat was tight, my heart pounding. Riley had taken a risk, coming to work, bringing me here. He had believed deeply enough in his feelings to expose them to me, and I was overwhelmed by how amazing that was. I wanted to give him that back, to try to figure out how to crack open my heart and display it for him.

I wasn't sure I knew how, but I was going to try.

He came over and held his hand out for me. I took it, and we strolled up the stairs, the night air blissfully lacking in humidity, a warm breeze rising off the river. My thighs started to burn by the twentieth or so step, but I didn't care.

"This is such a cool view," I said, hair blowing across my face. The air smelled like summer, like trees and a faint tinge of something sweet that I couldn't identify.

"It's even better at the top."

It was. When we finally reached the last step, me panting a

little from the effort, the lights of the city were spread out in front of us, reflecting off the river. "Wow, it's amazing."

"Yeah, it is, isn't it?" Riley took me onto the platform in front of the church and we leaned against the railings. "When I'm up here, it's a whole different perspective on the world. Down there." He pointed in the direction of his neighborhood. "It's not a pretty place on the ground. Life gets a little ugly in the details, but up here, taken as a whole, you realize the world can be pretty awesome. When I need to remember that, I come here and climb these steps."

"I can see that," I said, my fingers gripping the railing, eyes following the curve of the river, the water shimmering and softly lapping against the shore.

"I'm not a deep guy," he told me. "I have my GED and I'd rather talk about music than politics, and I have a temper that I try to control, but sometimes it gets the best of me. I'm not really a good catch for a girl like you, I know that. But . . ."

"No, don't say that." I put my hand over his mouth to stop those words, knowing they weren't true, but Riley caught my hand in his and pulled it down.

His brow furrowed with the serious determination of his words. "I may not have a college degree or a six-figure income, but I will love and respect and cherish you with everything inside me, and when I fuck up, I will apologize. So what I'm saying is that I was wrong, and I have no right to be jealous. What happened before me is none of my business. I acknowledge that, I understand that."

"Thank you. And for a guy who claims to not be very deep, you have an amazing way with words." Something was happening in me. With each word he spoke, he removed a brick from the wall I'd built over my heart. I was breathing hard, sucking air in and out of my lungs almost like I was having a panic attack, but it wasn't that.

I realized that I knew exactly what it was. I was in love. I had gone and fallen completely in love with Riley and the swelling inside me, the tidal wave of emotion that was overwhelming me, was the single most profound experience of my life. It felt . . . epic.

"Riley . . ." I took his face in my hands and I stared up at him, wanting to memorize this moment, to take in every tiny detail of his face, his mouth, his eyes. "I love you."

I had never told anyone that. Sure, I said, "Love you!" to my besties and on very rare occasions to my parents. But never to a guy. Not once. It felt like I just delivered myself into his care with those words. Like I had given him everything of value that I owned.

"Jessica," he breathed, taking my mouth in a soft kiss. "I love you, too. Will you marry me?"

I'm not sure who was more shocked—me or him. I gasped and he started. Riley Mann wanted to marry me. He wanted to be with me forever. He thought I was worthy of being his. It made me feel like everything in me was rising and swelling with pure joy.

"I didn't actually know I was going to say that," he said, with a little laugh.

I started laughing, too, my heart beating fast in a way that couldn't be healthy. I was giddy, and I asked, "Are you taking it back?" It didn't matter to me if he did. I was just glad that he'd said it. He loved me, that was totally obvious.

"No, absolutely not! We should get married. It's the best idea I've ever had, besides letting you stay in the house when the boys were gone."

"That wasn't your idea."

"Shh." He kissed the corners of my mouth. "Don't ruin the romance."

"Me? Please!"

Riley grinned at me. "Come here, sit down." He dropped to the ground, dangling his feet over the edge, patting the spot next to him. "It's a perfect night."

"It is a perfect night." I sank down beside him, awed by what was happening between us. "The best." This was the night that was going to change my life. Because I already knew. "Riley, I will marry you."

For someone who had never thought much about marriage and who had never been in love, the moment it was there in front of me, it was so obvious, there was no denying what had to happen.

The smile fell off his face. "Are you serious?"

"Yes."

His response was to kiss me deeply, his tongue sliding across mine, his hand burying in the back of my hair. When he finally pulled back we were both breathing hard and my fingers were curled in the front of his T-shirt.

"Luckiest. Guy. Ever," he said, then cocked his finger. "Write that down."

I laughed. "You're crazy."

"Crazy in love. And I'm going to permanently ditch the princess nickname. It's not you. A princess wouldn't do the Warrior Dash or tear up carpet or give up everything in that big house your parents own on principle. I'm sorry I ever misjudged you."

He was right. I wasn't a princess. I never had been. "Thank you."

He cleared his throat. "Hey, I have a confession to make."

Needing to lighten the intensity of the moment, I couldn't resist teasing him. "You're really a woman?"

He laughed. "Kiss my ass, Jess. No, the thing is my number is actually slightly higher than yours."

His number. He meant sex partners. I smacked him. "Are you kidding me? All that and your number is higher? I thought you'd been with like two girls and were madly in love with both."

"Well. I didn't mean to give *that* impression. I mean, that would be true for the last five years, you know, once I settled down a little." I swear his ears were actually turning pink. "But I got an early start."

"How early?"

"Thirteen."

Holy crap. I tried not to show any sort of reaction.

"And you know, that number racks up quicker than you'd think."

I raised my eyebrows at him. "You are such a complete ass."

"I accept that description in this particular instance. But for the record, the only girl I've been madly in love with is you." He smiled at me. "Cross my heart." And he did it. Just crossed his heart with those fingers that I knew so well, that had moved over my body with such tenderness and had held my hand when I needed strength.

"You're the only guy I've been in love with, madly or otherwise." I leaned against him. "I wish that I hadn't done anything with Tyler," I whispered. "I'm sorry for that. I am. I wish I could undo it."

He was silent for a second and I waited anxiously for his response. "I know," he said finally. "You couldn't know the future. It's not what I wanted either, but I trust him with my life, and you with my heart, so it's all good."

That meant more to me than just about anything. "I won't hurt you," I promised. "That's the last thing I want." I looked out at the river. "We should celebrate, you know? We're getting married." I felt insanely happy just thinking about it.

"I wish I had been more prepared. I could have really done something romantic here."

"What, like serenade me with Justin Bieber's 'Boyfriend'?"

"*Hell*, no."

"Take me to the bow of a cruise ship and tell me I'm flying, like in *Titanic*?"

"Uh, no."

"Salsa dance with me to perfectly choreographed moves we magically know while a band suddenly appears behind us?"

"Absolutely not."

"What could be any more romantic than those things?" I asked.

"I was thinking something simpler—like it would have been nice if I'd had a ring and some hooch."

I laughed. "Hooch? Because the thought of marrying me makes you want to drink?"

"No, to toast with."

"I think you're supposed to do that with champagne."

He made a raspberry sound with his lips. "That stuff tastes like shit. It's like asking for diabetes it's so sweet, and besides, you pay fourteen bucks for a bottle and you only get four glasses out of it. A twenty-dollar bottle of whiskey will get you forty shots."

"Classy," I remarked, leaning on his shoulder in the dark, the lights of the city spread out like a blanket. I was feeling so in love, the night so delicious and perfect, it might as well have been Paris down there. It was just as romantic, in my eyes.

"The classiest thing about me is you," he said.

That was a sweet thing to say, but I thought about it and wondered. "I don't know how classy I really am. I think that was part of the 'girl they wanted me to be.' I think the real me is more the girl with bare feet in Zeke's bar or chasing the vacuum thief around the yard. Jayden said I was a baller and I like to think there's truth to that."

"Damn straight. I wouldn't want to mess with you, that's for sure. So you're a classy baller. You should form a bowling team with that name."

I laughed so hard I started snorting, which made him laugh.

"I don't know how to bowl," I said, leaning backward.

"So learn. We got nothing but time."

We did. The whole future, stretched out before us, just like downtown below.

## CHAPTER NINETEEN

EASTON STARED AT ME LIKE I WAS THE BIGGEST IDIOT HE'D
ever encountered in his life. "That's not going to work."

"Sure it will," I said cheerfully, even though I had no idea if I
was right or not.

My thought was twofold. One, I was going to attempt a different tactic to get Easton to like me, because let's face it, I was in this
house for good and I didn't want him glaring at me at random
intervals. My angle couldn't be Rory's—I wasn't baking any pies,
and I couldn't be counted on to give stellar advice or keep from
swearing. But I could show him fun in a positive way, one that
didn't involve dirty magazines or throwing snack foods at people's
butts. Two, it was only mid-June and my skin was breaking out
from being in a constant pool of sweat. Easton and Jayden were
ripe, seemingly oblivious to the awesome merits of deodorant, so
we all needed to cool down.

With all of our nerves stretched taut because of Riley being at
the courthouse for the final custody hearing on Easton, I had spent

twenty-five bucks on an inflatable Slip 'N Slide. Only when we got back to the house, I realized the ancient hose in the garage was cracked in about six spots. Not willing to be defeated, I went and found the roll of duct tape and was wrapping it around the hose to plug the leaks.

It was Friday, five days after Riley had proposed to me on the top of the church steps, and I was happier than I'd ever been. I loved being with him, and I felt like I was stepping up and tackling challenges instead of passively moving through my life. It may seem basic to some people, but taking on a busted hose was a personal triumph for me.

"Where does the water come from?" Jayden asked, chewing his fingernail as he watched me.

"The faucet." I was sweating, hair flopping in my eyes. I kept checking my phone to see if Riley had called, even though it was in my pocket and I would feel it vibrate. I wasn't sure what would happen if the judge ruled against Riley, but it wouldn't be good.

Tyler was working a drywall job he had picked up, and I had wanted to go with Riley, but he had wanted me to stay with Easton, who was well aware of what was happening. I was supposed to be a distraction, and in that regard, I supposed I was being successful. I had driven them to Walmart in Tyler's car and it had taken us almost an hour of debating, well, me debating, which slide to buy. I was a little concerned about the whole inflatable bumper thing but they all seemed to have that now. I guess the head injuries from crashing into the garage were a thing of the past.

"Do we have a faucet?" Jayden asked, looking around.

Huh. "That's a good question." I had changed into my bikini top on pure optimism and heat exhaustion but I regretted not snagging a hair tie in mine and Riley's room.

"There it is," Easton said, pointing to the wall next to the back door.

Thank God. That would have been the ultimate fail.

"Does it work?" I asked.

Jayden twisted it and water sprayed out all over him. "It works!"

"Excellent." I eyed the hose and the Slip 'N Slide, which I had yet to inflate. "What end goes where?"

"Read the directions," Easton said.

"Nobody reads the directions," Jayden said with a scoff.

Yeah, I had a hard time picturing Tyler or Riley flipping through instruction manuals. The only thing they flipped through were the channels on the TV. I didn't think it was that offensive of a statement, but Easton shoved his brother.

"Hey!" Jayden said, shoving him back.

Realizing that Easton was feeling anxious, I didn't think it was the time for Jayden to go head-to-head with him, so I stepped between them. "Jayden, come here and start blowing this up, please." I was fairly certain that my breasts would distract Jayden from Easton and I was right.

He appeared dazzled and didn't even bother to hide his gawking. "Yeah, okay," he said to my chest.

A few minutes later, I left the duct tape roll dangling from the hose, sure I'd gotten all the cracks, and was heading to the faucet with one end to screw it in, Jayden swearing he was going to pass out after blowing up approximately five percent of the slide walls. Easton was throwing acorns at the garage.

Riley came around the corner and came to a stop when he saw us. He was wearing his least abused jeans and a plaid button-down shirt that looked like he'd borrowed from someone it was so foreign to his usual wardrobe. "What are you guys doing?"

"It's a Slip 'N Slide," Jayden told him.

"Jessica took us to Walmart and got it," Easton said. "She bought us deodorant, too."

I gave a sheepish shoulder shrug, trying to gauge his mood. He didn't look upset, but he didn't look ecstatic either. "I thought it would be fun." The Slip 'N Slide, not the deodorant.

"Wow, awesome," he started to say.

Then suddenly, without warning, his face crumpled. He put his hands on his thighs and bent forward, like he was having trouble breathing or he was about to be sick.

"Riley," I whispered, my heart sinking. Oh, God, no. It couldn't be. I started toward him, dropping the hose. "Are you okay?"

He shook his head and when he glanced up at us, I could see the tears in his eyes.

"What's the matter?" Jayden yelled in his overly loud voice, sounding terrified. I don't imagine he'd ever seen his brother cry, except maybe at their mother's funeral.

But Easton knew what it was. He bent over and picked up the Slip 'N Slide and threw it at the garage yelling, "No! No, they can't fucking make me go! I won't! I'll run away, I'll go to Canada! I'm not leaving!"

He kicked the hose, the dirt, the picnic table, and it snapped Riley out of his paralysis.

Riley start yelling back, "Hey, hey, calm down!" He went over to his brother and grabbed him by both arms.

Easton punched and kicked at him. I bit my lip, no clue what to do. I reached out for Jayden's hand, needing to get and give comfort.

Riley pinned him against his own chest, getting his leg between Easton's to prevent him from kicking, yanking his hands down to his sides. "Hey! It's okay, stop! No one is taking you away from me. Not now. Not ever. The judge gave me full custody of you."

The breath I didn't realize I'd been holding escaped my mouth with an audible whoosh. I squeezed Jayden, feeling relief so huge I felt woozy.

"What?" Easton stopped struggling, and Riley loosened his grip on him. He turned around and looked up at his brother. "What do you mean?"

"I mean, I have custody of you. Legally, I'm your guardian and you're not going anywhere." He grinned at Easton and rubbed the top of his head. "What do you think of that?"

Easton had tears on his face and he wiped them, sniffling. His voice was shaky. "Oh. Okay. Cool."

Then Jayden said, "Oh my God, why did you look like that? You scared the shit out of us!"

My thoughts exactly.

"Sorry. I swallowed my gum and I was choking."

That was the biggest lie I'd ever heard. He didn't even chew gum. But he obviously didn't want them to know he'd gotten emotional.

"Well, that's awesome news!" I said. "We should go out to eat when Tyler gets home and celebrate."

"That's a great idea, Jess," he said, shooting me a grateful look. "So what do we have going on here?" He bent over and inspected the hose. "Huh."

"It's going to work," Easton told him, yanking it out of Riley's hand and dragging it toward the faucet. His confidence touched me.

"I'm sure it will," Riley said, helping him screw it onto the faucet. He nudged his brother and gave him a grin. "Dude, Canada?

What the hell was that? But I have to admit, it was kind of awesome."

Easton shrugged. "I don't know. It sounds far away. And I figured if I got there, you would come and get me, no matter what the stupid judge says."

That made my throat close up.

Riley held his fist out for him, and they did a bump. "You bet your ass I would. You're my brother. We stick together. No matter what."

It was a sentiment that made me love him even more than I already did, and I hadn't thought that was possible.

Then he finished blowing up the slide while I screwed the other end of the hose into the plastic liner.

"Turn it on," Riley told Jayden.

The water shot up, only I didn't realize there was a sprinkler feature at the end, right where Easton and I were standing. It got us both and I jerked with a shriek. "That's cold!"

Jayden and Riley thought it was downright hilarious. "Isn't that the point?" Riley asked.

I stuck my tongue out at him.

While Easton and Jayden stripped off their shirts and started their inaugural slides, yelling the whole time, Riley and I sat down on the picnic table. He lit a cigarette and I didn't complain, knowing he probably needed something to calm him down in the aftermath of the hearing.

"So what was that about?" I murmured, reaching for his free hand. "You seriously scared the piss out of me."

He shrugged. "I don't know. I was so relieved, so excited to get home and tell you all, and then I came around the corner and I saw this . . . I saw this perfect little fucked-up world we have going on here." He took a drag. "I mean, what could be better than the girl

I love hanging with the brothers I'd do anything for? I felt so damn lucky that it just overwhelmed me. This could have gone so much different."

"I understand." I did. "And I bet that somewhere up there in heaven, where there's no heroin, your mom is watching and she's proud of you and happy."

He pursed his lips and rested his chin in his palm, smoke drifting over his face, his eyes dark and serious and luminous. "Yeah. You're right. And thanks for understanding that I don't wish her dead. I never have."

"I know."

"I hit her once," he said quietly. "She was waling on me, using an unopened beer to just clock me in the head over and over, and I was trying to push her off, and I nailed her right in the face without meaning to. I feel so guilty for that."

And that was why I loved him. One accidental contact on a woman who had abused him for years, and he felt guilt. "She forgives you, just like you forgive her. Her life was a painful struggle but look at what she left behind . . . you and the boys are a beautiful legacy."

He smiled. "And you're beautiful." Leaning forward, he gave me a quick kiss. "Do you know that I need you? I don't just want you, I *need* you."

My heart squeezed. "I feel the same way," I murmured. "I feel like with you, I finally know who I am."

For a second, we just stared at each other, the words settling in, the future mapping out.

He gently kissed me again, then gave me a grin. "Why don't you go and jump on that slide? I really wouldn't mind seeing you in a wet bikini."

"Perv." Not that I minded in the slightest. We were inching ever closer to total completion of our relationship (read: sex) and all this extended exploration and anticipation had given us an intimacy that I hadn't even known I was capable of. If he wanted me soaking wet, well, I could totally manage that.

WHEN TYLER GOT HOME, HE FIST-BUMPED ALL HIS BROTHERS with a big grin, having gotten the text from Riley. "Hell, yeah," was his opinion. He rubbed Easton's head. "I'm going to get you the next Harry Potter book with my next paycheck."

I was lying on the picnic table getting some sun and I rolled onto my side. Riley was sitting on the bench behind me, his hand lazily stroking my thigh below my shorts.

"Cool!" Easton was a little high on life, running around the yard, soaking wet and clearly relieved. "Riley says we're going out for burgers and milkshakes!"

"I know. You guys go and change and by the time you're ready Rory should be here."

"Rory's coming?" Easton started doing some sort of jump and spin thing.

"Yep. She figured today is an important day, man, she wants to be here for dinner."

"Excellent," I said, genuinely pleased. I missed her and I had a lot to catch her up on. "I won't be the only chick for a change. Having all these sexy guys around me is starting to spoil me."

Riley made a rude sound. "If that's a hint, sell it somewhere else, because I ain't buying."

"I am," Jayden said.

That made me laugh so hard I'm sure my breasts gave him enough jiggle to fuel more than one fantasy.

After an awesome and rowdy dinner at the burger joint we came back to the house, laughing and talking. I hooked my arm through Rory's as the guys dropped down in the living room on various surfaces. "Come on, I want to talk to you privately."

"Where are you going?" Riley asked.

"Our room. Rory and I want to do girl things." I meant paint our nails and gossip.

But he raised his eyebrows and said, "If you two are going to make out, can I watch?"

"Riley!"

"Dude," Tyler said to his brother. "Seriously?"

Rory was blushing. I threw a couch pillow at Riley.

"What?" Riley asked Tyler. "I mean, come on, if they were going to make out, wouldn't you want to watch? Seriously, be honest."

Tyler grinned. "Yeah, I can't lie. But I meant, you know, maybe you should watch what you joke about it in front of certain people." He jerked his head toward Easton.

"Oh, yeah. Sure." Riley made a face. "Oops."

"Jesus Christ," Tyler said.

"I'm working on it!" Riley protested.

"We're going away," I said firmly. "Come on." I pulled Rory. "You have to see our room."

When I opened the door, feeling triumph, Rory started laughing. "Oh my God, Jess, this is awesome! I mean, I can't believe what you did with the whole house, but this is classic. I can't believe Riley, of all people, sleeps here."

I jumped on the bed. "Sit down. It's a freaking water bed, can you stand it?"

We climbed up by the headboard and leaned on it, our knees up. I had unpacked my boxes from our former dorm room and I had discarded the weird horse blanket dirty thing that had formerly resided on the water bed. It had been replaced by my purple floral comforter with hot-pink fuzzy pillows. The pattern was actually called garden floral, and it was like juicy daisies on acid. There was an orange throw at the bottom with dangling pom-poms that I had learned served as serious entertainment for the cat at three in the morning. Over the bed I had hung my giant white J (okay, I made Riley hang it) next to which Riley had taken a Sharpie and drawn a huge R, right on the wall. So we were JR.

On the nightstand I had replaced the brass lamp with a purple blown glass one, and on the dresser next to the picture of his mother, I had set a ceramic hand, to hold my jewelry. The first day after I put it there, I kept finding it in weird places, like sticking out from under the couch cushions, and in the fridge. But once his amusement with using it to scare his brothers wore off, Riley started cramming his wallet between the thumb and index fingers and left it in place.

"I miss you," I told her. "I'm glad you're here for the weekend."

"I miss you, too. It's cool to see my dad and everything, but it's just that I feel like my life is here now, not there, you know?"

I nodded. Rory was wearing a cute and very short dress, the feminine and floral print one only she could pull off. I would look like a giantess trying to squeeze into a toddler's dress if I wore that. "I get it, trust me. I mean, I am upset about my parents, but at the same time, as long as they're still willing to talk to me, and my dad is, what difference does it make if they cut me off?" I had thought about it a lot, and there were worse things than being forced to grow up a little. "My mom will miss me eventually, but right now maybe we don't belong in each other's worlds."

"You seem really happy, Jess."

"I am. Riley asked me to marry him."

"What?" She turned to me. "Holy shit, what did you say?"

"Yes." I gave her a confident smile, enjoying saying that out loud. "I don't know when, but I just know I will, at some point. I figure there's a reason I never fell in love before." I was waiting for him. "So do you think you'll marry Tyler?"

"I would like to, eventually, but Tyler has this fear that I'll become a doctor and ditch him. He needs to see that I'm going to stick around."

"The Mann brothers have a lot of pride," I said. "It's got them through some nasty shit. But it also makes them loyal."

"Totally. So we're like sisters-in-law in a way." She tossed back her auburn hair and gave me a grin. "I feel like such a girl saying this, but I love that we're besties and dating brothers."

Laughing, I said, "I know. It totally rocks." It was petty to admit it, but when she and Kylie had been going on and on about how much they loved their boyfriends, I had felt left out of their friendship. Like I couldn't share in their giddy secret. But now I got it.

"I can't believe you did a Warrior Dash. I could never do that."

"Tyler would go in front of you, clearing your path of everything. He likes that he's the tough guy to your girly girl."

"That's true. Maybe that's why our educational imbalance works out, because he likes to take care of me."

"Riley likes me to tell people off. I think it turns him on." I laughed.

"Then I guess despite the sheer number of human beings on the planet, we both found our perfect mate."

"I love it when you sound like a scientist."

"That isn't science. Though arguably, we were following evolution and both sought out a partner we perceived was a strong candidate, who could protect us."

Evolution had nothing to do with the gushy-gush I felt when I looked at Riley. "Whatever. Let's paint our toenails."

"Yeah, I don't believe it either," she said with a laugh.

"Hey, I was thinking of getting a tattoo. What should I get?"

"A portrait of Riley's penis," she deadpanned.

Seriously, sometimes Rory killed me. "I haven't even seen it," I told her.

Her jaw dropped. "Are you serious?"

"I mean, I've touched it, but I haven't seen it, seen it, and it hasn't been really all that close to my body. Yet."

"Wow," was her opinion. I knew what she was thinking, but she didn't say anything, and I loved her for it.

"Pink or purple?" I asked her, pulling open the drawer to the nightstand. I held up the polish bottles.

"Purple. You must match your purplicious bedroom."

"One night when Riley is sleeping I'm going to paint his nails."

# CHAPTER TWENTY

I THOUGHT ABOUT RILEY WAKING UP WITH HOT-PINK FINGER-nails as I curled up next to him in bed that night and I couldn't prevent a giggle.

"What?" he asked. "Are you plotting something with Rory? You two looked damn pleased with yourselves."

"We were just catching up. It's good to see her and today is an awesome day. I just feel happy for you, for Easton." That was definitely true.

"I'm pretty damn happy, too. Even if I'm living in a teenage girl's dream bedroom."

I laughed, sliding my leg over his. I liked the scratchy feeling of his leg hairs over my smooth skin. "It's not that bad."

"Oh, yes, it is. But I don't give a shit. I'd sleep in an igloo with you."

For some reason, my laughter evaporated. I told him sincerely, tilting his heads toward me, "Riley, I love you. You do know that, don't you?"

"I do." He kissed me softly, then studied me. "I love you, too."

The soft glow of our new night-light gave a warm tone to his skin. Riley had decided we needed a night-light because he wanted to see me in our bed but didn't want to keep the hall light on because of his brothers. I liked it like this because there was nothing anonymous about what we did, what we shared. It wasn't bodies moving in the dark, it was eyes locked together.

So when he slid his hands down my back and over my ass, the soft touch already raising goose bumps on my flesh, I fought the temptation to close my eyes, wanting that connection. He rolled me gently onto my back and brushed his lips over my collarbone, burrowing into the neckline of my tank top, tongue flickering over the swell of my breast. Our breath mingled, my sighs unguarded, every reaction natural and intimate.

When he kissed me again and again, my lips swollen and damp, my body tightening everywhere, fingers tracing the muscles in my back, I could feel his heart beating in his chest, pressed against me, an anxious staccato that matched mine. Riley sat back and lifted off my shirt, tossing it on the floor. The way he looked down at me, as if I were the most beautiful woman he'd ever seen, had my lips parting on a sigh, nipples tight. He bent over and took one into his mouth and I arched up with a cry. He licked and tugged until I dug my nails into his hot skin, heels moving restlessly on our bed.

My body was moist, aching, when he flicked his tongue lower and lower, carefully peeling down my sport shorts and panties, studying me as he exposed inch by inch. Then he took off his own boxer briefs and I sucked in a breath. He rested his hands on either side of me and asked a very poignant, "Can we?"

I nodded. "Yes."

But he didn't press inside me. Instead, he covered himself with a condom from his nightstand, then rolled onto his back and pulled me over him. "I just want to feel you for a minute," he murmured.

We kissed and rocked together, our bodies pressed in all the most intimate ways but one. He entwined our fingers together so we were clasping hands above our heads, tongues tangling, my legs open on either side of his, moist inner thighs pressed against the thickness of him.

It was enough stimulation, hips rocking my clitoris onto him, breasts brushing, his mouth taking mine, that I shuddered in a slow and emotional orgasm. "Oh!" I said. "Riley . . ."

"Baby," he breathed, gripping my ass and rolling us both over so that he was astride me.

Then with his eyes fixed on mine, my body open entirely to him, he pushed inside. We both groaned and I swallowed hard, the sensation overwhelming as he rested there, throbbing. It was like . . . everything. Like there was just him and I and this moment.

"Jessica," he breathed. "God, I love you."

Then he started to move and something inside me shattered. I started to cry, tears rushing down my cheeks as I clasped his hands, waves of ecstasy lapping over me.

"What's wrong?" he asked, nuzzling my cheek with his. "What's wrong, am I hurting you?"

"No, God, no." I tried to explain. "I just . . . it just . . . it's so . . ." I didn't have the words for it.

But he understood. "I know, babe, I know." He moved faster, his grip on my hand tightening, his jaw tense. "Oh, God, you feel perfect. Perfect."

Our bodies moved together, our hands clasped, and I didn't know where he began and where I ended.

When he came, I came with him.

\* \* \*

SITTING ON THE TOP OF THE PICNIC TABLE AFTERWARD, SO
Riley could have a cigarette, a cliché that made me smile in secret
amusement, I put my bare feet on the bench and looked up at the
dark sky.

Everything had changed. But then, no, it hadn't. It was just
fuller, more.

His arm came around my back.

"There are no stars," he murmured. "Light pollution."

"Make a wish anyway."

"There's nothing to wish for. I already have everything I want."

God. The tears rolled down my cheeks, two damp rivers, as I
sniffled.

"I've never seen you cry," he said, puzzled. "Not even at your
parents' house. And now you cry twice in twenty minutes."

"It's because I finally let you in." I wasn't talking about sex.
And he knew it.

"I do have a wish," he said softly. "That you'll look at me like
that every night for forever. It's the sweetest expression I've ever
seen. Almost as sweet as you."

"Believe me, I will." There was nothing I wanted more.

"Oh, I believe you," he said, the corners of his mouth turning up.

I nudged his knee with mine, starting to smile myself. "You'd
better."

"I said I believe you. Pita."

And we both laughed.

Keep reading for an excerpt from

the third book in the True Believers series

from Erin McCarthy

# BELIEVE

*Available now from InterMix!*

# ROBIN

I SPENT MY SOPHOMORE YEAR IN COLLEGE PARTYING. I WASN'T even original about it. Just the totally typical pattern of skipping class and going out every single night. If there was a keg party I went, if there was a shot I drank it, if there was a guy I made out with him. I wore short skirts, showed as much cleavage as I could, and I felt sexy and confident while having the time of my life. I threw up in more than one toilet, made out with a taxidermied deer on a dare, and came home without my shoes, dorm key, or phone on a regular basis.

Later, I tried to look back and figure out why I had slid so easily into party girl, but all I could come up with was maybe I just wanted a louder voice, and drinking gave me that. I wanted some attention, I guess, or maybe just to have a good time where there were no rules. Or maybe there was just no reason at all.

It all seemed normal. What you do in college, right? You party. You make superficial friends. You drink. Do stupid things that you laugh about the next day and take pictures that will prevent you from ever being a senator.

It wasn't anything I felt bad about. I mean, sure, I could have done without some of those hangovers, and I did end up dodging a few guys who wanted to date after I spent a drunken night telling them they were awesome, but nothing to make me feel ashamed.

Until I hooked up with one of my best friends' boyfriend when she was out of town.

Then I hated myself and the existence of vodka. Because I wasn't one of *those* girls. Or I hadn't been. Never, under any circumstances at all, would I have come even remotely close to doing anything with a friend's guy sober, so why would I do that? How could alcohol make me cross a boundary so high and thick and barb-wired? I wasn't even hot for Nathan. I never had been. I mean, he was cute, whatever, but it wasn't like I nurtured a secret crush or anything.

So how did I end up waking up next to him on his plaid sheets, his arm thrown carelessly over my naked chest? I came awake with a start, head pounding, mouth dry, for a second wondering where the hell I was and who I had had sex with. When I blinked and took in the face above that arm, I thought I was going to throw up. Getting to the apartment, sex, it was completely a black, yawning hole of nothing. I didn't remember even leaving the party. No idea how Nathan and I had wound up in bed together. All I had were a few flashes that suddenly came back to me of him biting my nipple, hard, so that I had protested, my legs on his shoulders. Nothing else.

As I lay there, heart racing, wondering how the hell I could live with this, with myself, the horror slicing through me like a sharp knife, Nathan woke up.

He gave me a sleepy, cocky smile, punctuated by a yawn. "Hey, Robin."

"Hey." I tried to sink down under the sheet, not wanting him to see me naked, not wanting to be naked.

"Well, that was fun," he said, smile expanding into a grin. "We should do that again before we get up."

The thought made my stomach turn. "But Kylie," I said weakly, because I wanted to remind him that his girlfriend was back at her parents' for the summer, but she still very much existed. His girl-friend. My best friend.

"I love Kylie, but she's not here. And we're not going to tell her." He shrugged. "I didn't expect this to happen, but it did and we're still naked." He pulled my hand over his erection. "No reason we shouldn't enjoy it."

And he leaned over to kiss me. I scooted backward so fast, I fell off the mattress onto my bare ass. "I'm going to puke," I told him.

"Bummer."

Grabbing my clothes off the floor, I stumbled into the hallway, hoping his roommate, Bill, wasn't around. In the bathroom, I leaned over the sink, trembling, eyes that stared back at me in the mirror shocked, the skin under them bruised. I didn't get sick. I wished I would. I wished I could vomit out of myself the horrible realization that I had done something terrible, appalling, unfor-giveable, mega disgusting.

I couldn't use vodka as an excuse. And now I knew Nathan was an asshole on top of it all.

Without asking him if I could shower, I turned on the water and stepped in, wanting to wash away the night, the dirty, nasty smell of skank sex off of my skin. I felt like a slut, like a bitch, like someone I didn't even know, and my tears mixed with the steady stream of water from the shower as I scrubbed and scrubbed.

I spent the rest of the summer sober, far away from parties, guilt nibbling at my insides, making me chronically nauseous, and I avoided everyone. I begged Nathan to stop when he kept sending me sexy texts and I ignored my friend Jessica, who had stayed in town for the summer and who kept asking what was wrong.

By August I was consumed by anxiety and the fear that someone knew, that someone would tell, that I would be responsible for Kylie having her heart broken.

I slept whole days away and I couldn't eat. I thought about getting meds from the doctor for sleeping or for anxiety or for depression or for alcoholism or for sluttiness. But what was done was done and a pill wasn't going to fix it. Or me.

When Jessica called and said Nathan's friend Tyler was picking me up whether I liked it or not and we were going to hang out, I tried to say no. But then I decided that I liked to be with myself even less than I liked to be with other people.

Besides, once Kylie got back in a week, I wasn't going to be able to be friends with any of them anymore, and this might be my last chance to spend time with them. I couldn't be in the same room with her and pretend that I hadn't betrayed our friendship in the worst way possible. I wasn't going to be able to sit there and have her and Nathan kissing on each other, knowing that he had spent all summer trying to hook up with me again.

I was going to have to find a new place to live, and disappear from our group of friends.

If only it had been that simple.

If only I had walked away right then and there.

Then I never would have met Phoenix and my life would never have changed in ways I still don't understand.

**TYLER WAS A GOOD RIDE, BECAUSE HE DIDN'T NEED TO TALK.** He just drove and smoked and I stared out the window, my art supplies in my lap. I had promised to paint a pop art portrait of Tyler's little brother Easton, and I had to do it tonight because I might never see him again if I had the guts to follow through with my plan to move out of the apartment. I hadn't painted all summer. I wasn't inspired. And I didn't want to now, but I had promised I would back before the morning after with Nathan.

So since I couldn't explain any of that, I stayed mostly silent. I did say, "Rory gets back tomorrow."

It was a stupid comment. Of course he knew his girlfriend was coming back to school. But I wanted to make some sort of effort. It was hot, even for August, and the windows were open, air rushing in and swirling his smoke around in front of me.

"Yep. I missed her. A lot."

I didn't doubt he had. And I didn't think for one minute he would have betrayed her the way Nathan had Kylie. Even if he wasn't living with his brother and Jessica, who were also dating. Tyler just wasn't that kind of guy. Both Riley and Tyler were loyal, and I wondered why I always seemed to attract the wrong kind of guy. The liars, the cheaters. My boyfriend freshman year had been a douche, flirting with other girls in front of me, laughing it off when I complained. My high school boyfriend had told me he wanted a girl who had her life together, who had goals. What kind of goals was I supposed to have at seventeen? At that point I already knew I was going to college to study graphic design, wasn't that good enough? So apparently his way to fix my deficiency was to hook up with his ex at a party and humiliate me.

It was hard to believe that someday there would be a guy in my life who would love me the way my friends' guys loved them.

Of course, I was never going to find that guy at a keg party. Another reason I had stopped going to the frat house all-nighters. I didn't have the stomach for so-called living in the moment fun since I had woken up next to Nathan. So maybe I didn't have my life all mapped out, but I knew that I was done with the superficial crap. I knew that I had crossed a line I never wanted to cross again and if that meant giving up alcohol forever, then that's what I was going to do because I had gone from being cheated on to being the cheater, and I could barely live with myself.

And if I couldn't live with myself, what guy would want to?

When we went in Tyler's house, there was someone sleeping on the couch. I couldn't see his face since he was turned away from the room on his side, but he had black hair and a serious lack of a tan. "Who is that?" I asked Tyler.

"My cousin, Phoenix. He's crashing here for a while." Tyler kept walking past him to the kitchen. "Do you want a beer?"

"No, thanks." I hadn't had a drink in ten weeks and I didn't even miss it.

Jessica was in the kitchen, heating up food in the microwave. It was weird to me that she lived there with her boyfriend and his three younger brothers. I had never been to her parents' house but I knew she had grown up with a lot of money, and this was no spacious colonial in the suburbs. The house was small and dark and hot and rundown, but truthfully she seemed the happiest she'd been since I'd met her. Riley came in from the patio and kissed the back of her head, looking at her like he thought she was the most beautiful creature the world had ever created.

"Want some?" she asked me, dishing up rice and vegetables onto four plates.

"I'm good."

She switched out plates in the microwave and said, "Then let's go in the other room. I want to talk to you alone." She touched Riley's elbow. "Can you put these in for the boys?"

"Got it."

I followed her back into the living room and she sat on the floor by the coffee table. "Sit. I want to talk to you about what the hell is going on."

I did want to tell her. I wanted to get the awful truth out and ask her what I was supposed to do about Nathan. But I couldn't. All I could tell her was a small portion of the truth. I looked nervously at the sleeping cousin. "He can hear us. I feel weird talking in front of him."

"He's totally out. He just got out after five months in jail and he's been sleeping for two days."

"Jail?" I whispered, a little horrified. "For what?" How could she say that so casually, like it was no big deal?

She scooped rice into her mouth. "Fuck me, that is so good." She closed her eyes and chewed. "I'm going to have to step up the workouts but I think carbs are worth it."

I didn't say anything, sitting down on the floor next to her, drawing my knees up to my chest. I was wearing a sloppy T-shirt and I dragged it over my bare knees, making a tent, cocooning myself.

"Okay, so what is going on? Seriously. You won't drink, you won't go out. You've lost weight. You don't answer my texts. You're even dressing differently. I'm totally worried about you."

I was worried about me, too. I couldn't seem to drag myself out of the anxiety that had been following me around. "I'm moving out of the house as soon as I find a new place to live."

"*What*? Why the hell would you do that?"

Tears came to my eyes before I could stop them. "I just have to. I need to stop drinking."

"But, it's not like Rory is a big drinker. And I'm sure Kylie would respect it if you said you wanted to chill with the alcohol." She looked hurt. "We would never pressure you to party. God, that's so not us."

"I know." It made me feel even worse. "It's just I feel like I need to be alone for a while. I was even thinking about moving home and being a commuter. It's not that far to my parents, only like a forty-five-minute drive to class."

"You would seriously want to move home? That just blows my mind." Jessica stared hard at me, tucking her blond hair behind her ear. "Besides, this is going to leave Rory and Kylie with a whole house to pay for since we've both bailed on them. I feel really bad about doing that."

So did I. But I felt worse about screwing Kylie's boyfriend. What would I do when Nathan came over to hang out? I couldn't play it cool, like nothing had happened. I wasn't drawn that way. "Didn't Tyler say he wouldn't mind moving in with Rory?"

"Yeah, but I don't know if he can actually afford it." Jessica frowned, picking up her fork. "I guess I can ask him. I guess maybe Nathan could move in there, too, with Kylie. Bill is moving into the engineering frat house."

I dropped my knees, alarmed. That was not what I wanted to happen. I didn't want Kylie to become even more dependent and more in love with Nathan.

"This is so weird," she said. "This is totally not what we planned. It's like complete roommate shuffle. What happened?"

Rory fell in love with Tyler. Jessica fell in love with Riley. I blacked out and had sex with Nathan.

Not exactly the same happy ending for me. I wanted to tell her so desperately I swallowed hard and clamped my mouth shut. Telling her would only mean she would have to keep a secret from Kylie. From Riley, too. Telling Kylie would only hurt her to appease my guilt.

I couldn't do it.

Shrugging, I said, "Things change."

"Robin."

"What?"

"If you got attacked or something you would tell me, right? You know you can tell me." She reached out and touched my arm, expression filled with concern.

And it went from bad to worse. Now she thought I was a victim. I nodded. "I would tell you. It's nothing like that, I swear."

"Because it seems like you started acting strange after the party at the Shit Shack. Something is obviously wrong. So if that Aaron guy did something to you, tell me."

"No, he didn't." I shook my head emphatically. Aaron had just been a guy I had danced with, flirted with, kissed. Before he ditched me and somehow I ended up going home with Nathan.

"Did something freaky happen? Did you do something you regret, like anal?"

Not that I was aware of. I couldn't prevent a shudder. "No. No anal." Though I did do something I regretted, more than anything else I'd ever done. The person who said that life was too short for regrets clearly had never done something super shitty.

"Jessica!" Jayden called her name from the kitchen. "Can you come here?"

"Yeah, I'll be right there, buddy." She set down her fork. "Be right back."

Jayden was eighteen but he had Down syndrome and I knew that Rory and Jessica both cut him a lot of slack. If he asked for attention, they gave it to him, and I was totally grateful for the interruption. I wasn't sure how much longer I could lie to direct questions.

As Jessica went into the kitchen, the guy on the couch suddenly coughed. I turned and saw dark eyes staring at me. He had rolled onto his back and was sitting up on the arm roll, his hair sticking up in front. My palms got clammy and I stared back, horrified.

Not only was he completely and totally hot, he had obviously been awake for more than thirty seconds. He looked way too alert to have just opened his eyes.

"Uh, hi. I'm Robin," I said, my hands starting to shake. What had we said? Nothing incriminating, I didn't think. I hadn't admitted anything. Though I had said anal out loud and that was awkward enough. All those nasty jokes about prison popped into my head and my cheeks burned.

His expression was inscrutable, but he nodded. "Phoenix."

"Nice to meet you," I said, because that's what you say even if there was zero truth to it. It wasn't nice to meet him. He was a criminal and I was a lying cheat and I was way too preoccupied with my own self-hatred to have anything interesting to say to him.

"Yeah. Sure." He sounded about as enthusiastic as I felt.

Agitated, I sat down on the coffee table next to the couch, wiping my hands on my denim shorts. "Sorry if we woke you up."

He shrugged. "No big deal."

I wasn't sure what to say after that. He wasn't wearing a shirt and like his cousins, he had tattoos covering his chest and arms. The one that caught my attention was the bleeding heart. It looked severed in two, the blood draining down his flesh toward his abdomen. It was beautiful and creepy and bold. Was it a metaphor? It seemed a little poetic for the average guy, but something about his steady stare suggested he was no ordinary guy. His dark hair stuck up then fell over one eye, so it felt like he had an extra advantage, that he could watch me from behind that cascade of hair.

Jessica hadn't told me why he had been in jail and I decided I really didn't want to know. Phoenix was trouble and trouble was exactly what I was trying to avoid.

"I'm not a big fan of anal either," he said.

Giving or receiving? I couldn't tell if he was making fun of me. He didn't seem to be trying to lighten the mood with a joke for my benefit since he still looked stone faced. It made me super uncomfortable.

"We thought you were asleep."

"What difference does it make? You didn't confess to a crime."

Thank God. "I don't like just anyone hearing my personal business. You don't even know me."

"You're right, I don't." He threw back the blanket that had been covering him below the waist and he stood up. He was in his underwear, black boxer briefs that clung to his thighs. "Robin." He added my name at the end like it was an accusation.

His body was lean and wiry, yet muscular. He looked like he worked out constantly, but had been born with a raging high metabolism, so he would never be bulky, but every muscle was obvious, the V of his hips so defined it made my mouth thick with saliva in a totally inappropriate way for the situation. He bent over and picked up a pair of shorts off the floor, stepping into them and drawing them up. But he left them partially unzipped and the belt clanked against his thighs as he moved out of the living room and down the hall into the bathroom without another word to me.

I watched him, unnerved. There was something hard about him, mysterious. His name suited him, unusual and intriguing. Annoyed with myself, I went into the kitchen, where Jessica was clearly laying out the situation for Tyler.

"So what are we going to do? Kylie and I were supposed to share and Rory and Robin each had their own room, but now there's an empty room completely."

"Can you guys just break the lease?" Riley asked. "I mean, what difference does it make? Everyone can move out."

"My dad and Rory's dad are the ones who signed the lease. I don't think either one of us needs to piss our dads off any more."

Riley frowned. "No. That's no good." He looked at me. "I guess you should find a replacement, since you're the one moving out."

Hovering in the doorway, I crossed my arms over my chest, miserable. "I'll just move home and I'll pay my portion of the rent. I can cover it with my paychecks from waitressing."

I was trying to be fair. To not stick them with either a bigger rent or with a roommate they didn't know and may not get along with, but Jessica's eyes narrowed in suspicion.

"Wait a minute. So you'd rather live at home with your parents who are like sixty years old, and your ancient, evil-eye-giving grandmother, while paying rent on a place you don't live in, than room with Kylie and Rory? Okay, I call bullshit. What the fuck is going on?"

When she put it like that, it did sound insane. "Nothing is going on. I just need time to . . . reevaluate."

But Jessica was tenacious. "There is something going on and you need to tell me what it is."

Phoenix strolled into the kitchen, scratching his chest, and went to the fridge. "I think if she wanted to tell you she would have already," he commented.

That about summed it up.

"And who asked you?" Jessica said, whirling to glare at him as she yanked Jayden's empty plate out from in front of him and started scrubbing it aggressively in the sink.

"Just an observation."

"Well, mind your own business."

"I think Robin would probably say the same to you."

They stared at each other and I felt the tension between them. Phoenix being in the house obviously upset the balance of Jessica being house princess. She was a strong personality, and she enjoyed being the only girl in the house. Somehow Phoenix was challenging her, and it was obvious to Riley, too. He held up his hand.

"All right, chill out. Both of you."

"Please don't fight because of me," I pleaded, feeling even more horrible with each passing second. "Just please don't." And to my horror, I started crying, tears welling up and rushing out of both eyes silently.

Everyone looked at me in shock and no one seemed to have a clue what to say. I wasn't known for being particularly emotional. Fortunately, Easton intervened. "Hey, aren't you supposed to draw me?" He tapped the canvas Tyler had propped on the floor next to the table. "When are you doing that?"

"Now," I said, taking an empty seat next to him and wiping my face, concentrating on drawing my breath in and out, slowly, evenly. "I just need some space."

That was definitely a metaphor.

Jessica went into the other room, clearly agitated, and Riley followed her, murmuring in a low voice. Tyler encouraged Jayden to go outside and shoot hoops with him. It left me at the table, methodically squeezing my oils into my paint tray, Easton across from me, bouncing up and down on his chair, and Phoenix leaning on the counter eating rice straight out of the container.

He was watching us, but I ignored him. Yellow, pink, blue. Squeeze, squeeze, squeeze. If I just focused on one thing at a time, I could function.

And it actually felt good to have my brush in my hand, the smell of the acrylics familiar and soothing. I felt calmer.

There was a knock at the back door and Easton jumped. "Who is that?"

"It's probably my girlfriend," Phoenix said. "Or my ex-girlfriend if this conversation doesn't go well. She's supposed to come over."

So of course the gorgeous bad boy had a girlfriend, despite his incarceration.

Phoenix opened the back door and I have to admit, I tried to pretend I was busy working, paintbrush in my hand as I used a bold magenta to do the outline of Easton's head. But I snuck a glance up at the girl who walked into the kitchen and I tried not to be judgmental. She looked hard. Older than she probably was. Bad dye job, turning naturally brown hair bleach blond, drying the texture out. Lots of eyeliner. Bad skin. Her jeans were too tight in the waist and too big in the butt. Not the prettiest girl I've ever seen but maybe she was super sweet. And who was I to judge?

"Hey," she said and tried to kiss Phoenix.

He shifted out of the way and rejected her effort. "Why didn't you come see me when I was locked up?" he demanded with no other greeting. "Not once. I didn't know what the fuck was going on, Angel."

Oh, God, seriously? Her name was Angel? I threw up a little in my mouth. I couldn't think of a name less suited to a girl who looked like she could beat the shit out of me if I looked at her wrong. Carefully, I set down my paintbrush and pushed my chair back. Clearly this was a private conversation and I had enough drama of my own. I didn't want to be involved in someone else's.

"Who are you?" she asked angrily, shooting me a glare as the noisy scraping sound of the chair made her aware of my presence.

"I'm just going in the other room," I said carefully, not wanting to go a round with her. I had no doubt I would lose, especially in my current emotional state. Easton obviously felt the same way. He bolted into the living room without a word.

"Good," Angel said, playing with the ring in her nose.

"She doesn't have to leave," Phoenix said, gesturing for me to stay. "This is only going to take a minute. So what did you want to tell me, Angel?" He crossed his arms and leaned on the kitchen counter.

I stood up anyway, despite his words.

"I'm pregnant."

I couldn't prevent a gasp from leaving my mouth. Yeah, I should have left the room. But Phoenix didn't react at all. His face never revealed any surprise, and the only movement he made was to flick his eyes over her flat stomach.

"You don't look six months pregnant to me."

"I'm not. I'm only two."

He'd been in prison more than five months. Jessica had said that. I knew that. What I didn't know was why I cared one way or the other about it being his baby, but I felt horrified for him that he'd been cheated on, and a little bit of relief that he wasn't the father.

"Then I don't need to know that." Phoenix went and opened the door. "Bye, Angel."

"Don't you even want to know what happened?" She looked disappointed. "Who the father is?"

"No. All I wanted was to know for sure that we're broken up, and we clearly are, so good luck. Lose my number."

"You're an asshole," she said.

I wasn't sure how he qualified as the jerk in this situation, but I kept my eyes on the canvas as she stomped out the back door, and he slammed it loudly behind her.

"Well, now I guess we're even," he said.

I glanced up, curious to see if he was going to rage or look upset. But he didn't. He looked . . . neutral. "Even how?" I asked.

"Now we both know each other's personal business."

I finished my brush stroke. "True. And I'm going to stay out of it, like you did with me." I just wanted to paint, to lose myself in the wet sound of sliding paint.

He came over and looked down at my canvas. "You don't need Easton here to paint? You're doing it from memory?"

"Yes."

"Cool."

He watched me for a minute, and I didn't actually mind. I didn't need quiet or solitude to paint pop art and it felt good to lose myself in the narrow focus of creating lines on canvas. But while I wanted to respect his privacy, I also knew that it had to have hurt him that his girlfriend hasn't visited him in prison, that she had cheated on him. I also felt guilty that I was a cheater, that if it ever came out, I would be the one causing pain. I hated that.

"I'm sorry," I told him, glancing up, hoping he would understand.

"For what?"

I didn't want to be specific. I didn't think he would appreciate that. "For what I heard. For what you heard."

"That you heard it? Or because it happened?"

"Both. But mostly that it happened. It hurts, I know. And I'm sorry."

Phoenix shrugged. "I'll live. I've survived worse."

I wanted to say that she wasn't good enough for him anyway, that she was a liar and a cheat and a shitty girlfriend who didn't deserve him, but did I really know that? And if I was no better than her, did I have any right to say anything?

"Sometimes we do stupid things." Very stupid things. Sometimes we needed forgiveness.

"Yeah. Some of us more than others." Phoenix pulled out a chair and sat down across from me. "I've never painted before. I sketch. It must be hard to get the subtlety of the lines and the shading in paint."

"You sketch?" I asked, amazed, then not sure why.

He nodded. "And I do tattoos. I guess the difference is with oil paint you layer on top, right? With a tattoo you do a little, but mostly it's about precision and shading."

"Do you have pictures of your work?" I asked, curious to see it. The idea of tattooing someone with a needle scared me. There was no retracting a mistake.

Sort of like life.

"Nah. But I did the original design for my cousins' arm tat, the one they all have, and I did Tyler's dragon on his leg."

"Cool. That dragon is beautiful."

"Thanks." He drummed his fingers on the table. "We're a fucked-up family, you know. We haven't always gotten along, depending on whose mom was hooking the other on what drugs."

"Why aren't you living with your mom?" I finished the outline of Easton and started shading in his strong features. Even in the brilliance of yellow and magenta, I wanted to capture the deep sensitivity of his eyes.

"I don't know where she is. She didn't leave a forwarding address."

So not only had his girlfriend cheated on him when he was in jail, his mom disappeared and neglected to tell him? I wasn't sure I could be so casual about it. In fact, I knew I couldn't. My parents were all about family. They loved me and my older brothers in a way that was almost smothering, and I was grateful for it. "Oh my God, I'm sorry."

He shrugged. "She'll turn up eventually. But Riley and Tyler are being cool and letting me stay here."

I wasn't sure what to say. "Family seems important to them."

Those fingers increased their rhythm, but the rest of him stayed completely still. The only movement seemed to come from those anxious fingers and the intensity of his stare as his eyes raked over both me and the canvas. I was never still. My mom had always commented on that. I fidgeted and shifted and couldn't stay in a chair longer than ten minutes without creating a reason to get up for a task before sitting down again. I struggled to sit through movies, and I hopped up and down off a bar stool, going out on the dance floor and outside to smoke cigarettes I didn't even like. Even now I was bouncing my knee hard up and down and chewing rapidly on a piece of gum. His immobility fascinated me.

Which may explain why I said, "Do you want to paint? I have another canvas and brush."

Again, there was no reaction. I wondered what it would take to draw emotion out of him. "Nah, I don't want to waste your supplies."

"It's a cheap canvas. It was only five bucks."

But he just shook his head. Then a second later he asked me, "Do you have a boyfriend?"

"What?" I almost dropped my paintbrush. "No. Why?"

His phone slid across the table toward me. "Then give me your number."

"Why?" I said again, which was a totally moronic thing to say. But I didn't get any vibe he even liked me, let alone was interested in me.

For the first time, I saw the glimmer of a smile on his face. The corner of his mouth lifted slightly before he controlled it again. "Why do you think?"

For a split second, I felt like myself, and I said the first thing that popped into my head. "So you can send me honey badger videos?" I joked, because it seemed like a safer response. He was just out of prison and he had just broken up with his girlfriend ten minutes earlier. So not a good idea to get involved with him. I wasn't up for dating anyone, let alone him.

"Yes. And kitten memes."

"Well, in that case." I took his phone because I wasn't exactly sure how to say no. It seemed super rude, and I doubted he was actually going to ask me out. He would probably send me a typical guy text of "hi" or "what's up?" and I could say "hi" back or "nothing" and we'd be done with it. Guys put no effort at all into communication or pursuing a girl. If you didn't go into a huge long text of explanation of what you were doing and dug deep into their text to get an adequate response back, the conversation just died. A big old waste of time, that's what most texting with guys was.

So I typed my number into his phone with my name. It was an old smartphone, with a cracked screen, like he had dropped it on the pavement. I set it back on the table.

Tyler came back into the kitchen and looked over my shoulder at my work. "Hey, that's cool so far. You got Easton's nose just right."

Out of the corner of my eye, I saw Phoenix palm his phone and put it back into his pocket, tossing his hair back. Then he just stood up and left.

My phone buzzed in my own pocket as Tyler went to the fridge and started rummaging around. I pulled it out and saw it was a text from a number I didn't recognize. When I opened it, there was a honey badger video. At your request was the message.

I smiled for the first time in what felt like weeks.

Way better than writing "hi."